I0723984

Red

by

Evelyn M. Exley

A Novel of Alameth

exleybooks.com

EXLEY BOOKS

EXLEY FANTASY

TALES OF KING JUSTICE

King Justice, The Legend Begins

The Scarlet Lady

First Knight

The Silver Knight

Captain of Dragons

FATIMA'S STORY (YOUNG ADULT)

Book 1: The Forgotten Palace

Book 2: The Forgotten Prince

COMPANION NOVELS:

Guardian of the City (A NOVELLA)

NOVELS OF ALAMETH

Red

Legend of the Hunt

Creation

EVANSWOOD SERIES

Part I

Part II

CHRONICLES OF IKE:

A Prophet Named Ike

NOVELLAS:

Elue

CAVALCADE SERIES:

Book 1: The Nepa Republic

EXLEY LEGACY

The Warm Planet

Blood Moon

To the one
who gave me the cloak

1.

"The Dark Wood is dark," Gran used to say, "But it's my home."

My Gran was the first person I remember in this life, and she'd been living in the Dark Wood her life-long. She was already old when I came to live with her at three years old, after the accident that claimed my parents' lives. The woman seemed ageless. I was too young and my surroundings too new to understand the tragedy that happened, so it did not affect me and didn't seem to affect Gran either. I did understand eventually, however, that the accident had occurred in the Wood; all manner of accidents happened here on a frequent basis and were not a surprise to the People of the Wood, only tragic.

I lived with Gran in a little cottage on the edge of the village of Huntsville, and it was there my life began. As the village's only seamstress, she was hard-working and well-known. She saw quickly enough I would never be a seamstress, at least not with the skills she possessed, so she was relieved to discover I was good with injuries, herbs, and poultices. I had a good bedside manner, and was patient with difficult people. This could be put to good use in our little community and was a good way to earn a small living for myself, as she often encouraged me as I grew older.

Eventually she discovered my skill went beyond just a Healer's regular interests and abilities.

"You've got a bit of Fumi in you," she'd say, though this was never explained very well.

This meant, I surmised eventually, that I had a supernatural gift. One that moved beyond this realm into another one, where power worked in an unusual way to produce abnormal results. If you had asked me, I would have said I was only applying bandages and mixing herbal potions.

The size and depth of the injuries I took on grew over time. Our community learned to place more trust in my abilities, young as I was, though they never called it magic or Fumi's influence as Gran did. They were just thrilled to have a Healer who had a decent skill at it and required modest payment. Most of them paid in rabbit meat or garden vegetables, or bolts of cloth for Gran, or a new roof for our tiny cottage. This was an ideal, comfortable arrangement.

I quickly understood why Gran believed I had some rare gift at healing. Within only a short time of living with her, I learned that there is a motherly pride in your child because you love them and your heart rejoices at their every success, and there is a pride that needs your child to succeed so you can feel successful... A mother who hungrily takes credit for your accomplishments because she so desperately needs them. Gran needed badly to be well thought of.

These moments weren't all the time, some seasons worse than others. But even as a young child I became aware there was a slight gleam in her eye when she behaved in this way — a yellow glint that sprang up in her gaze. I didn't know what it was I was seeing, but it was there. At its weakest, she simply tossed her hair to others, pitched her voice unnaturally high, and bragged on me. No one believed the exaggerated notions she claimed, but everyone smiled. They all believed, like all people do, that she was simply a proud parent. She adored me.

At its strongest, the yellow eyes flickered at me behind Gran's for a moment. In the atmosphere around her I swore I could hear the raspy sound of animal breathing... There was always the strong feeling that I was her possession at these times. At any moment, I felt sure, she would fly into a verbal fit if I dared to dispute her, dared to take from her what was rightfully hers.

As a child, I felt I was being siphoned somehow. Nothing I did and nothing I was was my own — it was hers. I inwardly cringed every time she introduced me. I knew instinctively if I showed any resistance to her or made any comments to others about her behavior those present would quickly correct me. They understood she was a proud parent, they would say. She did this out of love for me. She wanted the whole world to know I was her treasure. From their perspective, I should be grateful. But something about it left me uneasy. Something wasn't right.

Then there were the People of the Wood. The Dark Wood held several villages; I learned all of them with time. From a young age I hauled my little basket packed tight with medicines and hand-made bandages far and wide, roaming over the dark winding trails of the forest on foot. Everyone needed a Healer... and I was a good listener too. They all had a story to tell. Some wanted me to come just on that merit alone.

I don't suppose they knew I was listening as keenly as I was, nor watching so closely. Every one of them had been affected by life here somehow, I realized. I grew certain of this from a young age.

Like Old Man Samson, for example. He lived in Huntsville and often called on me for herbs to relieve neck pain he had had for most years of his adult life. He preferred to call me Healer, rather than Red. He was the one who taught me about manipulation.

He was a cranky man, largely unfriendly. He loved to sit and talk for hours about his life. He had gone on great adventures outside of the Wood and told me about a world I had never known. Through watching him — even at times through my own arrangements with him — I learned he could never admit what he wanted, even when asked directly. For him, it was easier not to talk out an arrangement with others. This took time, and risked that the end results would not get him exactly what he wanted. So he'd make up some woeful or complicated reason to get his way. He'd always pretend to go along with the discussed arrangement, and then at the last moment create a story that guaranteed he got exactly what he wanted. Part of his technique was to take advantage of the social generosity of others. He preyed on the naive, the innocent, the giving. Never in big ways, and only from those people whom he believed had it to spare, especially his family. It was a harmless kind of stealing that he justified entirely.

Of course I knew he was manipulating me when it happened. I wasn't deceived and never fooled. I let him have the fruit of his efforts — not to reward him, but because I knew how suddenly mean and accusing he would become if I spoke up. He was viperous. I had often witnessed him react viciously with his family and various members of the community; I could sense the tension there between us if I dared to protest or asked him to clarify his commitments. There was no one to protect me, and no high ground to run to should he lash out. I was just a girl, and a small one at that.

At the same time, during this I also saw Samson's great pain, a pain that left him vulnerable, just as my Gran was, to that yellow light in his eye, to that heavy-breathing monster that was somehow involved. I saw his great need for relief that extended well beyond the neck pain he was living with. Most of all, I held my peace because I saw he needed some person not to let him go. He was old and alone, and very few people liked him.

All the People of the Wood were similar, all of them carried some inner pain or hungry need that was then fueled and encouraged by the Unseen Presence. I didn't know what that Dark Presence was. I didn't know what it was after, and the People never spoke about it, as if they were unaware of it. I could see they agreed to its influence. They were the ones who turned the power over to it. But I never really knew what it was.

These woods were a dark and difficult place to live. Deep with shadow, cold, rife with mystery. Home it was not. Unlike Gran and these people, it was never home for me here. I wondered if it was truly home for anyone.

I first learned about the wolves from the Huntsman, and only incidentally. He was never one for words, that one.

I met him at fifteen years old. My Healing duties had taken me into a deeper part of the Wood that day, so deep in fact that through parts of it I had to light a little lantern which I carried with me on days I knew I would be traveling farther from home. It was an uncomfortable temperature here, an odd mix of both cold and heat which was common in the Wood. As usual, I wished I had more than the short shabby little cloak around my shoulders. It was growing thin from years of use and had become nearly useless. My only saving grace was the long woolen skirt and sturdy leather boots, the latter of which had been payment from Huntsville's cobbler for doctoring a broken arm he suffered for falling off his roof.

Danner never did tell me what he had been doing on his roof. He had no need to be up there, considering he was best friends and next door neighbor with the local thatcher. There were many things patients kept from their Healers out of shame or other unknown reasons. I suspected this accident had to do with a dare between the two men which they did not want to reveal to me... or to anyone else who asked over the ensuing weeks. But I received a fine pair of boots out of it, and that was good enough for me. I was hopeful the shoes would last for several more years, now that my feet had finally stopped growing.

I was on my way home now, tired and ready for the little lunch I had packed in my basket before departing the cottage that morning. It was this desire that took me off the path momentarily. I saw sunlight through the heavy trees to my left and thought I could take my lunch where the shadows were not quite so deep or thick.

Skirting massive trunks, stepping over a tangled web of roots spread out on the forest floor, I moved delicately for the light. This was tedious work by use of the lantern, but I knew it would be well-worth the reward to sit in some semblance of sun after a long morning in the darkness. My patient that morning had not been a difficult one, thankfully, but he had hardly needed the urgent care which I had been called such a distance for. I spent most the morning listening to his personal woes, eager to make my way back home.

It was then I heard the unexpected gallop of horse's hooves in the distance just ahead. This was a single horse, riding too fast through these dense forests. The sound startled me and I froze to listen, reaching for the lantern instinctively to dim it. There was no sense in giving away my presence until I was ready to alert them.

Surprisingly, the rider gave a sudden shout, one I interpreted as playful and urging the horse on, which was just as odd in these parts of the forest, particularly here in such thick undergrowth. I could hear the animal leap over an obstacle, and his hooves came down heavily on the hard earth. Then a crash occurred, followed by a terrible tangle of foliage, forest undergrowth, and a human body meeting disaster of some kind. The rider let out a painful yelp... and then there was only the silence of the forests.

My first instinct was as a Healer. Where there was an accident, there was most likely an injury. The silence was telling that something negative had occurred to the rider, particularly as the quiet stretched out. Not even the horse was shuffling around.

Quickly, I re-lit the lantern and moved forward. I followed where I had last heard any human sound, picking my steps. My heart was pounding, but I ignored it. I'd seen enough serious injuries now to not let fear or uncertainty impact my mission.

Soon enough, I saw a flash of white and picked out the image of a horse through the broken web of brush and trees. He came more into view as I approached, a massive animal of purest white. I realized his long neck was bent over his master at his feet, nibbling on the man's collar, hoping for a reaction of some kind.

It was then I let my steps be heard, so the animal would not be startled. He looked like a horse that was capable of defending himself and his rider if he thought they were being attacked. The gold pommel of a sword could be seen at his saddle. For a quick moment this distracted me. I'd never seen anything like it in my humble upbringing...

Then my eyes were drawn back to the rider, who was sprawled on the ground unconscious. His dark clothing was as rich as the saddle and gear strapped to his horse, sewn with tailoring that would make even Gran supremely envious. I approached closer, keeping my steps tentative until I was certain the horse had seen me and accepted my presence.

Enough light broke through the canopy of branches overhead to set the lantern down on the ground and kill its light, then I stayed bent, examining the face of my patient, keeping on the far side of the horse. He was a young man — only a year or two older than myself — with a chiseled face and olive complexion. Certainly he was not one of the People of the Wood. No one in the Wood was tow-headed, not one. I suspected he was not a commoner of any kind in the Land of Hadithi.

Just as I reached for him, he moaned suddenly, stirring. He opened his eyes and shook his head, immediately intent on sitting up.

Without thinking, I placed both hands on him. *"Easy. Easy, my friend.* You came off your horse hard."

He didn't obey me, though my voice and words did slow him. He rolled to a seating position. In only a moment he had already taken in his surroundings, the horse bent over him, and me at his side with my hands still offering support.

"Where did you come from?" he asked. He sounded dazed and in slight pain, but aware enough.

"I'm a Healer," I quickly assured him. "I've been out seeing a patient and heard you take a fall. Are you alone out here in these forests?"

"No. I slipped away from my party." He laughed a little as he gave this confession. He was amused by his actions. "Here — help me to my feet, would you? I'm a little dizzy."

This young man had none of the self-consciousness I was accustomed to in boys of my own age. Without thought, he placed an arm around my shoulders. Taking for granted that I would assist him, he leaned on me as I pulled myself to my feet.

As soon as we struggled to a stand, he stepped away, still shaking his head dizzily. "My thanks."

"Are you able to see clearly?" I asked him. "Do you have especial pain in your head?"

His half-laugh returned, but again this seemed directed at his own daring, not at my questions. "I'm fine. Nothing serious. I just need a minute to clear my head. Hey, boy —" His attention was turned for a moment by the white horse, who was nuzzling now on his master's collar in concern. The young man patted the animal's withers affectionately, reassuring him. "I'm fine. Shouldn't have tried that leap in the dark."

The young man's eyes returned to me. It was true, with every second he was on his feet he seemed to gain more coherency. He was focusing in on me now, taking in my clothing with one broad sweep, as well as the little basket and lantern at my feet. "You're just a girl. You're a Healer, you say?"

If I was just a girl, he wasn't much more than a boy, I thought. He had a rakish look about him, and appeared as though he spent a great deal of time laughing. The blue eyes that were on me were already alive with sparkle.

"I am," I told him. "I live here in the Wood."

"I'm Prince Desi," he announced, but even this was pronounced casually, as though he took no especial merit in it.

He paused as though he expected me to return the greeting with my own name.

I was a little more taken aback than he was, obviously. The most important person I'd ever known was Huntsville's mayor, who conducted business in his smithy barn with the glowing forge at his back and manure usually at his feet. We were not a very formal people.

The most I knew about the Royal family of any kind was in connection to the White Palace, one of their summer homes located along the southeastern edges of the Wood, just fifteen minutes' ride from the cottage. The Royal Family was rarely there, and when they were local people were not made aware. We neither knew when they came or left, which they had managed quite successfully for all the years of my life. When they did hold leisurely activities or hunted, they remained within the insurmountable stone wall around the circumference of the Palace property. They brought their own staff and shipped in all of their own supplies. We as a community were very politely ignored.

"You escaped the White Palace?" I asked him with surprise.

His eyes filled with pleasure at this thought. He laughed aloud. "Only to irritate my bodyguard... I won't do it again." He winced as his hand came up to the back of his head in reminder. "He warned me the Wood was too dark and tangled for fast horseback riding, along with a thousand other precautions. I should have listened. Look, do you need a ride somewhere? If you get me back to the road, I'll take you wherever you need to go..." His brows drew together briefly. "I still don't know your name."

"Red."

This stopped him temporarily. He gave a frowning smile. "Red?"

I shrugged with a small smile. "It seems no more strange to me than meeting a prince in the forest." He was a very unassuming prince, whoever he was. I liked him. I had always presumed Royalty was high-minded and lofty. He might have been any of the village boys of Huntsville, who were less affected by the darkness of the Wood and were not quite to manhood enough yet to take on the sobriety of responsibility and hardship. They were fun and free and often too playful for their own good.

The Prince grinned at my words. "All right, Red. I need to know where the road is. Can you show the way?"

"Of course."

I stooped for my basket and lantern, intending to lead him on foot, but he stopped me with the wave of one hand. "I'll take those. You can climb up behind me. We'll move faster if we both ride."

This caused me to pause briefly as I considered his offer. He seemed harmless enough. In fact, he was not like the people here at all as I gave thought to it. He was clean somehow. Untouched. Full of light even and void of shadows.

At my nod, he tucked the basket and lantern away in his saddlebags, mounted easily by use of the stirrups and horn, and extended one hooked arm down to me for climbing up.

I paused, considering once more. Sitting astride the horse in this position above me as the Prince was, I thought to myself, *He is not quite a boy*. He sat square-shouldered like a man and had an ease upon the steed that spoke of hardened experience. I told myself he probably knew well what to do with the sword at his saddle too.

Nevertheless, I did take his arm and allowed him to swing me up on the steed, finding him unsurprisingly capable. I immediately clung to the low cantle rather than his form, avoiding close contact with him.

In another moment, I was pointing in the direction of the road. "There. You'll have to pick your way through the forest a little, but the road is just ahead."

He obeyed these instructions easily enough and we soon found the path. The way was heavy with shadows, but the dirt-trodden roadway was clear. We began an easy trot towards the south.

I'd ridden a horse many times, of course. Travel on horseback was still faster and easier, especially in the Wood. Gran owned an old nag much more worn and simple than this marvelous piece of horseflesh; occasionally, when she did not have use of it for her own travels through the forest, I begged to borrow it. This horse, by comparison, was elegant and well-trained, his every step placed on the worn path with the greatest carefulness for our optimum comfort. I wondered what Gran's reaction would be when we rode up to the cottage together, the three of us.

After a moment, the Prince suddenly said, "They call you Red because of your scarf?" He had guessed the origin of my nickname.

"Yes. My Gran raised me. She dressed me in red scarves from the moment I came to live with her at three, and everyone in Huntsville began calling me by the name. Back then it was Little Red, which, thankfully, I have finally outgrown."

"What's your given name?"

"Isobel."

This gave him pause for a moment. "A queen's name. Stunning."

I did not know this fact, nor had I ever given my name much thought. The pragmatic in me quickly did not see how this could possibly make any difference to my identity or future. Only a Prince would have the luxury of stopping to consider the beauty in a name just for the sake of its beauty.

"Seeing as I am not a queen, I don't see how it makes much difference," I said.

The Prince shook his blonde head in front of me, giving a muttered laugh. "You sound like Jacobe."

"Jacobe?"

"My bodyguard. He thinks I'm too winsome and poetic. A dreamer, he says. He's been trying to cure me of it for years."

"You sound as though you don't get along very well," I suggested.

"Not at all. He's like an older brother to me. He's taught me nearly everything I know. I've known him most of my life."

As if discussion of the man suddenly brought him, a rider broke onto the shady road just ahead and at first sight of us plunged into a well-trained gallop. Upon reaching our side, his horse slid to an impressive halt, forcing us to a hasty stop. His mount was a fiery red color I'd never seen in a horse, more stunning by far than a queen's name or even a steed like the Prince's beautiful mount. I'm sure my mouth dropped a little at first sight of the animal, and then at first glance of the man commanding it.

He was a fierce, wild individual. Strange feathers clung to his long stream of dark hair, and he bore deep scars across one cheekbone that divided it in rough partitions. Even in the shaded lighting of the forest path, I could see both of his temples were inked in azure blue with chaotic artwork that hinted at animal eyes, broken shapes, and smoky images. His tall muscular form was outfitted in shapeless tiger pelts and soft boots — certainly not clothing or an image one would expect in a Prince's bodyguard, nor a Prince as refined as this one. Across the man's back was the long wooden stem of a broad-axe.

Wildest of all were the set of almond-shaped eyes that immediately fixed themselves upon me. He addressed the Prince first, however. "I've told you for years not to leave the Palace grounds. The Dark Wood is dangerous unless I'm with you."

The man had a sharp, near-menacing voice to match his appearance. I'm sure I was still gaping. He was from another land, another place foreign to me, one which I could not place or understand.

Desi was obviously much more accustomed to him. "Dangerous how?" he argued with brotherly familiarity. "It seems fine — unless you're speaking of Red here, who, as you can see, is quite harmless." The Prince glanced back at me, eyes laughing.

"There are wolves," the man responded bluntly. "Packs of them." He was still staring at me with a curious intense gaze.

His words struck me, even in spite of the uncomfortable circumstances. *Wolves? I'd never seen a single wolf in all of my life. And yet...*

The Prince continued to argue, shaking his head with a wry smile. "Red here travels all over the woods by herself. Yet she seems completely unconcerned."

The man's fiery-colored steed was a restless one. His hooves danced for a moment next to us... until his master clinched the reins with tight control. Desi's bodyguard was still eyeing me.

"Red is unique," he announced.

I wanted to say outright, *"I am?"* And yet, somehow, in just that instant, I knew that too.

The man's response seemed to catch the Prince for a moment. He glanced back at me quickly, trying to see what it was his bodyguard was discerning.

Clearly, Desi spotted nothing out of the ordinary. I could see the thought pass across his face. I was only a girl, and a young one at that. He dismissed Jacobe's words.

"Shall we get on our way?" he asked. "I agreed to take Red home."

"I'll take her home," his bodyguard broke across. "We should drop you off at the Palace first, Desi." His wild eyes met mine and he bent his head just the slightest, yielding respectfully. "If the young lady feels comfortable with me as an escort, of course."

"She doesn't know who you are," Desi objected, though his intentions were unclear. I thought possibly he just wanted to delay a return to the Palace... or secretly desired to harass Jacobe.

His bodyguard's steely gaze kept mine, undisturbed. "I'm the Huntsman," he explained. "I am Desi's bodyguard. I've been a gladiator, a soldier and a spy. I work personally for the kings of two countries. Is that enough information to content you?"

It should have terrified me, I thought. But instead, I found myself nodding silently, agreeing.

Nothing particularly eventful happened after that. The Prince disappeared through the quiet gates of the Palace with a friendly goodbye, and the Huntsman delivered me home with nary a word. Gran was not at the cottage when we arrived, so there was no dramatic scene as I had secretly hoped for. Today not even anyone from the village was walking past. After the Huntsman's departure this afternoon, this would end my encounter with him and the Prince, absent of any proof or witnesses that I'd ever seen them.

Upon arrival, Desi's bodyguard swung me to the ground at the front edge of our tiny yard and nodded down to me. His silence during the journey had not been cold, only focused. Quickly, he handed me my basket and lantern from his saddlebags.

"Thank you for your assistance, young lady," he said.

I didn't know whether to curtsy or flee his presence. His voice had the quality of authority that could make a strong horse shiver.

Instead, I chose to hold my ground. I nodded back, smiling up at him. "It was good to meet you, Huntsman."

He gave me one final stare. Just at that moment his unruly steed chose to dance once more on his hooves. I took a quick step back. The horse swung in a restless circle twice, until his rider gave up trying to take command of the fiery animal. Wild gold-flecked eyes broke away from mine as the man heeled the stallion and thundered away without a word.

And that, as they say, was that.

The next day around mid-afternoon Gran came pounding on my bedroom door. The suddenness of it startled me. I should have been accustomed to her occasional impulsive behavior after so many years of living with her, but my quiet nature had never adjusted entirely. I looked up from a pile of hand-made bandages I was bent over, now scattered across the tiny bed that held me up nightly.

"Gran?"

She sounded unusually excited when she answered. "Red, you have a visitor at the door."

This was not so uncommon. We had a constant stream of visitors at all times of day and night, either asking for Gran's business or my services. I was mildly confused as to why she was stirred up.

I abandoned my project and exited the room, which opened directly to the central room where we ate, cooked, and received visitors. Our only door stood open just now and a tall figure stood within its shabby wooden frame. Yes, I could see why Gran's gray hair was wild and her eyes stirred with excitement. She could barely stand still on the opposite side of the table between us.

There within the doorway stood the Huntsman. He was dressed in a new costume, this time as a gladiator, with polished pauldrons, breastplate and girdle. In our tiny cottage, he was a massive, intimidating figure. Just as yesterday, he was a character of another time or land, or even of an ancient world. The brass across his chest and in the strips below his waist carried a hieroglyphic design that surely said words of importance... if one knew how to read them and understood what they meant. At his back was, once again, the long-stemmed battle-axe, ready at a moment's notice. Beneath this, attached to the leather at his neck, a full-length cloak the color of red draped to the floor.

His intense eyes caught sight of me at once. "Red, I have asked your grandmother if the White Palace could have use of your services for the summer. We will pay you well and ensure your safe passage to the Palace daily. I have assured her you will never be in any danger within the Palace walls should you agree to the position."

A heavy tension was in the central room of the cottage. Gran, I knew, was secretly thrilled and fascinated. She would have a dozen questions on her lips as soon as he disappeared from whatever other-world he had arrived from...

For a moment I had nothing to say. He was so very focused and tight-lipped, so strange and unique. I took a moment to smile slowly at him. "Hello, Jacobe. Welcome to our home. How are you today?"

I think his mouth nearly dropped open. Yet in the next instant there was a sharp thought that passed over his face. He announced at once, "I'm well, as I hope you are, young lady. Forgive my lack of greeting. I'm eager to return to the Palace and my place at the Prince's side."

At this I said, "I presume the position you are offering has to do with my healing services?"

"Yes. The Prince and his guests are a rambunctious lot and they often fall prey to bumps, bruises, and strains. You have a fair amount of King Fumi within you, which are the only kind of Healers we use. Since you are local, this makes you excessively convenient. We would like to keep you on retainer at the Palace during our stay here."

Again he was so very direct, without explanation, possessing knowledge and opinions I had never before heard in my life. He announced them as if they were common and commonly understood. I could not help but turn and stare sharply at Gran, who had been the only person to declare similar things over me. Even she had mentioned King Fumi only in half-hearted passing through the years, as if he was a magic or a person she but thinly believed in. *What could this man possibly mean by all of this?*

Gran's inner excitement was growing. She burst out in a shrill ecstatic voice, "Of course she'll take the position! She needs the work. Go on, Red, get your things together. *Now.*"

She wasn't going to accept any response but immediate obedience. Without word, I did as she commanded, returning to the central room within only moments armed with my little basket. Once again I had my short cloak on and the red scarf securely tucked in place around the crown of my head. The Huntsman barely gave me a glance.

"Very good. My horse is outside." He nodded at Gran, who had found her voice and filled his ears with conversation during my absence. "Good day to you, Seamstress. I will return Red this evening, as promised."

It seemed to me he fled the cottage as if hounds were nipping at his heels. This almost made me smile, though I refrained.

Unaware entirely, Gran followed us out into the yard, still talking. She was filled now with last-minute instructions for me that seemed to suddenly occur to her. She hadn't done this in years. Today she seemed most concerned about my manners. Her shrill voice echoed across the yard and filtered down the street, as if she desperately hoped someone — *anyone* — would take notice.

Quickly, Jacobe leapt upon his waiting steed and reached a hand down to me. I took this almost as swiftly as he offered it. He paused only a moment to take the basket from my hands and tie it in some obscure way to the saddle horn, where it balanced against his knee. He also removed the double-edged axe from his back and slipped this into a scabbard that hung conveniently from the saddle.

Then we were wordlessly thundering away from the cottage, leaving Gran behind, her voice still streaming down the road after us.

At first I did not touch the Huntsman as we rode, instead clinging to the bucking saddle with clenched teeth. Yesterday I was able to ride like this successfully, I told myself. But for a hard mile or two he did not reserve speed, until I found myself regretting my decision to avoid — at the very least — tucking my hands in the back of his heavy leather belt. Surely touching a man foreign to me and as wild as he was still a better option than this.

So I did. I reached out without permission, brushed aside his heavy cloak, and tucked all of my fingers in the wide belt at his waist. This was much better. It did position me closer to him, and occasionally my forehead bumped his rock-hard shoulder, but my stability on the horse returned while we traveled at such driving speed.

His head turned just the slightest at my touch, but he said nothing. I sighed a little in relief. He was intimidating, but apparently not an entirely unreasonable man.

Fortunately, he slowed after a time. I immediately found myself less jarred and relaxed.

"Red, I have a question for you," my escort announced suddenly. This must have been the purpose for his slowing, I realized.

"Yes?"

"Have you lived with your grandmother all of your life?"

"Yes, since my parents died. I was just a toddler."

He sounded thoughtful temporarily. "Interesting." He added nothing more.

I was too young then to ask anything further unless he offered it, especially of a man like him. I thought maybe with time I could learn what thoughts he held about me. For the time being I abandoned the subject and so did he.

That afternoon marked a new era in my life. One never seems to know this at the time it happens in life, and when one does sense a change, as I did that day, one cannot determine the size of the change or the amount of the impact.

But I did sense something that afternoon as we passed over the same dirt path that divided and wound in a thousand directions all through the Dark Wood, then even stronger as we rode alongside the stone wall of the Palace. The wall itself was made with the same material as the Palace — white, sterile, smooth-stoned. It revealed nothing, shielded everything. I had always been curious what this place was, who lived here, why no one in the village or on the road passing by ever heard a sound from within its grounds beyond the wall. Like all the village children, I'd been madly curious about the kind of life lived here when the Royal family was in attendance. The wall had long been considered protected by magic in the eyes of the local village boys, who claimed they could never steal into it no matter how hard or concerted their efforts. No one I knew had ever been within its confines.

As we came upon the palace gates, the Huntsman pulled his horse in with impressive skill. This sharp action was so unnerving I loosed my hands and tensely wrapped my arms around the man's girth, forgetting he was a stranger and a wild man. I clung to him desperately as the horse skidded to a halt on his hoofs.

I didn't realize I'd also buried my face in Jacobe's back until I heard him say quite calmly, "We're there, Red."

I pulled away slowly, seeing we had indeed come to a successful halt only feet away from the gates. Tentatively, my hands returned to his belt, no longer confident even after his announcement.

The Huntsman turned his head, as the horse danced restlessly beneath us. "I'm sorry I startled you."

I gasped, "I'm not used to horses, especially not like this one — I'm sorry I couldn't be a braver passenger — "

His head turned back to the front. "I disagree. You are one of the bravest individuals I've met."

There was no explanation to this. He merely waited, staring up at the gates.

The gates before us were solid dark wood, ornate, held in place with wrought-iron hinges of such beauty and complexity that none of the local smithies could have possibly fashioned them. In another instant, with Desi's bodyguard giving no signal or sound as far as I could determine, they swung open wide, allowing us quiet entrance.

Yes. Small or large, wide or tall, my life was on a new course… and I had no idea where it would take me.

I released a fascinated little breath as we entered a stone courtyard. This held a round pool with a statue in it of a king, both made of the matching stone of the courtyard, the palace, and its surrounding walls. The man's image was what took my attention first. His stone-carved face held a warm expression, with a cravat held at the throat by an elegant dress jacket, along with long boots and a small crown atop his curly-mopped head. Through his hands flowed a stream of water that fed the pool. My eyes, for no reasonable explanation, could not help but remain fixed on him for some time.

Behind the mysterious king was the Palace — four stories high at its highest peak in the center, designed as a pale half-moon circle with a bevy of dark quiet windows. It was, in my simple experience, *magical.* Baskets and pots filled with glowing blossoms hung draping from the windows; hedges and bushes skirting the structure burst with the brilliant color of a dozen kind of flowers. Overhead, songbirds trilled and warbled from towering trees, announcing happiness and joy beneath a distant sky of softest blue. I had never known such a place of light or open space.

To the right were the stables, which the Huntsman took us to at once and promptly helped me dismount. This handful of low buildings, also made of stone, contained the sound of restless horses and braying livestock of a smaller variety — domestic sounds that did not steal from the quiet peace here or take from its elegance, and instead seemed somehow to add to its beauty.

Without word, two servants exited from the interior of the closest building. One calmly took the fiery horse from the Huntsman, nodding to my escort formally, while the other man stood by with arms folded behind him, waiting for any instructions to be given. Both men looked identical, like two kittens from the same litter — same livery costume of royal blue colors and gold fringe, exact short height, strong facial bones and brown hair thickness. Being a medical person, I wondered how it was they could be even the same weight.

Quickly enough, though, my attention was caught away, back to the King and the Palace, then to Jacobe, who wordlessly began clipped steps back across the courtyard, expecting me to follow. There was that continued sense of intense focus about him which inspired anyone in his presence not to dawdle… though of course a large part of me wanted to.

He led the way around the back side of the mansion on the northern side of the courtyard. I had hoped he would take us straight through the front door, but he did not. That opportunity, I hoped, would come eventually.

Here, on the opposite side of the Palace, the quiet grounds fell away into an open spread of beautiful gardens and pale-stone walkways, revealing a wide open lake beyond. A small white-stone sitting wall separated the lake from the gardens, curving around the bay, extending in both directions as far as the trees and low hedges would allow one's eye to see.

The waters of the lake were still and quiet, sparkling in the farthest distance like the color of a million jewels. No one from Huntsville had ever laid eyes on it, it was forbidden. The lake and all the grounds surrounding it belonged strictly to the Royal Family. The loch was, strangely enough, also extremely hard to find. I'd tried once, sneaking into the Wood just past where the wall ended and trying to find a way in from the northern trees. So had a dozen other village children who wanted a peek at the famous waters. We all discovered the same thing — the wall protected the entire property.

Now, staring at the lake's beauty, I wished I had found it a million times as a child. This piece of property was the most beautiful place I had ever laid eyes on in my humble fifteen years. It lay free of the tangled brambles of the Wood, spacious, blanketed in a dozen shades of green. It was as if every tree and hedge, every flower and bush, politely made way for its neighbors on either side, allowing for sunshine and ample floor space. The gardens were alive with color and filled with the song of a dozen birds.

Almost at once I heard the sound of laughter and happy voices. My eyes were pulled to the water's edge on this side of the property where a display of half-circle stone benches were settled. These faced the lake in a humble little setting under the shade of a towering cottonwood, discreetly hidden from the windows of the Palace by heavy low branches. The sharp echo of young voices rose up from this secluded corner of the property.

"The Prince and his company are on the lake terrace," Jacobe explained. He paused and turned to me then. "I will introduce you as a Healer on retainer. You should be aware, Red, that they will be well-mannered, but most likely their kindness won't extend much beyond that considering you are not a guest of the Prince or known by them. Do you understand?"

I nodded, *yes.*

He surprised me when he scanned my clothing with a quick eye. "You'll already be younger than all of them. Not all of our friends are as warm-hearted and free of social constraint as the Prince."

"You are thinking of my clothing now," I told him.

"Yes. It will leave an impression. I think I should speak to the household steward about a uniform of some kind for you while you are here."

The Huntsman did not strike me as a man who would be aware of the social games people played, nor caring of how well a servant adjusted here. I gave him a frowning smile.

"I thank you for considering me," I responded. "I am not familiar with the Prince's class of people, it's true, but my work as a Healer has put me in very delicate situations with all genders and ages for years now. I think I will be prepared, proper clothing or not."

He considered this briefly, then nodded. "Very well. We will go down now and see about the uniform later."

Immediately he turned and led the way towards them through the low gardens. As we went, a dozen aromas and fragrances took my senses, filling the air. I was surrounded by a beauty I had never known. I told myself I could endure a great deal of social mistreatment for the opportunity to walk in this garden every day.

Within only a few moments more we came upon the little group. They were a colorful gathering of ten or twelve, dressed brilliantly in fine silks and satins, a mix of young men and women all slightly older than myself. I'd never seen anything like them, either. They were as beautiful as the gardens.

A slight difference in years is a huge difference to young people of that age, the Huntsman was right. I could see at once, just as he had warned, that I would be politely ignored during my stay here until they had need of me. Maybe even then. Of those who had observed our arrival, all had already turned away, seeking entertainment in one another.

But Desi suddenly turned, noticing Jacobe, then his eye fell to me.

"Red!" He broke through the little group and rushed over to my side, face aglow, smile bright. Without thought, he took my hand in both of his and held it kindly.

Suddenly every eye on the terrace turned to us now, curious and watching.

"Jacobe talked you into it," he declared, "I'm glad! We will have need of your services — one of us is always getting hurt." He laughed.

Unsurprisingly, Desi was dressed as brilliantly as the day before, this time in a tailored leather tunic with tiny seamless stitches, held firm over a linen shirt and leather breeches. He carried no weapons, just a delightful and charming expression. He leaned towards me conspiratorially. "Have you seen any wolves out there?"

This made me smile, I couldn't help myself. We both cast a glance at the Huntsman, who entirely ignored the comment and instead moved across the terrace to take up a quiet standing position behind the little group.

2.

That first summer I spent more incidental time in the Huntsman's company than I did the Prince or his companions. They had fewer injuries than Desi or Jacobe had asserted, at least this summer, and this left me nearly always located a short distance from whatever activity the group was indulged in. Jacobe, as it happened, was in a similar position, lingering back, a tall silent figure on the outskirts of daily events, who occasionally barked commands if the Prince or his guests over-stepped their bounds.

Two days after I arrived, one of the household servants — there was an entire fleet of them who maintained the Palace during the Prince's stay, I learned — presented me with a uniform. This was a black cotton dress flowing well past the ankles, and a white shirtwaist trimmed in lace. The dress shouted a clear message, just as the Huntsman had said I would need. I was now an official member of the household. Along with the dress a pair of black patent leather slippers were included and dark nylon stockings to cover skin. I'd never seen nylon before, nor heard of it, and the same little maid had to explain its use before I knew how to slip these on. She was not *unkind,* I observed, only busy and distracted with responsibilities as everyone seemed to be here.

Jacobe was the only odd one. He neither dressed nor behaved like any of them. The Prince's guests and household staff were what I imagined a Palace household to look and feel like; he, on the other hand, was mysterious and wildly strange here among this civilized group. I could imagine, as I watched him covertly during my long hours of waiting, that he had once been precisely what he claimed to be — a soldier, a warrior and a spy. His stalwart manner never changed or wavered at any time as he interacted with the group of young people, and his eye as he watched the prince's movements from afar was keen and alert, ready to spring into action at any time. He often interacted with the household staff in matters concerning the Prince, and these instructions and communications were as resolute and unbending as he was with Desi. I wondered what had brought him to work for the King's son as a bodyguard.

Because he was so foreign to me, I found his age difficult to place as well. *Twenty-five or thirty?* I guessed, judging from his eyes, not even certain of this theory considering how inked his skin was. Such a tender age was difficult to believe of him, especially of a man who had his rich history and behaved as he did. Desi had said he'd known him most of his life.

Eventually, as the long hours and days turned, Jacobe turned to me and said, "Red, do you read?"

I looked over at him in surprise.

At the current moment we were stationed outdoors on the terrace, while the Prince and his guests roamed the gardens around us. They had quieted some as the afternoon wore on and the sun grew warmer; a few had disappeared inside the Palace for refreshments. I was seated in the shade of the cottonwood on one of the half-circle benches, demure, privately thrilling over the fragrances that the dry summer wind swept down from the gardens and over the still lake waters. My companion — if you could call him that — was in his usual position, standing in full sunlight without change of expression, his face towards the water and his ear towards the group behind him.

I tried to answer him, realized my voice was dry from disuse and warmth, coughed, and said, "Yes, I read. And write. I completed all the levels our local school has to offer."

Immediately he turned towards a small stone table nearby, which had been laid by the Palace staff earlier and held an array of dried fruit that would keep in the sun, along with a silver pitcher of water just now beading with sweat. The Huntsman reached for an unused wooden mug, poured water into it, and took the few steps to my side to offer this.

"How long ago did you complete your schooling?" he asked.

I hadn't presumed the comestibles were for me and had already run through the water and small tidbits I had brought from home that day. I took a long thankful drink and settled back against the trunk of the tree behind me, still holding the mug. "I was ten; I'm fifteen now."

In keeping with his usual reaction to my statements, Jacobe fell ponderously silent. He was always thinking something. Then he said, "How long does your schooling usually take?"

"Eleven years. I finished several years early."

A slight frown line creased between his brows. "You must be accustomed to much greater activity than this."

I smiled up at him, silently laughing. "Yes. Much greater activity than this. My Gran thinks I'm going to grow heavy and slow if I keep this up for long."

He had already moved back to his guard position several feet away, but his gold-flecked eyes were still studying me. "She seemed very eager for you to take the position, and shows an eagerness every evening I drop you home. Has her attitude changed towards your job here?"

How to explain to him that it was not the job she disliked, she was only expressing her jealousy? That her eagerness every evening was towards him and his proximity to the Royal Household?

"She has not changed her viewpoint towards the job," I assured him. "We need the money, and she feels confident that I will do my part well here. She is only tired of all of the villagers complaining at our doorstep because I'm not available this summer and they are forced to travel to the far north of the Wood where an animal healer is attempting to treat them." This was a half-truth, but it would do.

"Ah." He accepted this, or appeared to. A silence fell.

My eyes were already beginning to drift back to the lake, presuming our conversation was over, when he suddenly announced, "Red, the Palace has a library. Would you be interested if I brought you some reading to pass the time?"

My heart leapt at once. My eyes turned and caught his. *"Yes."*

The following day he brought me a handful of books. Though I am certain his motivations included providing me with mild entertainment while I passed the time, each volume he selected for me opened my mind in a way I could not have imagined. His action, I felt sure, was intentional.

All of the books he delivered were ancient and heavy, leather-bound, the pages dog-eared and browning from age. I quickly devoured their words. From the reading I was soon caught up in the exotic history of a country called Alameth. No one in the known world knew where it was located, and only those who were educated in the secret methods of traveling to and from Alameth did so. It was in this land, the books revealed, that all the laws of science and understanding changed. Many things were possible that were not possible anywhere else. Men and women of rare ability often settled within Alameth's borders, called and invited by the spirit of King Fumi himself.

It was Fumi who made Alameth famous. He was, surprisingly, a poor local boy from Hadithi who was given a secret map as a child and learned how to access Alameth. Over time he won a famous competition in the land offered by the King and was awarded the throne. His descendants had ruled since.

After reading this, I found myself observing Desi's facial features over the next few days from the distance I sat. We had very little interaction with one another; after our initial greeting, he had busied himself with his guests and care-free summer and seemingly forgot my presence. But he was nearby enough to compare his face to the statue in the front courtyard of the Palace and make my guesses.

He didn't seem unique, I thought to myself, as I sat under the shade of the cottonwood considering the books' claims. None of the household staff or its guests appeared anything but ordinary. My eyes flickered to the Huntsman. *Jacobe, on the other hand...*

It took a few days to summon the courage to speak up. I didn't know if Jacobe would show resistance, or if his entire intention for offering the reading was to provoke questions, but I couldn't help myself any longer. One afternoon — once again after the Prince and his guests had quieted in the warmth of the summer sun and were lazily picnicking under the heavy trees behind me — I brought up the subject.

"Is it magic?"

Jacobe's sharp eyes met mine, pulled away from where Desi was located just at the edge of eyesight beyond my cottonwood. He knew instantly what I meant.

"No. Not magic. Some of who we are and what we do is science. Some of it is... power."

"What kind of power?" I asked him. "Dark arts? What is it?"

He shook his head. He was dressed in his pelts and soft boots again, standing with a strength that was intimidating and ferocious. Along with the broad-axe across his back he wore a curved sheathed sword today at his waist.

"Nothing like that," he explained. "Our power is *creative* power. It is the life that exists in all living things. We release it through our speaking, through the works of our hands. Everything we create is fueled by the power of life."

I did not pause to consider these profound words, I would absorb them later. Right now I had a half dozen questions that had been brewing for days. "Am I related to Fumi? Is that why you said I had a great deal of him in me?"

"No, I was using spiritual language. You carry a great deal of his spirit in you — his gifts, his uniqueness, his values. It is obvious to anyone who knows our people, and who has experienced Fumi personally. In Alameth we would consider you his *spiritual* descendent."

I was staring at him now. "Desi and his guests seem quite —" I was grasping for words.

The Huntsman nearly smiled. This was the first time I'd ever witnessed it. I was beginning to think the man only had two expressions — dead-pan sobriety, and a stern ferocity that still made me tremble even after days in his company.

Just now he managed to rein his amusement in, hardly giving expression to it. "All of his guests are quite normal, yes. We have a large contingent of regular citizens who live within our borders. They are as much a part of us as anyone else. Desi, however —" Jacobe paused and grew cool with displeasure. "Desi is young and self-absorbed. Hopefully he will outgrow it in time. Fumi is there within him, though, particularly seen in his humility towards others. He does not consider himself above his fellow man."

Then he changed the course of the conversation slightly, his eyes returning to the picnic in the distance to take note of his charge. "As you have probably already guessed, Fumi was Desi's great grandfather. Alameth has stayed in good standing with the current rulers of Hadithi and keeps a summer palace here, as you see. This is the first time the Prince has been allowed to come without his parents."

I couldn't help myself, though I knew my next inquiry was more personal and probably shouldn't be asked. I blurted out, "The Prince told me you were like an older brother to him and have taught him nearly everything he knows."

Jacobe's eyes flicked back to mine. He could hear the question in my statement and understood it. "That would be true. I was commissioned by the King to train and guard the Prince until he comes of age at the end of next summer. At that time he is slated to join the military for several years. My time will be over in service to him then."

"And — are you from Alameth?"

He answered this with the same unflinching straight-forwardness, letting me empty myself of all my curiosity without rebuke. "I have my own homeland, but Fumi called me long ago and I became a citizen of Alameth. I make my residence there, yes… when I'm home. I have often been called away on assignment by the kings of Hadithi and Alameth, or by Fumi himself."

It suddenly occurred to me how much information he was so willingly giving me, both about himself and Desi's country. No one of my people would ever do such a thing, and I especially hadn't expected it from him, truth be told. I paused a moment and considered this, wondering, allowing my bedazzlement with Alameth to pass momentarily.

Eventually I asked him, "Why have you told me all of this? These seem like secrets kept from Hadithi and other parts of the world. I'm just a girl, and an unknown one at that."

I didn't expect the answer he gave, bluntly. "They are not secrets, but we are discreet about who we tell and what we say. For me, I want you to grow to trust me, Red. It's important that you feel safe around me. In order to judge whether I am trustworthy or not, you need information and context. Can you accept this?"

There was no way to tell clearly what he meant by this. He was too mysterious and cryptic for a girl my age to fully comprehend, I presumed. But I could sense his sincerity underneath his stern resolve. He didn't want me to be afraid of him, as no doubt most people were who came into contact with him.

I nodded. My words came out quietly. "Yes, I can accept it."

The summer carried on uneventfully for me as a Healer. Desi and his guests remained injury-free, and I was left to sit in my usual spot and listen to them as they scattered over the grounds. On some days later in the summer, when their activities were lazy and light, the Huntsman offered to let me walk the grounds around the lake.

"You can't get lost," he assured me. "If you find yourself in unfamiliar territory or you become tired, call the name of the Palace and it will be just ahead."

At first I took him up on his offer simply so I could see this phenomenon, but I was also understandably thrilled at the opportunity to explore. These were beautiful forests, full of light and calm, so different than the Dark Wood. Soft grass grew in abundance underfoot; the lake waters were always visible through the trees, sparkling in the sunlight like a sea of gems. I never met anyone, and — just as Jacobe had said — I could "call" my way back to the

Palace easily no matter where I found myself. After such a sedentary summer, these walks were wonderfully refreshing.

After that first afternoon of conversation, Jacobe and I spoke little about Alameth. He offered a few more volumes from the Palace library, but these subjects covered the fascinating topic of inventions that had been introduced to the country by its scientists and did not stir questions for me, only wonder and imagination. The current queen and Desi's mother, Greta, was herself an inventor who had originally been invited to the country by Fumi and had contributed to the compilation of the inventions presented. I was equally thrilled to discover that the books included pencilled illustrations, which captured my attention entirely. Sometimes I took one of the volumes with me on my walks and found some cozy spot in the grass-bed beneath the trees to read for hours.

By far, that summer was the most restful I had ever known. But eventually, it did come to an end. The days grew less hot, the sunlight softened, and the cicadas began their mating cry from the tops of the trees just before sunset.

As the final day of the Prince's stay approached closer, I understood from the conversations around me that they would be returning the following summer. However, I did not count on the Huntsman asking for my services, particularly since there were no injuries for me to treat this year. The Palace could just as easily call on their own Healers, I reasoned, and spare themselves both the money and the presence of a young unproven stranger.

I had already prepared Gran for this eventuality when Jacobe brought it up one afternoon.

I was standing in the shadow of a great oak tree, watching the Prince and a male companion wrestle some distance away on the forest floor east of the Palace. All of the other guests were gathered around them with enthusiasm, cheering, calling out in excitement. Two of the other boys on the edges were already demanding their turn as soon as the winner emerged.

This was a new sport they had decided to indulge in. I rather suspected, from becoming familiar with Desi over the past two months, that he had grown restless at the thought of returning home tomorrow and needed some way to expend his unhappiness. They had created a set of rules in advance of the match and one of the young ladies had been designated as the umpire. Thus far Desi and his opponent had obeyed the guidelines, but seeing as it was the most physical contact the group had tried since my arrival, I quietly positioned myself closer in the case some unforeseen tragedy occurred.

The Huntsman was stationed closer to them at first, then upon sight of me, made his way over to my side. We watched together in silence for a brief time; then, when it appeared nothing immediately alarming was going to occur, Jacobe spoke.

"We leave tomorrow," he announced.

I nodded, my eyes still on the rowdy match. He knew I knew this.

"I have spoken to the household steward, Red. If you are in agreement, I would like to employ your services again next summer."

I turned and looked up at him quizzically. He was a *little* less intimidating now. "I didn't do anything this summer. Wouldn't it be just as well to save yourself the funds and call on your own Healers as needed?"

"The others talk too much." His answer was direct, as usual.

I laughed out loud, which was rare for me. It was true, I sat in silence for most of the summer. The quiet was a welcome break after years of constant conversation from the People of the Wood. "Very well. I agree."

He seemed relieved, though I had no proof of this. I only suspected it. "Good. I had thought you might have a strong duty to your patients and refuse."

"I *do* have a strong duty to my patients. They will have me all fall, winter and spring," I answered.

This made him smile. I'd seen that smile slip out a little more in the last month. "Very well."

"Very well," I repeated.

Inwardly, I rejoiced. There was nothing I wanted more than to return next year. The work was easy, but even if it had been difficult, I was well-treated here and experienced a great freedom I had never known.

That evening the Huntsman delivered me to Gran's little house for the final time. He did not linger. Gran was already barreling out of the front door and making her way over as if she had been expecting us, announcing herself in a loud voice as she came. This had easily become her favorite part of the day for the past two months.

Tonight Jacobe ignored her.

With his eyes still on me, he turned his fiery steed towards the direction of the Palace. "Goodbye, Red. Be careful."

I smiled up at him and nodded. He was ever the defender and protector to those around him.

Then, with a subtle signal using his heels, the two shot off like lightning, both rider and horse thundering down the road.

I turned sixteen over the winter, though I hardly took notice. The People of the Wood more than made up for my absence by keeping my schedule so busy I hardly had a full night of sleep. The only event worth remembering in the midst of the dreary litany of house calls and visits to the herbalist for more medication was a chance encounter with Jamie in Huntsville.

The month was January, the coldest part of the winter season in the Wood. Ice and snow did somehow penetrate the dark forest and still managed to pepper our village streets and wooded roadways. Frigid air and small gusts of freezing wind were the largest combatants of the season. I had only my thinning short cloak and woolen scarves to protect me and often used whatever pennies I had to buy hot tea or warm cider in the local villages in order to endure the long walks to and from my patients.

It was after one of these particular visits in a little shop in Huntsville that I stepped out into the cold downtown street, grateful for a warm belly and the past few minutes by a fire. I was headed home at the end of a long day and hurried forward without too much consideration of my surroundings, aware only of the darkening sky which predicted increased cold and impending nightfall. Gran had refused to go out today and promised she would have a warm supper for me when I arrived. As I had grown older she provided this benefit less and less, and tonight, I thought, I would be exceedingly grateful for it.

Distracted by these thoughts, I didn't see the dark figure approaching until he was already upon me. Too late, the uneven patches of ice and snow underfoot did not allow me to stabilize myself. The tall stranger was forced to reach both hands out in order to save me from falling.

"Whoa there! I'm sorry — " He stopped as I lifted my face to his and exclaimed with enthusiasm, "If it isn't the good Healer herself — Little Red!"

Steadied now, I stepped back from his grasp, shaking my head. This would be Jamie. Not a stranger after all. I'd known him since we were children. We had attended the same local schoolhouse together until I finished my courses; then I only saw him at village gatherings and events when I had the time to participate, or like this, in chance encounters. I had never paid much attention to him. He was a village boy, full of energy, good teasing and small pranks. Over the years, in all fairness, I had often heard how well-liked he was in Huntsville, popular among the adults as a responsible, yet entertaining young man. He was a man grown now. But I still had no time for him.

"Hello, Jamie." I moved around him and kept walking forward. "Good day to you."

"Red!" He was protesting my indifference. He took a long-legged step or two to catch up to my side. "What did I do to offend you? I'll fix it. Was it the use of *Little Red*? I'll drop it this very moment and never use it again."

"That would be nice," I murmured.

He took a few more hurried steps with me and then shot me a quizzical expression. "You haven't been around much. Even less so than normal, in any case. I hear about your great exploits often enough but never see you."

"Most of my patients this winter have been in the Northern part of the Wood," I explained.

Truthfully, I wished he would just be on his way. Conversation slowed my steps and I was eager to get home.

His breath manifested in a white cloud next to me as he spoke. He was dressed a great deal warmer than I was in a heavy coat, woolen gloves and fur hat. "I'm fortunate to have a position here in Huntsville only two blocks away from home."

He paused, waiting for me to inquire what his work was, but I ignored the invitation. He went on anyway. "I'm an apprentice for the cobbler, Danner. It doesn't earn me much money yet, but it will. I've decided to either take over Danner's business when he retires in a few years, or else save my pennies and start my own in one of the villages up North."

Out of social obligation entirely, I murmured, "How nice for you."

He still wasn't catching the trail of hints I was leaving him… or he was choosing not to. He kept moving in my direction down the street, matching his long steps to my short quick ones. "Your Gran says you were working in the Palace this summer."

Ah. *So that was it.*

I shook my head, not bothering to look over. "You know Gran…"

He did know Gran. She was always talking, and quick to let her neighbors know when something of significance happened to her household. Some individuals, especially the young people in the village who were not as afflicted as their seniors, understood a few of her methods. She loved to exaggerate the details.

"Yes," he agreed, with a short laugh. "I know your Gran. But there was something about this story that struck me. You were gone all summer, and there were rumors from others…"

This made me stop in my tracks entirely and turn to face him. "And why is my business so important to you, Jamie? You seem mighty curious today."

He could have said he was raving curious about the White Palace and its occupants. Perhaps he was. But he didn't. Instead he looked down on me from his lengthy height, completely unbothered by my blunt remarks, and smiled with a confident air. "I like you, Red. Always have. Haven't you figured that out yet?"

Quickly, I smothered my surprise. I hadn't expected that answer. It rang of sincerity and was delivered with a directness I was unaccustomed to.

I considered for a moment. It was true, being the local Healer had aged me somehow, moved me past the behavior I'd seen in village girls my age who held an over-abundance of fascination for kissing, romantic interests, babies and marriage. Gran had a great distaste for the village men (and boys) and had always declared she was opposed to my marrying any of them. These two factors had kept me focused away from them, and my indifference in their presence kept me safe from conversations like this one.

"Well, I guess that would explain a few things about you," I said then saucily.

This made him laugh at once. Apparently Jamie was not among those who were so easily dissuaded.

He had an infectious laugh that rang out. I joined him, unable to contain it. A few villagers, just now leaving a shop across the street, turned and observed us briefly as the sound filled the still wintry air.

Jamie noticed them… or perhaps noticed me taking stock of them. He turned back to me and shrugged laughingly. "I just thought you should know. Then possibly next time we crash in the street and I ask you imposing questions, Red, maybe you'll answer."

He waited for my reaction to this. That merry light in his dark eyes had only deepened with humor.

I gave him a slow amused smile, shaking my head again. "Maybe."

He grinned, and then we parted ways.

Gran heard about the encounter from someone in town only a day later. She probably wouldn't have cared if they hadn't told her Jamie and I were laughing together. This required a clear explanation and she was determined to get it. I had little to tell her, as was the truth, but she still suspected trouble was afoot and declared she much preferred for me to work at the White Palace, safe from masculine interest. Sixteen, she claimed, was a dangerous age.

At these words I found it difficult to believe Gran had ever had an encounter with Fumi or knew his people well enough to recognize his spirit in my ways. I remembered well what Jacobe had said and had often considered this truth in moments like this one, when she and I clashed the greatest. I would have liked to ask her about the areas of her past which I did not know, but I dared not broach it. Something in me — that same inner instinct that had always led me with her and the other villagers — held me silent.

As I left the conversation with her, I thought, with a weary tiredness, that sixteen did not feel like a dangerous age, just another year passing... another year of difficult patients and eternal trots through the forest. Jamie's few harmless words and the single shared laugh had been a little light in the cold darkness. I was greatly looking forward to the White Palace next summer, where things were vastly different.

Spring arrived early a few months later. I was grateful for it, though this did not impact the Wood with much beauty and made no change in my driving schedule. With the change in weather also came seasonal colds and minor illnesses that all the local children and families passed between each other. I was kept busy making rounds and soothing unhappy patients, with no thought on the summer as yet.

So it was a great surprise to me in mid-spring when I exited our little cottage around noon, my basket in hand, and heard a rider thundering down the road from the east. Very few villagers in all of the Wood owned a horse, and even fewer ever rode them with such passion. Still, this peculiarity did not distract me from my purpose. I paused on the edge of our front yard, waiting for the rider to pass before I stepped out into the road.

He slowed as he approached our little house. I knew him at once.

Jacobe's fiery red steed was more recognizable today than he was. Sitting tall and imperial on the horse, Desi's bodyguard was outfitted in a tricorn hat in deep blue, now sitting cock-eyed on the crown of his head. A sweeping cloak in the same color fanned out behind him and trailed over his mount's croup and tail end. Beneath his cloak was a linen scarf bound at his throat and tucked in a pale silken waistcoat that fell below his waist, meeting form-fitting breeches of the same cloth, and heavy knee-length boots. Surprisingly, he was bereft of his axe today and only a simple sword hung from a thin belt at his waist. I'm sure I was staring at him like a child watching a colorful parade ride by. In my wildest imaginations from youth, inspired by the few storybooks our simple school had to offer, I could only imagine the captain of a grand ship or an important nobleman sporting such a look.

The set of flashing painted eyes beneath the hat were still Jacobe's, however. He announced, "You've grown very thin, Red."

I sighed, nodding. "I have not slept much since I saw you last."

"Your patients?"

"Yes." I gave him a frowning smile. "You're *here*."

"We arrived early. Desi has been in a foul mood for weeks and his parents suggested it. I came at once to see when you could begin work."

"Ah." I accepted this, heart pounding suddenly. This was good news for me.

To my surprise, the Huntsman swung one leg over his horse and jumped off. He took the three steps between us in one. "Will you come with me to the Palace now? You need rest."

He towered over me quite intimidatingly, yet I realized in that instant somewhere in the long brutal months since my work at the Palace I had grown unafraid of his powerful physical presence and abrupt manner. I didn't know how this was possible or what had caused it — perhaps because I had spent a great deal of time walking in exhaustion through the wintry forest considering his small kindnesses and those two wondrous months working at the White Palace. But nevertheless, not a trace of hesitation was left within me.

"Yes," I told him. "I will come."

"Where is your grandmother?"

"Out measuring someone for a dress they ordered." I stepped away and moved towards the cottage. "I will leave her a note and fetch my uniform."

"Leave the uniform, Red. We will have new dresses made for you this summer." His eyes fell to my clothing. "You are wearing the same clothes Desi and I found you in last year. Do you not own anything else?"

I answered him honestly. "No. There's hardly been time or money. I'd have to make them myself. I would have worn the uniform, but thought I would need it for this summer and didn't want to soil it. My work is quite tolling on clothing."

"What happened to the money you earned last summer at the Palace?"

I shrugged. "Gran is saving up to open a shop in town. She's hoping to do so by the end of this summer with the wages I earn. This plan will bring in more income for her and will allow me to have my own cottage here. I don't mind. If she moved out, I could tend to some of my patients here and this would make my practice easier to manage."

The Huntsman considered this briefly, grunted, and turned back towards his horse. "She's a seamstress, yet you are dressed like *that*. Leave the note too, Red. I will send a servant from the Palace to tell her."

I obeyed him, grateful to depart so impulsively. The action felt like the shedding of a dead winter skin. In another instant Jacobe had mounted his horse and effortlessly pulled me up behind him. He tied my basket to the horn of his saddle.

"All set?" he asked, as I adjusted the long folds of his magnificent cloak between us.

He wore no belt to cling to this year. I hesitated for an instant.

As if he sensed the reason for this, he added, "You are welcome to hang on any way you like. *Thunder* and I do like speed."

I smiled to myself. We had both learned a little since last summer. Quietly, I leaned forward and placed my hands on either side of his hard mid-riff, gripping the material of his waist-coat, then balanced my chin between his shoulder blades comfortably. He felt warm against the cool spring air around us.

Thunder was dancing restlessly beneath us, past ready.

"All set," I assured him... which instantly inspired Jacobe to wheel the horse around to the east and tear down the empty road towards the Palace.

That summer was very different than the one before it, though no less impacting.

In the first few days of my arrival, Jacobe ordered a small wardrobe for me. I was measured by a tailor and his two assistants, who had obviously been transported from Alameth for this express purpose, and within three days more a handful of dresses and accompanying accessories were delivered. Jacobe instructed me to wear them when and where I pleased.

They were not uniforms, I took careful note. These were simple, beautiful gowns capable of being worn even at home if I chose. Two were made of linen for the summer months — one in egg-shell blue, the other in antique white — and the final two were designed for cooler days by making use of heavy dark cottons. All of them permitted activity and freedom of movement, an additional gesture which I was grateful for. I happily buried away my red scarves and ragged clothing, briefly considered the absurd idea of asking everyone I knew to call me Isobel now, and began at once to wear the new wardrobe at all times.

Even Gran approved. But then, anything issued by the Palace was going to win her approval.

At first sight of me in the blue gown, she grunted and said, "About time you took a little care. You're nearly a woman grown now, not to mention the folks at the Palace are Royalty and you should look your best in their presence. I'm glad they ordered them. Just don't go gettin' any ideas," she added. "The men around here are *hounds*. Steer clear of them, because *they won't be steering clear of you*."

Another change from the previous summer was that Desi's guests were not at the Palace when I arrived. There was no explanation for this, though within a short time I could safely ascertain this was due to the Prince's current frame of mind. I did not see him at all my first week there. Long before I arrived each day he set out for the other side of the lake to hunt — information told to me by Jacobe — and did not return to the Palace until after I had left for the day.

For these reasons there were also fewer servants, and a quiet resided over the Palace and grounds that was both relaxing and new.

I was accustomed to the constant busy activity here, the noise of Desi's guests. As soon as the first day, the Huntsman sent me on long walks or ordered me to lie in the sunlight somewhere on the grounds. His attitude suggested that he did not require accountability or anything else of me except rest. Throughout my time I walked freely all over the immediate property, inside and out of the Palace, often without anyone knowing at all where I was at, delighting simply in the glorious freedom that was suddenly mine without cost.

It was on one such "required" walk that I found myself a week after my arrival, armed with a heavy volume on the subject of Alameth and my little basket, which was just now filled with picnic foods provided by the Palace kitchens. I had chosen the antique white dress today and was feeling deliciously lovely for the first time in my young life, carefree and unfettered after many years of obligation and hard responsibility.

Soon, after a mild amount of searching, I found a quiet spot at the foot of a red oak just on the western edges of the lake and settled there. I stripped myself of my shoes and stockings, buried my toes in the soft cool grass around me, and read until I grew drowsy. The forest was heavily shaded here by a canopy of branches overhead, bereft of the sounds of birds or insects. Brilliant sunlight sparked off the still waters before me. A gentle breeze, faintly tainted by the aroma of newly blossoming flowers, swept over me. How very different this experience was compared to the last several months. A great sense of peace and safety fell upon me. Laying aside the book, I let myself curl up on the blanketed forest floor and finally slept.

I don't know what awakened me. Certainly nothing alarmed me. I simply came awake and aware of my surroundings and opened my eyes.

There was a man standing some feet away, I realized, though even this did not jolt me. He stood under the shadow of a neighboring red oak, leaned against the wide trunk in a relaxed pose with ankles crossed and blue eyes fixed on me. He smiled a handsome smile as soon as he saw my eyes flicker open and register his presence.

"Hello, Red."

I sat up at once and took him in.

Desi had changed in the past year. A quiet had fallen over him, a thoughtful sobriety that was obvious to me even in these few seconds of study. He was also more handsome than ever, there was no denying it. Today he wore a hunter's costume with leather yoke, forest green tunic, and black leather leggings. He was well-built from his training with Jacobe and the physically active life he maintained, certainly more fit than the young men I knew at his age who were lanky and thin, and this showed starkly just now.

It was easy to see what he'd been doing. His brown ankle boots were made with soft cowhide for moving through the forest quietly. At his feet was a leather quiver full of trimmed feathered arrows, while buried in the grass nearby I could *just* see the wooden curve of a bow where he had tossed it down temporarily. I thought the look of a discreet, light-footed archer suited him well in his current mood.

"Hello, Desi," I returned.

"I should have awakened you when I found you, I know," he quickly said, along with a smile, "but you looked so beautiful and peaceful I didn't have the heart to disturb you."

Desi had an easy way about him, more so than anyone I'd met at any age. He could deliver compliments with just the right amount of flattery and flirtation. The young women last summer had adored him for it. I thought possibly this trait came from being a Prince. I also suspected, from watching him many hours last year, that he had a great deal of experience with women for a man so young.

Just as quickly, I was suddenly conscious of my new-found beauty. He had obviously been admiring me when I woke and this was a very new feeling. To cover for this, I quickly reached for my stockings and leather slippers.

"How are you?" I asked. "Jacobe told me you've been hunting."

He straightened and moved towards me, dropping down a foot or two away. "I've been *pretending* to hunt. Really I've just been wasting arrows and brooding about my future." He sounded disgusted with himself.

I turned my head and smiled at him kindly. "You *do* seem rather sober."

At this close distance he took me in again, thoughtfully, eyes sparking. "Where's the red scarf? Or that terrible uniform Jacobe put you in last year? I didn't recognize you at all when I first came upon you. I thought our forest might be inhabited by a fairy, or a mer-maid who had climbed out of the waters for a brief nap."

I smiled. Now that my feet were properly clad, I stood, planning to gather my things and leave.

"I have abandoned the scarf for good," I told him with satisfaction.

The Prince released some murmur I didn't catch and I looked down on him with a quizzical smile, wordlessly asking for an explanation.

He shook his head up at me in a quiet sort of wonder. "You are really beautiful, Red. I don't know if anyone has ever told you that, but you are. You were so hidden before. Why do you keep your hair so short?"

If he hadn't asked a question of me I would have been struck speechless entirely. I could feel my face flush and heat rise to my cheeks. He was right; no one had ever been so straightforward with me, particularly not someone as attractive as I considered him to be.

My hands reached for my hair, which dangled at chin-level flat and straight in the color of coal. "It won't grow any longer," I explained.

Desi was sharp and experienced enough to see my discomfort over his attentions. He smiled a little to himself.

"No matter," he said gently, "It doesn't detract from you at all. Shall I help you with your things?"

3.

That summer was destined to be the most eventful one I'd had in life — not because of outward adventure, or new inspirational discoveries, or threat of personal danger. Those years would come, and would soon be upon me. This year was eventful because my heart came alive, slowly at first, but then with great rushing momentum, rather like a trickle of water that grows into a mighty river thundering downstream at torrential speed. If I hadn't before been aware that there was a heart within myself capable of admiration, of longing, of love and even passion, then I certainly became aware that season.

Desi was the cause. The one who, in his desperate need to avoid staring into the face of his future, saw a wondrous distraction and decided I could save him. I was his deliverance, and he was the most glorious being I had ever encountered in my humble little existence. He brought me to life.

Jacobe had to know what was happening. Not even a blind man could overlook it, though Desi and I were ourselves too young to recognize the truth at first. Love in all its glory was upon us before we knew it.

At first the Huntsman held his silence. As was his way, he merely watched. The Prince and I spent every day together, laughing, talking. We hiked; and Desi attempted to teach me archery; and we explored every room in the Palace. We filled our days with youthful fun, giving no thought to what tomorrow held or how we would face it.

And Jacobe watched. Sometimes from a distance, sometimes absent altogether, trusting in our innocence in those moments even if we were ignorant of what was happening within our hearts. When I was in his company alone, Jacobe behaved towards me as he always had — resolute, informative and kind. But his eyes held a thoughtful expression often enough in those days, calculating the behavior of his charges, our growing closeness, the obvious chemistry between us.

He did not speak until the day Desi and I went boating on the lake.

This activity was my idea originally. The Prince pounced on it with enthusiasm and for an afternoon went in search of a dinghy he swore was located somewhere on the property. After some doing, he managed to find it and put one of the capable man-servants at the Palace to work preparing the vessel for sea-worthiness.

Only a day later the wooden skiff was prepared and ready, and the two of us launched our craft mid-morning from the shallow waters near the lake terrace with spirits high. We were in full view of the back windows of the Palace, but gave little thought to this as we rowed happily around the sun-drenched lake. I had never had such an abundance of time or play, and Desi — who had experienced an over-abundance — enjoyed my delight over everything. He was easy to share the moment with.

After some time, Desi rowed us to the center of the lake and we settled there temporarily. He was caught up in telling me of a hunting expedition he'd been on with Jacobe a few years before in which they had tracked and killed a savage bear in the mountainous regions of Alameth. To properly demonstrate his story, at the point where he described the bear's death by a hail of arrows, Desi stood in the little watercraft and declared the tragic ending with a loud voice. Quite unbecoming of a Prince, he had earlier stripped himself of his shirt, boots and socks as relief from the heat and now stood looking like a half-naked wild man.

I laughed at him, which he had been hoping for and encouraged him even further. At one point he gave a small jump in the skiff boat and I shrieked laughingly as the little vessel bobbed wildly.

Unable to resist the temptation, Desi repeated the jump with an even louder shout, but this time the rowboat retaliated by turning on its side, sending us both tumbling into the lake waters.

This accident should have made for an easy recovery. Desi was a strong swimmer; I was adequate. The small boat had only to be turned over, which the Prince was also capable of, and together we could throw ourselves back into the little craft. Even the water itself was calm and the temperature wonderfully refreshing after the few hours of sitting in the sun. But as soon as my body tumbled into its depths and I began the scramble back to the surface, I felt a resistance against my ankles. I struggled against this briefly, not certain what was happening, but the pull grew even stronger, dragging me down into greater depths.

At first I reached down to feel if I had become entangled in something which I could loose myself from, but there was nothing there. I looked around wildly, eyes wide open, breath held. The waters at this level were dark and visibility was low. *What could possibly be happening?*

Again I struggled hard, using my hands and the strength of my body to fight towards the surface, but the invisible leash held me firm in its iron grip, continuing a long slow drag to the bottom of the lake. Panic began to quickly build within me, the uncertainty of not knowing what to do or how to do it. My heartbeat thundered in my ears. I wondered how long it was before I ran out of breath... before Desi realized I had not surfaced and began to search for me... before I lost consciousness altogether. I wanted to scream, but couldn't.

A dozen imaginations flashed through my mind as I realized the true danger of my situation. *Gran getting the news... Desi's devastation and self-blame... Jacobe's fury and shock... My life coming to an abrupt end, without any future at all...* I would have sobbed hysterically if the situation had allowed for it.

Then, just as I felt hope giving way within me, a brilliant light appeared in the murky depths before me. A face formed in the cloud of light; strong hands reached for my arms.

I recognized this face, I told myself. He looked like Desi. But he was not Desi. This man was not young. He was ancient, timeless, possessing a face that held many secrets.

His hands were gentle; I could see he was smiling. *How lovely he was...* A great peace came over me and I stopped struggling.

I could feel myself losing consciousness, almost spent of breath. The fight to free myself had required a great deal of my small quantity of air. *Perhaps I was experiencing a delusion due to lack of air...*

This thought was the last one I remembered before the world around me went black.

I came to consciousness slowly, seeing flashes of light and murky indiscernible images, hearing a voice speak to me but unable to determine what it was saying. I lay there and allowed sentience to happen, not struggling against it.

After a moment the light morphed into the brilliant sky overhead... into the hard ground beneath my soaked exhausted body... and the author of the voice became Desi, who was kneeling over me in a desperate panic.

"Red, don't die on me. Don't die on me, Red. Don't die on me..."

He was soaking wet; strands of his hair dripped on my face. I opened my eyes fully and blinked at him.

He saw this at once and broke into a small relieved sob. *"Red —thank Fumi —"*

Then a commanding voice crashed over him. "Is she all right?"

This was Jacobe now, who was suddenly towering behind the Prince with a stern expression. He was staring down at me. I found I could not respond to either one of them.

Desi turned at the sound of his voice. "She's conscious," he said, though he sounded worried.

"Move aside, Desi."

The Prince was quickly obedient, standing back, while Jacobe stooped at my side and took me in. "Red? Do you know who I am?"

I tried smiling at him but was uncertain if I was successful. I did find my voice, however. The soft words emerged. *"Hello. Where did you come from?"*

Even the immovable Huntsman looked a little relieved after hearing me speak. Still, he was insistent. "Say my name, Red. Please."

The words were there more easily now. *"Jacobe, Jacobe, Jacobe."*

This response made him break into a smile, quickly there, just as quickly gone. His strong voice lowered. "Can you sit?"

"I think so."

He assisted me as I made the attempt, and then kept one steadying hand on my shoulder as I sat upright. Recent memory was beginning to return now — boating with Desi, the fall overboard, the dark shadows pulling me down into the depths of the lake waters. I shivered suddenly. "Some — something tried to drown me."

Jacobe answered gravely, "I know."

He exchanged a quick glance with Desi, who still stood hovering on my other side. The Prince's expression was impossible for me to see from this vantage point.

"Something Evil from the Wood has trespassed and made its home in the waters," Jacobe explained.

Desi murmured, "It wasn't there last summer when everyone went swimming. I'm sorry, Red. I managed to get free of it."

Jacobe nodded. "I will see to it right away. Meanwhile, Red, you need to rest for awhile at the Palace. We should get you out of the sun." He paused, obviously considering the best course of action.

"I can walk," I assured him.

"It's quite a distance, I think not."

"Could we call the Palace and it would appear?" I wondered why this wasn't suggested immediately.

Jacobe shook his head. "You are too exhausted for that kind of transition. So the only thing to be done is — "

I remembered nothing after that. The darkness of sleep fell over me as quickly as the Huntsman's words cut off.

In my dreams I had the strangest sensation of movement, as if my body was being gently rocked or jostled. Or carried. And then I was awakening again... this time to find myself in a private room at the Palace.

The small room they had brought me to was elegant and richly decorated, as all the rooms in the Palace were. Long windows surrounding the head of the four-poster bed were thrown open; a warm summer breeze wafted over my head and circulated through the quiet bedroom.

I understood immediately what had transpired, why I was in this room and where I was at. Fumi's face lingered in my mind, and I realized he had been the one who saved me, the one who had reached into the black depths of Evil and pulled me free. This left me in quiet awe. Why had he come? Why had he rescued me? What did this mean?

I remembered too, faintly, that after his rescue I floated naturally to the top of the waters. This was when Desi found me and pulled me to the shore.

As he tried to revive me on the tree-filled banks of the lake, I could now remember some of Desi's words to me — words that had spilled over me in a mindless swirl and were lost at the time. The desperate situation had forced out of him what had been growing unknowingly in his heart these past several weeks. He admitted his love for me, and begged me to return to him. I was the best thing that had ever happened to him, he said; no one had ever filled his life with such joy.

Remembering this now, I was moved. Tears threatened to spill. No one had ever spoken such words of gratitude and love to me. Gran's love was expressed through her acts of service and her faithfulness to provide for me until I could take care of myself. Even through this she had been too troubled and far too busy to make her motivations clear. I had had to guess her heart. Desi's tender words were like balm, like a sweet nectar that filled my soul and flooded my being. As a Prince with many opportunities, he could have loved anyone, but he chose *me*. I was flattered, I was honored, I was baffled, and I was softened to the core. *He loved me...*

As I stirred slightly, a servant emerged at the foot of the bed and darted away, obviously dashing off to report the news that I had awakened. This caused me to blink a few times and move each of my limbs a little, experimenting. Strength had returned while I slept, thankfully. I realized someone had stripped me of my blue linen dress and re-clothed me in a long cotton nightgown.

I also understood — without knowing the time or having the ability to properly read the intensity of sunlight that was pouring in through the soft curtains around me — that I had been asleep for some time. The Huntsman, somehow, had put me to sleep.

In only a short time Desi entered the room. I heard him come and smiled at him as he strode, soft-footed, to the side of the large bed. He was dressed now in dark pants and a pale blouse, plain comfortable fare after the troubling activities of the day. His sun-kissed face still reflected that trouble, but he took my hand with relief.

"Red."

I was suddenly shy, suddenly nervous, but my joy at the sight of him over-rode this. I smiled fully and sat up. "Desi — all is well now. See? I'm fine."

This caused him to smile a little, though the cloud did not lift entirely. He sat on the edge of the bed facing me and brought my hand to his lips. He brushed my knuckles with a sweeping kiss. "I'm glad you're all right," he said quietly. "You were floating face-down when I found you. I — I didn't know —"

"The danger is past now," I assured him. "I can feel my strength has returned and my mind is clear, both good indications that no harm has been done."

He seemed to accept this. He nodded. Then his expression slowly changed to a quiet frown. "The Evils here are not in Alameth, Red. I forget sometimes, though Jacobe has warned me enough. This is the first time One has slipped over the wall. I should have paid closer attention."

"You couldn't have known, Desi," I told him, then reconsidered my words. I did not know what Alamethens were capable of, after all. "Could you?"

Desi shook his head and shrugged. Troubled. Guilt-ridden. "Jacobe tells me I could have — *should* have. He's been filling my ears while you slept."

I recognized now the source of trouble. And my instincts told me there was more, more than he was saying. Jacobe had appeared out of nowhere as I came to consciousness on the shoreline. It was possible that he had overheard the Prince's confession to me.

I asked quietly, "What else did he say?"

Desi's gaze cut across mine. Took in my face and form. Restlessly, he stood to his feet and moved away from the bed. "Do you really want to know? It involves you."

"Yes."

He moved to the window nearest me next to the bed, turned back the pale curtains in his way, and glanced outside momentarily. "He thinks I've begun to single you out among the rest of the girls I've known. Possibly among all women. He warned me that you weren't like the others, in the case I hadn't already realized it. He said you have a very un-spent heart, and a soul that is older and wiser than most; he claims we are vastly out-matched. I should take care with you, he said, not mislead you any, either through words or deeds. He didn't think I was serious enough, and certainly shouldn't be about you. And of course he rebuked me royally for endangering both of our lives today. The Evil you encountered could have done serious damage to you even if it hadn't been able to drown you." He glanced back at the bed broodingly. "He doesn't approve of my pursuit of you, Red. Not that he approves of any of my decisions recently," he added dryly.

My heart leapt at these last words, I couldn't help myself. "*Are* you pursuing me?"

Desi was not like other people I had known, not even like the Huntsman, who held his thoughts as long as he could and rarely expressed emotion. The Prince's heart was nearer to the surface. He was a dreamer. Privately, I didn't think this quality in him made him unwise; I thought this made him a beautiful soul. He had not been hurt or injured by life. I liked to think even if injury did happen in his future he would still keep dreaming, unable to change or harden.

The Prince turned to me now and took me in for a moment. "I —
I want to be careful what I say to you, Red. Jacobe's words — he's
always been right about everything. *Irritatingly*." He added with a dry
mutter, "My parents trust him far more than they trust me."

I said nothing to this. He hadn't answered the question. So I
simply waited.

Desi knew I was waiting. He broke into a laughing smile. He
turned away from the window and resumed his place on the edge of
the bed.

At last he confessed quietly, "I will always love you, Red. I know
myself well enough to know that. It will last far beyond today, and
beyond whatever the future may hold. You see me better than anyone
has."

These sweet words naturally brought a deep emotion to my face,
and Desi quickly moved closer. His warm arms surrounded me;
gently, he kissed my forehead and the bridge of my nose. Then I
found myself responding, caught up in a warm tide I had never before
experienced. He felt like gentle sunshine to a parched soul raised in
the dark.

Sensing my compliance, his mouth moved for mine. These were
simple kisses that slowly deepened. As they did, his hands moved to
my face and cupped it.

I had no idea if Desi had had much practice kissing, but his heart
was in his affection and I trembled at the feel of it. In return, I gave
him all the love we had grown in our little time together.

At last he pulled away. Smiled into my eyes. He put his head on
my forehead, hands still cupping my face, and we both closed our eyes
for a moment.

"I love you too, Desi," I murmured. "You're so easy to love."

Two days passed before I had the opportunity to speak to Jacobe. I had deliberately looked for a moment when we could speak alone and Desi was safely distracted elsewhere. The Prince still had obligatory physical drills and other measures he rehearsed daily, both as a way to maintain his fitness level and in preparation for his military training and service beginning in the fall. Sometimes I watched him; on this day I excused myself and returned to the Palace to locate the Huntsman.

As I entered the back entrance to the Palace and paused just inside its doors to allow my eyes to adjust to the dim lighting, I realized how familiar I had become with the mansion and its grounds. I had no official place here, but somehow, in spite of that, it had become home to me. In the evenings, when Jacobe once again swung me up on the back of *Thunder* for our traditional jaunt back, I often had to force myself to return to the cottage and to Gran. Especially now, I had no desire to be anywhere else but here.

I suspected that the Huntsman was located in the library. This was a comfortable room where he could often be found during the warm summer afternoons indulging in reading material or penning letters. Desi told me the Huntsman kept a busy correspondence with many people from his past, as well as the King and Queen, when he was not on demanding assignments.

The library was a wide open room filled with long rows of heavy volumes and ancient books on two levels, located in the northeastern side of the White Palace. This room was lit by the inclusion of at least a dozen windows on the lake-side of the room, revealing the gardens beyond and a portion of the heavy forest. Beautiful arm-chairs, foot tables and stained glass lamps were assembled in little clusters throughout. This was called the Prince's Library, I knew, due to the arched wooden door that stood closed in the center of the floor-to-ceiling bookshelves. Through that unassuming door was Desi's private chambers — a security precaution that had been installed when he was just an infant.

The Huntsman was seated strategically. He had chosen a low arm-chair facing the lake and the gardens where he could view the property, also located under a window where the warm sun directly filtered through and lit the pages he was reading. Today he was dressed as he had been the first day he came for me this summer. The tricorn hat and heavy cloak were laid aside nearby, exposing his bent inked face and broad shoulders. Strangely, he looked as though he belonged here in a quiet, refined library, though from his rugged appearance and fierce manner I would have thought he'd always prefer *Thunder* and a long stretch of empty road.

He looked up at once upon my entrance to his left. "Red."

I smiled at him. My fear of him had never returned, even now after knowing his disapproving thoughts on Desi's interest in me. My only secret wish was that he would talk more. It was obvious that there were many things he knew which I didn't.

"I came to speak with you," I told him.

He did not seem surprised by this. Using a long-stemmed feather close by, he marked his place in the heavy volume he held and slid the book aside next to him in the chair. He motioned towards another deep chair to his left. "Please, sit."

I took the seat obediently, adjusted my linen skirts and settled back, studying him briefly. His eyes looked less wild today, his manner calm. With elbows resting on the chair's arms at his sides, he had locked both hands and was looking at me with a quiet patience. It was a good time to ask questions of him, I could see that.

"I was curious about how you suddenly appeared at the lake the other day," I announced.

He gave no change in expression at this. "Desi didn't tell you?"

"No, why would he?"

If the Huntsman could be wry beneath that deadpan expression, he supplied ample amounts of it with his next words. "I thought he told you everything."

A small smile pulled at my lips and gave way. I was grateful my cheeks did not burn and betray me just then. "He didn't tell me the answer to this, so I must assume he does not tell me *everything*."

Some thought crossed his mind, but it was obvious he didn't intend to express it. Jacobe merely shrugged as the beginning to the conversation. "I am not just a bodyguard."

"I assumed."

He half-smiled at my response. "You're getting bolder, Red. I am what they call a Dimensioner. I'm capable of teleporting myself and others between dimensions. For a few years that was almost exclusively what I did — escort kings and important individuals between Alameth and other countries. Eventually some of them asked me to teach them to hunt and we would find forests and other exotic places to hunt large game. Now, of course, my duties to Desi's parents have extended well beyond that. I am often brought in to keep an eye on certain individuals, or to escort significant persons to Alameth at the appropriate time, for Fumi's sake. I happen to also be a trainer and a bodyguard to the Royal Family."

His information was fascinating and made him further fascinating, but I only acknowledged it with a nod, not stopping. This was how it always was with me — I held my questions until they burst out like a hailstorm of arrows. Afterward, long after the conversation had ended, was when I would take all the information and absorb it thoroughly.

"And the Evil in the lake waters? You said it came from the Wood. Desi recently said there were many evils there. I heard you allude to this as well on the first day I met you. Why haven't I seen them before? I've lived in the Wood my entire life."

Jacobe did not hesitate. "I have often asked myself that same question. I'm not certain why you have thus far been immune from harm or contact with the many Evils that exist here. I'm also not certain why you nearly drowned the other day, suddenly. This shows you are not entirely immune, unfortunately."

"And do these evils have an appearance? How would I recognize them?"

"In these woods most of them look like giant wolves."

I shivered suddenly. "I've never seen them."

Jacobe's eyes were on me with quiet intensity. "*Yes*. Another mystery I cannot explain. I've seen many of them during our stays here on the occasion that I left the White Palace property."

"And they didn't attack you?"

His answer was succinct. "I've killed a few."

I asked myself why I had even asked the question. He was the Huntsman. Of course he'd killed a few. He was probably trying to spare me and had no doubt killed a far greater amount than that.

"Fumi rescued me," I blurted out. "He appeared at the bottom of the lake and released me from the Evil."

This news, though shocking to me, did not have a visible effect on the Huntsman. "I suspected as much."

"You did?"

"There was no other way you could have survived, frankly." Also another succinct answer.

I fell silent. Too many questions crowded my mind now, many of them unable to be expressed. I was baffled.

As if he suspected my state of mind, Jacobe added quietly, "You're special, Red, as I have said before. Probably more special than all of us can fathom. Be patient with yourself and the process of maturity. It will become clearer with time. Fumi will ensure that it does."

As it happened, he did not bring up the subject of Desi that afternoon. I was grateful, as I thought on it in retrospect. Not only would such a conversation have been too much after a full load of surprising revelation, but I would have had no thoughts to give him on the matter. I certainly couldn't provide him with any assurances that the Prince and I would not grow closer. We had already given our hearts... and there was no stopping the avalanche that had been set in motion, crashing and burying everything in its way.

Nothing more eventful happened as the summer wound to a close. Even Gran was quiet, her earlier concerns mollified now that I was safely removed at the Palace. She had no eyes to see the change in me and was instead distracted with her fall plans to move to town. She had already found an unused shop and had begun to ready it for business.

Hearing her evening updates, I began to think towards my own immediate future. Desi, too, began to consider the fall and its obligations. Naturally we desired to be together, but the circumstances had not presented any options but the hard truth that sacrifices must be made for both of us. For the first time, I dreaded returning to my practice and a weary life in the sunless Wood. Desi grew restless and irritable — never with me, but with Jacobe, who always had some instruction to give or a Royal message to deliver. The Prince grumbled nearly every time he saw the man.

There was no real way to soothe him. I understood well the challenge of accepting what is and forcing your soul to do what cannot be found in your heart, with little hope for another kind of future. I had fewer options than Desi and had tasted less freedom, so the idea was not as difficult for me. The Prince had little faith he could be a good king, given that he resisted all of its preparations and the dutiful life it required. He brooded about this constantly.

Jacobe began mentioning their return to Alameth more frequently, briefly at first to help prepare us, then with more insistence. The King and Queen had sent several messages which Desi conveniently ignored pertaining to his military duties and their expectations of him. Jacobe was not willing to let this pass by for very long.

One morning, after the Huntsman had delivered me to the Palace and had wordlessly disappeared into its depths as he normally did, I sought Desi out. I found him on the lake terrace as I did every morning, waiting for me. Today he was especially brooding and discontent; he filled my ears at once with a fight that had occurred between he and Jacobe the night before.

"I think we will never agree, he and I," he stormed.

He paced like a caged lion in front of me as I sat in the shade of the familiar cottonwood. The sun, already high, burned hot in the cloudless blue sky. Not even a gentle wind sweeping up from the lake helped bring any relief to the intense temperature.

"Jacobe has always been so vastly different than I am," he declared angrily. "*He* should have been my father's son. He always pleases the King, while I have *never* pleased him. You should see them together. The two laugh together even, if you can imagine that." Desi paused in his steps and snorted scornfully at the heavens. "I've never made my father laugh. I doubt I've ever brought him any joy at all."

I was quiet, watching him, listening. His face was red from the heat, and dark from emotion.

"It is entirely unfair that I am Prince. I have no choice in the matter. I've been told repeatedly it's the law that I should inherit — a law which is not even in the true spirit of Alameth or would have ever been carried out by Fumi. If I had *any* place to go, Red, I would." His anger had quickly taken on a darker note. "I'd run as hard and as fast as I could if there was some place to go. I'd never return to Alameth, *never*."

I had detected over the summer that he was much closer to his mother and quickly murmured, trying to distract him, "Does your mother have any thoughts on all of this?"

His voice burned with heat. "She has tried before to convince my father that another plan would be a better one for me, but he is immovable. Since then she has chosen to stand with him in his insistence that I follow this road out to the throne. Now she simply appeases me. I haven't spoken to her in weeks," he snapped.

I fell silent entirely at this. He had not expressed any of these thoughts through the summer. We had only had eyes for each other and that had been enough to hold his frustration at bay. Now, I made the choice not to add anything to the conversation. These matters were far outside of my experience, and something told me it was unwise for me in particular to interfere with the destiny of kings and kingdoms.

"*Jacobe.*" Desi was muttering again. His long-legged pacing took him to the edge of the terrace and back twice before he added more. "When I become king, I'm going to send the man on some mission in the most remote location I can find and fabricate ridiculous reasons to keep him there. *For years.*"

He didn't mean it. At least not this part. I knew him well enough to know that. Beneath his resentment and the restlessness caused by his impending future, Desi admired the Huntsman. The young Prince had become the man he was in large part due to Jacobe's teaching and companionship over the years. It had been obvious to me all summer how much the two enjoyed the company of the other man, even in spite of the clashes between them and frequent scoldings from Jacobe. They were, indeed, like brothers.

It took some time for Desi to cool that day. Little things set him off. I debated briefly whether to return home early and allow him time to think by himself, but he did settle eventually and we distracted ourselves in the library where the temperature was cooler. Thankfully, Jacobe was not in here today.

After some time of reading separately in silence, Desi grew bored and threw down his book, glancing over at me where I was seated in a chair apart from him. He didn't speak for a time, watching me. "You are so beautiful, Red."

He was, I had learned quickly, endlessly fascinated with me. I looked up from my book and smiled at him. "And you are terribly handsome."

He broke into a grin at this.

"*Desi —*"

This new, authoritative voice caused both of us to start slightly and turn towards the open door some distance behind Desi, where Jacobe stood within its frame. He was a tall strong figure that shrank even this sizable room with his presence. At that moment his face read that he had just heard the little interchange between us.

"I need to speak with you," he added.

While Desi had less self-control when it came to disguising his emotion, Jacobe carried a tension in these moments that was so cool as to be frightening. He was always reminding me in small ways what a dangerous man he was.

"I thought we discussed everything there needed to be discussed," Desi argued testily. "What else could you possibly have to say?"

"Apparently I have more," the Huntsman replied coolly. "I need to speak with you."

Growling, Desi jumped to his feet and stomped towards the doorway. "Fair warning, Red," he snarled, as the two departed together, "This could take awhile."

It did take awhile. So long, in fact, that I went in search of them. Outside of the library was a Great Room that extended the full depth of the mansion from front door to the back wall. From this, multiple exits led to different hallways and rooms of the Palace. I paused a moment and listened. There was no sound, no movement. Even the spare few servants working this summer had gone quiet, buried in some other part of the mansion. My instincts told me to check the stables, and I exited the double front doors and stepped out into the courtyard beyond. I had noticed that Jacobe took Desi out here for discussion if he thought the conversation would turn heated. He preferred that none of the household staff hear the words exchanged between them.

Sure enough, as I crossed the courtyard to the long low stables, I could hear their two voices raised in disagreement. They were located somewhere farther down, inside one of the stalls.

Jacobe's voice was, naturally, the more calm of the two. "She is not for you," he was arguing. "Red is not a queen. And her destiny is certainly not at your side."

I found a place against the outside stable wall and stood listening. These first words stung. This surprised me, seeing as I already knew he disapproved. I also had great confidence that the Huntsman valued and respected me. And they still stung.

They caused an angry burst from Desi as well. "Well, I'm not a king!"

"Desi —" Jacobe was warning him with that tone.

The Prince knew he could not win this point and changed tactics. "Doesn't Red have a say in her future? She's in love with me."

"You're certain of that?"

"More certain than anything."

The Huntsman was dangerously cool again. He was angry, I realized. "Then I predict many difficult years for both of you, Desi, unfortunately. You must still carry out your military training, and there are many more Royal obligations in your future after that. Red will be left here waiting for you."

"I could take her to live in the Palace at Alameth!" the Prince snapped.

"Yes, you could. And she will live there for some time as a complete stranger in a foreign land. Alameth is no easy place to adjust to without guidance, and there will be additional expectations required of her as your future bride. She won't even begin to know what these are. Have you considered these things at all?"

Desi was not prepared to give up yet. "The King and Queen will help her —"

Jacobe cut him off. "They will not be interested in the object of this year's summer romance. You know that's exactly how they will view it too, no matter if you are both very serious or not."

Desi snarled, "Then you can help her — You know her, you know Alameth — If you encourage them, they will listen to you —"

But Jacobe gave a brief laugh, though not one of true amusement. "I think not. I'm not endorsing this for you, or for her. Red deserves better."

These last words were said like a whip, and Desi must have felt them as such. He snapped out, "Better than me, you mean!"

Jacobe's tone did not flinch. "Yes. That's exactly what I mean."

An eerie silence fell then. I sensed even from this distance and in complete blindness to the two that Desi was considering coming to blows with his bodyguard. I could also imagine Jacobe's narrowed eyes and cold expression daring him to try, while half-way hoping he would. My heart was beating in my ears. *What would I do if the two began pummeling on each other?*

Desi made another choice, however. After a few icy moments of complete stillness, he snarled hoarsely, "*You* — are not my father!"

"No, I most certainly am not. You'd know it if I was your father in this moment," Jacobe growled back.

And then Desi was stalking out, away, down the wide runway that separated the two stables. He passed my position against the outside wall without seeing me and stormed across the courtyard.

I called out for him. He stopped short, turned round and caught sight of me. His face was thunderous. "I'm sorry if you heard any of that, Red. I'm sorry — for everything." Horrible guilt swept over his face... and then he was gone, spinning back around, gaining speed until he was running into the forest on this side of the gardens, like a mad man trying to escape the ghosts that haunted him.

The following day Jacobe didn't come. I rose early, as was my usual habit, dressed, said goodbye to Gran who rode away into town on some important mission, and waited at the usual time for the Huntsman to show. He had never once been late or absent. But today, *Thunder* and his master did not make an appearance.

This immediately gave me cause to be concerned. Yesterday had ended abruptly with Desi's disappearance into the woods. Jacobe had emerged, clouded and tense, and suggested that I return home early. He'd ridden me home with nary a word, and dropped me off in a distracted frame of mind.

And now, he had not arrived.

Mid-morning I finally decided to walk to the Palace and see for myself what was happening. There had to be some legitimate reason for Jacobe's unexplained tardiness — another fact even more concerning than his absence. His unknown reason frightened me before I ever knew its name.

Gran had taken our single horse, so I set out on foot. The day was gray and overcast, humid in the Wood as it always was. I took the lack of sunlight as a bad omen and hurried as quickly as my feet would allow without breaking into a run, which I refused to do. I would not panic, I told myself. There was a perfectly reasonable explanation for today's break in Jacobe's routine... and I was determined to meet it head on.

It was nearing noon by the time I saw the walls of the Palace arise in the distance. *That walk is far greater in length when one isn't atop a four-legged horse,* I thought to myself. Within a few moments more I approached the gates, stopped, and waited. Nothing happened.

I had always secretly suspected Jacobe held some invisible power that opened them, but had never asked him about this. I supposed today — and the fact that the massive gates weren't opening no matter how long I stood here — proved my suspicions. From there, I was at a loss as to what to do next. I could jump and shout, I reasoned; maybe that would garner someone's attention from within the Palace walls. Or I could return home and wait until Jacobe brought me the news I was seeking. I had confidence in him; he would ensure that I understood what had happened.

The latter choice was the one I made that morning. I was just turning back for home and moving from the gates when I heard them begin to open. This startled me. I turned round once more... in time to see Jacobe already riding through the partial opening atop *Thunder.* He was wearing his infamous gladiator's costume again, with the sweeping red cloak fanning out behind him.

He saw me at once and said with surprise, "I was just coming to find you. How long have you been here?"

"I just arrived."

He nodded, accepting this. One hand extended out for me as he brought *Thunder* alongside where I stood. "Climb on. We'll go inside the Palace walls and talk."

I detected nothing in particular about his mood or tone. I was only just now developing the ability to read him after two summers in his company, and today he gave nothing away for me to run with. Obedient, I used his hand and allowed him to swing me up behind him on the saddle. Once he could feel my grip locked in his belt and my chin between his shoulder blades, he heeled the horse back around to the open gates and shot through them.

I had no idea what to expect next. As the Huntsman pulled *Thunder's* rein to a halt before the statue of Fumi and wordlessly helped me dismount, I realized I was holding my breath. I quickly stepped towards the fountain, which poured water from Fumi's hands at all times, and took a moment to breathe in its shadow. Behind me, Jacobe dismounted more slowly and then joined me, also staring up at the statue before us. The sun had parted the clouds on this side of the wall and was streaming down on us as we stood here in the courtyard. My companion was silent for a long moment.

"I have something to tell you, Red," he announced.

Even quiet, the Huntsman was strong. His voice held authority as consistently as Fumi's fountain flowed with water.

I turned to him bravely and lifted my face to his. "Tell me quickly, please."

His eyes were dark — darker than usual — and he stared down at me with an unusual expression I could not define as he made the announcement. "I was late this morning because Desi left in the night with all the belongings he brought with him for the summer. I don't know if this is one of the things the Prince told you, but in the case he hasn't — he is unable to teleport, but I did teach him long ago how to travel back and forth from Alameth. He has never attempted it before, however. I followed him there to find him and soon discovered he had joined his regiment early. The next step, of course, was to notify his parents, which took some time as well. They had much to say on the matter, as you can imagine." He paused, still looking down on me with that strange expression, careful with his next words. "I did try and persuade him to return, Red, at least to say his goodbyes. I thought he owed you at least that. But he refused. His regiment plans to depart from Alameth early and immediately take up his training in another land they use for these exercises. It will be impossible for him to return, even for a visit home, for several years."

It could have been worse. Desi could have run off and disappeared. He could have been injured, kidnapped or killed. Instead, he had bowed his head and tucked his tail, resigned his rebellion, and taken up his duty. This impacted no one but me.

I was numb; I felt nothing. Not even the faintest emotion stirred in that moment. I simply stood there, my thoughts blank.

Jacobe naturally held the explanation for this. Quietly, he said, "This will be a shock to you, I know. I knew it would be. Desi's actions grieved me greatly for your sake. I wish there was something I could do to change this for you."

I still said nothing, not moving. There were no questions or insecurities for my soul to ask. I knew what came next. The answer was plain and clear. I would return home, the Huntsman would close the White Palace, and we would all resume our lives as though nothing happened.

Jacobe came to his next thought slowly. "Red, the King and Queen have an assignment for me they wish for me to begin at once. I, too, must fulfill my duty. During my return from Alameth this morning I tried to think of solutions for you, but none have presented themselves to me. I do not have the kind of lifestyle or resources to provide some place where you could start a new life of your own, away from the Wood. The people and places I know — the resources I have — are for other kinds of performances, not domestic needs. Sadly, I can't soothe this trouble for you or change your circumstance. That is the terrible fact of the matter."

It was too soon for me to consider these thoughts, too soon after the shock of what Desi had done. But I understood they must be said; he wanted to ensure that I knew he had tried, he had wanted to, and the honest truth that had come of it. There was no changing the inevitable.

I knew I should speak. At some point I was going to have to speak. I shook my head, then cleared my throat with a small cough when I discovered it had closed on me.

Jacobe's hand reached out for my arm and gripped it in a strong warm grasp. He had never touched me before. "Red, perhaps we should find a place to sit — "

I shook his hand off, shaking my head once more. "No, there's no sense dragging it out. We both know what needs to happen. I'm a

Healer. I've had many conversations like this one with families whose loved one is dying. It is best that they accept as quickly as they can and move on with their lives."

The Huntsman's eyes were still upon me, though his quiet commanding tone never wavered. "I find myself deeply uncomfortable leaving you here in Hadithi, particularly in the Wood. You've always been safe, there's no denying it, but still..."

I held my ground now, finding the strength from somewhere. "Fumi saved me before when I needed him. You said yourself there was something rare about me. There is obviously some destiny in my future which he is preserving. He will come to my aid again if I need him, won't he?"

Slowly, almost reluctantly, Jacobe agreed. "*Yes*. All of that is true. You have only to call his name and he will deliver you."

I nodded, as if that settled it. I couldn't smile up at him with any assurance, but I could sound resolved and determined. "Very well then. We know what must be done."

I almost choked on these last words, but stopped myself forcibly and smothered the pain. There would be time enough for crying later, I told myself. Now was the time to accept the truth with courage and do the hard part of leaving the White Palace, probably forever.

Jacobe was silent for a long moment. He glanced off, away, staring at Fumi's statue and the spilling water, then returning to me. He was making his decision now. One of his hands reached for a small sachet dangling from his belt, untied this with nimble fingers that did not require him to look, and extended the little pouch to me.

"Your wages," he said.

I took this, nodding again, and stood weighing it in my hands. This gesture was the final one.

"I'll take you home," he announced, to my bent head.

"No." I didn't look up at him, but my tone was set and clear. "I need the walk. I will walk home myself."

I knew he didn't agree; I could feel the objection emanating from his person. But he didn't protest, respecting my decision. "Very well. If that's what you prefer." He paused again. Our conversation was filled with heavy pauses now. "I wish you well, Red. I wish you every happiness you can find."

These words were numbing too, I discovered. There was no happiness I could find. If the Wood held happiness, I would have already found it.

I could only nod. I couldn't look up. I didn't have enough courage for that. "Farewell, Huntsman. Be safe."

As I took the first step away from him, he called out my name abruptly and said, "I forgot in the haste of the morning. Desi gave me a note for you." He was already reaching into a leather pouch at his belt and now pulled a folded note from its interior. He didn't make me take the step back; he came forward at once and tucked it in my hand.

"Perhaps it will bring you comfort," he said gently.

I had never heard the Huntsman so tender. I didn't know he was capable of it.

I closed my palm over the little note, nodded once more, and walked towards the massive gates. They opened outward and without hesitation, the well-oiled hinges making no sound as they did so. Everything of Alameth's creation was flawless. I stepped through them, past them, and to the other side. The Huntsman was still watching me walk away, I knew.

At this thought, as I took the first terrible steps onto the dark Wood road that would lead to home, I turned towards the open Palace gates. Jacobe was standing across the short distance half-way between Fumi's fountain and myself, his tall militant form bathed in the sun-filled light of the property. The hooded red cloak lay without wrinkle or catch across the broad width of his shoulders, falling in long length to the cobblestone behind him. Above his head, the pale-stoned Palace glowed with an other-worldly light. I lifted a hand in farewell.

The gates were closing now, sweeping shut. My last glimpse of him was as he returned the gesture, his scarred, tattooed face and wild eyes burning with angry suppressed emotion as I walked away. This was not how he had wanted it; he had warned Desi, who had not listened, and I was still departing with a broken heart, back to the shadowed and dangerous place they had found me.

And that, as they say, was that.

4.

It took days for me to find the strength to read Desi's note. I didn't want to hear what he had to say. He had not had the courage to speak the words himself before he left, nor to prepare me for his abrupt departure. He had not chosen to fight for the love we had found even in the least way. He had tossed it away as though, like the Huntsman suggested, I was merely the object of his latest summer romance. I didn't think I could read any tender words from him for awhile.

But eventually, as the time passed, I could not refuse my own heart. I still loved him. That would not die, nor fade. I needed to hear what his final parting words were.

One black night in the cottage, while Gran safely slept in the other room and a lonely fall wind exhaled in gusts at the shuttered windows, I lit a candle and pulled his note out from under a floor board of my tiny bedroom where I had hidden it. With my heart in my throat, I sat on the drafty floor wrapped in a heavy blanket and read his words in the shadowy light.

"Dearest Red," he wrote, "You will always be the most beautiful young woman I have ever known. Your face, with its sparkling eyes and quiet smile, will never leave my memories for the rest of my days. Your inner beauty filled my soul. I am sorry, deeply sorry, that our parting is like this. If things could have been different, I would have wholeheartedly taken you with me and committed myself to your happiness and your future. But alas, I am not in control of my life or what befalls me. I was clearly never intended for you. I only hope you can hold onto the good memories we shared. I know I will. I know the sound of your voice will haunt my dreams for a lifetime. ~Desi"

I told myself I wouldn't cry, but I did. The tears refused to stop for some time. I blew out the candle and sat in the darkness, weeping until my eyes were burning and dry.

Even apart from Desi, it was the ending that was shocking, disturbing. It was over. All of it. Reading his note marked the final end of it. Nothing would come of it, after all. Nothing had really changed. My life had not been altered. I was still going to have to return to my dreary existence and walk it out.

I had come away from this experience at the Palace empty-handed, with only the tormenting knowledge that an entire world of beauty, wildness and light was continuing without me. I had no part in it, after all. Not even the smallest part. I had been so certain that a new door had opened to me.

Even the Huntsman, focused as ever, had quietly moved on, moved ahead. Without the Prince he had no connection to me. Many years would probably pass before he ever again remembered me. No, what he would take with him from this was Desi's disobedience and cowardice, the Prince's failure to protect my heart in light of his own self-preservation. Jacobe's focus was on the Prince, and he would not soon forget the younger man's disappointing behavior.

The emptiness was almost too much to face. My daily life was here to resume. Money had to be made. Injuries had to be fixed. My part in the upkeep of the cottage still had to be maintained. But there was no hope now of another future. For two years I had stepped into another world, complete and beautiful, but this one in the Wood was the one I belonged to. And I found it devastatingly empty.

Worst of all, Desi was gone. His laughter, his life, his dancing eyes. I had been so convinced that he was a greater man than this. I had trusted that love, given myself to it. The Huntsman had been right all along. We both should have listened to him.

For a long while I missed the simple things — Desi's tiny kisses on my knuckles... The way he brushed the loose strands of my hair away from my brow in random moments... His endless fascination with me even when I was distracted or unaware. He had begun to fill such a huge part of my life. Even though I had never stopped long this summer to imagine what my future life would be like with him, neither could I imagine any life without him.

Days and weeks passed — numbing, blinding days in which I was unable to truly focus on anything but the pain and shock.

Gran took notice, even in spite of her busy activity. She had already begun hiring a few of the men in town to help her dismantle the heaviest of her things and load them onto her rickety wagon. She owned a framed bed and bureau, and planned to take the cabinetry from the kitchen, the long table in its center, as well as her heavy sewing machine and other materials that belonged to her craft. This would not leave me much, mostly three empty rooms, but I didn't mind. Right now the only thing I craved was time alone and to myself without her many interruptions.

Her sharp eye landed on me during the busiest of these few moving days, in which I helped as I could between patient calls. It was then, for whatever reason, my behavior for the past several weeks seemed to occur to her.

She was standing in our central room warming her hands by the fire when I arrived home, faithful wicker basket in hand, and greeted her briefly.

I planned to skirt past her at once and head to my room; this was where I had spent as much time as possible since the close of the summer. But her sharp voice caught me.

"You're thin again, girl. And you've not been sleeping. I've heard you shuffling around at night, don't think I haven't. You aren't talking neither." She made all of these observations as if she expected an explanation.

I paused a few feet from her and gave her a direct glance. She never seemed to age, Gran didn't. For as weathered as her face and hands were, she still had the energy and fortitude of a thirty-year-old woman.

"I've never been much of a talker, Gran, and my patients have been in demand again. I've tried to help you as much as I'm able with the move. I'm not sure I understand what the concern is."

She shook her head, not dissuaded. "I've got plenty of help aside from you. My concern is you. You upset because the Palace didn't ask you back next summer?"

I had to give her something, I was aware. She could be relentless when she thought she had landed on some interesting tidbit she didn't know. I sighed tiredly.

"Yes, that's precisely it. It was disappointing, and I could have used the money now with you moving to town."

She snatched the bait at once. "Well, there's no sense getting this down about it. I'd be sorry not to have the money or opportunity too, but the job was never going to last. You've got plenty of patients who keep calling you back and that's enough work to last a lifetime. You've got to bolster up. Have a thicker skin. It's too bad nothing more came of the Palace job, but we can't always sit around in the sunlight and wait for the wealthy to get sick."

"You are right, Gran," I agreed, trying to clear my face of the tiredness that was obviously driving this inquiry. I could have burst into tears right there. "I have enough work to feed and house me and that's more than many of my patients have."

"You're good at it too," she continued. "I was just saying it to Wendell Peterson the other day. You're good at Healing. Everyone thinks so. Don't you let me down now." This last phrase was delivered as a low threat. How quickly her mood turned dark when she felt that whisper of insecurity.

I nodded assuringly. "I won't." I moved now for the bedroom door, just in time for her to add behind me with a growl, "And get yourself some food! You're wasting away."

I didn't point out to her that there was no food left in the cottage. She had been taking her meals in town during this busy interval, particularly since, for the moment, she had extra funds after finding that my summer position had given her much more than she had budgeted for. Jacobe had paid me almost twice what he had the first summer.

I didn't mind that Gran took the extra funds she didn't need. I didn't want the money. Jacobe, I assumed, had only given the surplus of funds because of the terrible deed Desi had done. Let Gran have it, I thought; I would earn my own way in life. Aside from that, I was also looking forward to a life of independence on my own. I had made many personal compromises to live compatibly with Gran over the years, and after this summer I wasn't certain I could do so anymore. I certainly couldn't hide the depth of my struggle from her for much longer. It worked in my favor that she took the money and settled herself in town with as many initial comforts as possible.

I didn't eat supper that night. I collapsed into bed and slept the hard sleep of emotional exhaustion. This weariness clung to me the next day as well, though I did my best to shake it off. After a particularly trying morning spent on patient calls, I returned to the cottage in time to find Gran and a few of the townsmen loading the last of her items. *At last.* Quiet would return to my little life and I could begin, hopefully, to pull myself together in privacy.

The men had backed the wagon up to the front door and were loading a few remaining items. I could hear Gran's crackly voice escaping from inside as she gave stern instructions regarding the transport of her more expensive bolts of cloth. I approached the door, avoiding the wagon and its busy occupants, intending to slip inside and to my room.

It was then a tall figure exited supporting a long bolt of black silk over one shoulder. He nearly crashed into me and apologized profusely after realizing the accident his blindness could have caused. I stepped back, out of his way. Dark laughing eyes met mine.

"Why, Red! I didn't realize it was you. You just getting back in from calls?"

This was Jamie. I hadn't seen him since our minor collision in town almost a year ago. He looked as light-hearted and charismatic now as he had then.

He didn't wait for my answer. "Excuse me. Let me drop this off and then we can talk."

He turned and handed the heavy bolt to one of the men in the back of the wagon, who secured it somewhere in the midst of the load and quickly reached for another bolt borne upon the shoulders of a second man leaving the house. Quickly, to make room, both Jamie and I shuffled aside by a few feet, allowing more space for the busy operation.

Jamie turned to me. "How are you? It's been forever since I've seen you. Your Gran said you were working at the Palace again this year."

Not for the first time I was glad I kept Gran in the dark on many of the details of my life at the White Palace. She was a leaky spigot, that I knew well. "I'm back on patient calls," I told him, not quite confirming her information.

"So you'll be living here on the edge of town now without your Gran." Everyone I had greeted in the past two weeks had made this statement to me. This was interesting news for our little village. They would happily take any reaction I was willing to give them in response.

"Yes, I can carry out a great deal of my practice here at the cottage," I explained. "It works well for both of us."

"The winters are terribly cold," Jamie agreed. "I'm glad for you. Those who can travel to you, should." His eyes drifted to my dark cotton dress, far different apparel than the last shabby dress he'd seen me in, but his next words were not related to whatever thought passed over his face briefly. "If you need firewood through the winter, let me know. My father and I spent the summer clearing some of the property behind our cabin to build some fencing for more livestock. We have plenty I can sell you, and I could bring it by myself so you wouldn't have to go to the trouble. I know you won't have the wagon at your disposal anymore."

"Thank you," I told him politely. "That is very kind. I may take you up on it sooner rather than later. Gran will be taking the firewood supply we have with her for the shop in town."

He nodded. "I saw the shop already. She's done a fine job with it. I think she will get much more business on main street than out here. She should do well, I think."

The mood between us was friendlier than last winter, he could sense that. In truth I was glad to speak with him as long as it kept me away from Gran's watchful eye and sharp tongue in these final moments before she left. Our conversation was clearly within the earshot of the small handful of local citizens who were here to assist her, both inside and out of the cottage; she certainly couldn't disapprove. She believed in being neighborly. I had received numerous sermons and scoldings about this as well over the years when she observed me withdrawing socially.

"Red —" Jamie's tone had turned slightly. He lowered his voice as he stood over me. "Would you be opposed to me coming to check on you in a few days — make sure you're getting settled in all right? I know a thing or two about houses. I could see if there's any repairs the property needs before winter."

I didn't quite know how to respond to this. The only thing I'd been aware of lately was the desire to be alone. His eyes were kind and free of motivation. At a loss, I murmured, "Sure. Certainly. Evenings are best. I'm usually out on calls the rest of the time."

He nodded. "I figured. Then I'll be seeing you." He gave me a quick grin and raised his voice again to its normal volume. "I'd better be getting back to work or your Gran will dock my wages for standing here."

My first night in the cottage without Gran — indeed, my first night without her since I had come to live with her — was a strange one. The little house had been stripped bare without her belongings, and was even quieter without her presence. Glancing around the cottage at the end of the day, I was too weary to make any plans for my practice, as one might expect when new possibilities open up, but I did anticipate an excellent night of sleep. I prepared for bed early and stoked the kitchen hearth one final time, promising myself that I would act upon Jamie's offer tomorrow and re-stock my supply of firewood. My last task before slipping under the covers was to secure the front door. We had never bolted it before, but I did so now.

It was as I was drifting to sleep that I heard the sound. A high-pitched, lonely howl somewhere nearby, reverberating in the heavy trees, magnified in the stillness of night.

I was immediately jolted awake. *Wolves.*

The others, slowly and one at a time, began to join their leader from several parts of the forest around the cottage.

Theirs was an eerie sound, a haunting unforgettable melody that held no rhythm or consistency except chaos. The voices seemed to be calling out to one another, locating their pack in the black darkness, carefully assembling.

I was trembling. I'd never heard them before, not once in my life. *What could this mean? Why tonight, of all nights?*

They couldn't hurt me, I told myself, as their mournful baying continued. I was safe indoors and the door was locked. There was nothing to be afraid of.

But I was still afraid. All of Jacobe's words came back to me, his heavy concerns over leaving me behind. I didn't even own a solitary bread knife at the moment.

I told myself they were not nearing the house, they were moving away, and indeed they were. The sounds did not stop, but grew fainter and fainter... until the quiet stillness of the forest resumed. A gentle wind blew against the cottage, harmless and relaxing. It was as if the wolves had never come.

Sweeping aside my blankets, I reached for a candle-plate on the little stand by the bed and lit it by use of the box of matches kept there as well. There was no sleeping for awhile this night. I slipped my feet in my worn slippers, yanked the top blanket off the bed, and left the room for the safety of the kitchen fire. This was probably the only place I could hope to feel safe in the cottage tonight.

Gran had taken all the wooden chairs, and of course her cushioned chair, so my place this evening was on the hard wood floor. I curled myself up in the blanket and promised myself I would purchase a little rug and two sitting chairs for patients just as soon as I had the opportunity. The emporium in town could order these for me from one of the Northern villages of the Wood and have them delivered.

For hours that night I fed the hungry fire and wondered if the wolves would return. I jumped at the slightest sound outside the cottage, anxiously wishing for dawn to come. I had no idea what to make of what had happened. What did they want? Why were they here in the Wood? I had never asked Jacobe these questions. I should have.

There were a great many things I should have done, I told myself. This, at last, turned my thoughts to the abiding struggles within me right now. In light of the deep emotions this brought up, the wolves and their frightening appearance eventually dimmed and grew less ominous.

Desi's face was the last image I saw in my mind's eye before I drifted to sleep towards dawn, his quick grin and flawless features. He was easily the most handsome man I had ever seen and would probably ever know. I missed him sorely. But it was Jacobe I would have paid greatly to have with me on a night like tonight...

The next evening, well before dusk, Jamie rode up to the cottage in a buckboard with a load of chopped wood. His father was with him. Like his son, Brewster seemed to carry a merry spirit and had a light-hearted manner about him. I had not interacted with the older man much over the years; he and Jamie, who lived alone together on the outskirts of town in an opposite direction to Gran and I, had rarely ever needed medicinal services. Both were healthy and spry, as proven tonight when the two quickly unloaded the wagon into the little shed next to the cottage without pause. They made a good team and seemed to share an easy companionship between them.

Brewster knocked on the front door when they were completed and I allowed him into the warm kitchen while Jamie finished securing their team of horses outside. At once I could see Brewster was Jamie in duplicate physically, only an older version; his face carried some weathering and he was graying at the temples. He looked around the central room of the cottage, saw its emptiness, and moved for the fire to warm his hands.

"I heard your Gran moved into town," he said. "You've got an empty house now, I see."

I was standing over the small range nearby, stirring a pan of watered-down stew. I was in desperate need of groceries and had not had the time today to fetch them from Huntsville. At least, I thought gratefully, Gran had left me one pan and a stirring spoon, along with a meager supply of other cooking dishes. I doubted I would ever have too much use for them; when out on calls during the daylight hours, I joined my patient's families during their meals as a form of payment. The food was not always good, or even a very large portion, but it saved me the trouble of preparing all of my own meals.

"I am in need of furniture for my practice," I told Brewster. "I plan to buy a few chairs and an examination table. I'll use this room as the one for waiting, and Gran's bedroom to see the patients."

He stooped and threw a small log on the fire from the last of my supply stacked next to the hearth, sending sparks up the chimney. His back was turned away from me. "Jamie told me you didn't have much. We have a few extra wooden chairs in our barn, back from the days when Jamie's mother was still alive and entertained folks. They're a bit worn, but only a little. I'd sell them to you for a low price. Then you don't have to order new ones. Saves you money for your practice." He turned on one heel to catch my response.

I nodded at him. Not for the first time in the past several weeks, I thought how different life was here from the Palace, where everything was supplied by servants or already in place. The People of the Wood — and now myself — had to arrange painstakingly for every detail in life. "That's very kind of you. I can walk over tomorrow late afternoon and inspect them before purchase if you're agreeable to that."

Brewster's dark brows went up; a grin pulled at his mouth. "I heard you were real smart. Good for you, Little Red." He turned back around to the fire, the amusement still evident in his voice. "Jamie's wanted to get married for some time now, you know. Always going on and on about it. I'd like to see him settled soon. It troubled him for awhile that he couldn't afford it, but he can now with his job at Danner's. He'd do real good catching a girl like you —"

It was upon these terrible words that Jamie entered the cottage. His eyes quickly took in the scene. He had to have noticed the disturbed expression on my face because he announced at once, with regret in his eyes, "Pop, leave Red alone. Everyone in town has probably had this conversation with her, trying to matchmake all of their sons. She's heard it enough." He turned to me with a helpless shrug.

His father was undisturbed by his son's rebuke. Instead, he turned round on one heel and grinned up at me unapologetically. "I imagine it's only going to get worse now that you're living out here on your own. You're of a marrying age now, or nearly so. I say let Jamie take the whole problem off your hands —"

"*Pop!*" This was part-rebuke, part-groan. Jamie shook his head at me. "My apologies, Red. Sincerely."

I knew this was the part of the conversation where I was expected to graciously forgive Brewster's teasing comments with some laughing dismissive statement of my own. Either that, or issue a smart come-back as Gran often did when her neighbors teasingly rode her about something uncomfortable. But I had neither response to offer today. The incident with Desi was too fresh, my life and future felt too bleak, and I knew Jamie's father meant it. Whether good-hearted or not, he was using humor and teasing to disguise what he really wanted to get across.

I turned back to the stove quietly, took up the wooden spoon and began stirring the bubbling stew. "I'm sorry I don't have a warm meal to offer the two of you for your kindness in bringing over the wood. This is mostly water. You wouldn't find it very tasty, I'm sure."

The words were said without malice, but the two of them quickly caught the hint. Brewster stood to his feet and grinned widely at my slight offense. "Not much of a cook, huh? It's no matter. Doesn't matter that you're a little on the sensitive side neither. You've got other skills that will come in handy for the young man who catches you." He snickered. "See you around, Little Red."

After these raucous statements, he slapped his winter cap back on and took the few steps to the front door, leaving it open for Jamie to follow as he exited. As a result, late evening light streamed into the kitchen, brightening the room. Currently the three small windows facing the street were covered in heavy curtains. A chilly breeze blew in and around my feet.

Jamie did not immediately follow his father. He stood watching me, trying to decipher how much damage Brewster had done. "Red, I hope you can forgive him — he doesn't mean anything by it —"

I quickly turned my head towards him. "Yes, he does." To my surprise, I heard the icy words slip out of my mouth, "Is that why you've really come? To *catch* me?"

He hesitated only a second, taking in my expression and tone. He had proven he could handle my direct speech last winter, but I had never showed such strong emotion before. Probably no one in the Wood knew I was capable of it. The pale light streaming through the doorway illuminated Jamie's dark eyes and deeply sobered them. "I came because I thought yesterday that you looked sad and thin, and I saw how alone you would be here, with nothing left to you. I thought you needed a friend."

It took me a moment after his father's words for me to accept this. The older man had had no idea what pain he had stirred within me. I didn't want to be here, facing this life, dealing with this future. In the Wood, marriage was nearly the only option left to me. If I did make the uncommon decision to remain unwed, it would still be many years before the community's voices died down on the matter. And the choice would be a difficult one. Living alone in the Wood, as Gran had for many years before I came, carried additional risks and hardships.

"Very well," I said at last. "I thank you for your kindness. You've been very kind." The words came out stiffly, but they were coming. I did mean them, difficult as it was. "I can pay you for the cord tomorrow. One of my patients promised me payment in coins and I'm slated to see them then."

Jamie could feel the tension lifting. He seemed easier. He smiled a little. "That's perfect. I'll be home late afternoon on. Danner doesn't have a lot of business right now."

I nodded.

His eyes were humble. "Please forgive my father, Red. Everyone around here is like that."

I couldn't help myself, my tongue was loose today. I told him very directly, "Yes. They are."

With eyes still watching me carefully, Jamie detected that tone again and did not press the matter. He could see I wasn't going to excuse the People as he was. He nodded. "I'll see you tomorrow then."

I only nodded in return... and then he turned and shot out the door, pulling it closed behind him, hurrying to join his father.

Jamie did indeed prove to be a good and faithful friend. He aided me in hunting down unused pieces of furniture from the citizens of Huntsville and slowly stocked the cottage with everything I needed for a home and my Healing practice. Soon enough, I had a small kitchen table with chairs, cabinets for storage and workspace in both my Healer's room and the front room, as well as a myriad of other items I needed, such as a broom, mop, and eating utensils. These all came discounted or free of charge in exchange for medical services. As more people became aware of my plans, very quickly my little house was full of patients waiting during daylight hours to be treated.

Jamie also helped me keep up the property as I needed. He was handy with building and repairs, and winterized the little cottage before the cold winds and icy weather began. He never asked for anything except hot coffee, which I kept fresh on the oven range for all of my guests. And in the few moments he warmed himself inside, we shared conversation and a few laughs if I wasn't treating patients. I was grateful for this small bit of companionship, particularly since I was daily surrounded by a difficult People I often could not relate to or fully understand. My interaction with him was harmless and friendly, and eventually I relaxed in his presence without fearing he would attempt a romantic pursuit which I could not return. His father's words that had implied his son was anxious for marriage did not ever come up. Thankfully, Jamie seemed content.

These weeks and months were a welcome relief after the emotional hardship I had endured. I tried to put White Palace and its occupants behind me and worked hard at what was at hand, hoping, with time, that the pain caused by that other life would fade away altogether. The struggle was there beneath the surface and occasionally emerged with a force, but at least, I thought, the affliction and torment was not as acute. I was slowly improving.

With my practice held in the cottage, I no longer had to walk as far or as much and hardly ever traveled a great distance into the Wood. For me, safe inside now, this was the warmest winter I had spent in years. Sometimes my patients, who surprisingly enjoyed my home in lieu of their own for treatment, would bring me home-baked bread and other fare that supplemented my diet. Without Gran here this meant more for me, and I prospered for it. I put on weight instead of losing it and was glad for it. All of this, including Gran's absence, aided in my recovery.

My only apprehension that winter was surrounding the wolves. They continued to come every few nights, following the same pattern as they had the first time I heard them. The leader of the pack would begin the howl, followed by the others, one by one, until they located one another and disappeared somewhere into the Wood. In some moments I thought they circled the cottage before moving on, but I could never be certain. Every time they came I was held in suspension until their voices faded and ceased, wondering where they had come from, why I could hear them now, and what it was they searched for in the night. Those nights were the most difficult for sleep afterward, and it was no easy thing to wake the next morning and face the day.

I had yet to hear any mention of the wolves from anyone else in Huntsville and thought this was very odd. If the pack was dangerous, as the Huntsman had assured me they were, this was never discussed by the people in this village or any of the others. I never treated anyone in the Wood for wolf attacks, never once. But there had always been odd things about these People that had struck me over the years; I was not surprised by this mystery.

At one point I considered confiding in Jamie about my recurring visitors. He was the most reasonable person I'd found in the Wood, and he had a calm practicality beneath his humor which I thought would keep him from doubting me, overreacting, or running to the neighbors with the news. But for some reason I did not. After my experience with Desi, I was not willing to confide in anyone too quickly. I particularly didn't want to encourage closeness with Jamie. It was best I did not single him out any, I reasoned.

So life continued. The seasons began to turn, slowly at first, then more quickly. I was eighteen, and then I was nineteen. Through these seasons I barely looked up from work and the upkeep of the cottage. There was always some task to do, always someone asking for a Healer, always herbs or bandages to procure, and life did not slow.

As fall faded into winter only weeks before my twentieth year began, Huntsville began to prepare for its winter festivities. These were held every year during the holiday season. The few streets were decorated, several activities were planned which included a sledding party and a tree lighting ceremony on our Main Street. All of this excitement over a period of two weeks culminated in the final night of grand celebration — a dance held in Old Man Samson's barn, where pipers and mouth harpists and all other kinds of woodsy instruments were produced for entertainment purposes. Huge amounts of food were served, and everyone laid aside the hard work of the year to dance, eat and gossip with neighbors. Our little town had developed such a reputation for these events that even members of other villages would join, invited by friends and neighbors. The roads leading in and out of Huntsville were especially full on these nights with everyone attending.

For years now I had not attended any of the activities, this was how I preferred it. When Gran had insisted that I come, I found a reason not to. There were always sick patients to check on, or emergency calls during those days that I intentionally ensured would keep me out late. This year I didn't plan to behave any differently. Even better, I could remain home without an excuse, as I had for the past two years, and enjoy a quiet evening to myself. An independent life had its privileges.

A week before the night of the dance found me following my usual routine. With winter came huge amounts of small complaints and minor illnesses that kept the front room of my little cottage filled to bursting. That particular day I handled all of my cases until almost dusk and then, with several more waiting to see me, I announced that business was closed for the day. I had already observed there were no serious cases left, and informed them they could return tomorrow and I would treat them in the order that they departed. In the past two years I had followed this method to ensure I did not overwork myself as I used to, and to prevent individuals from taking advantage of my warm fire and free coffee during cold days.

Thankfully, within only minutes the little house was empty. It was this time of day I usually tried to get in a walk after such long hours in a small space. Usually this meant walking to the edges of town and back again, never deeper into the forest. I had avoided the Wood as much as possible since the wolves had surfaced at night... and because many of the roads nearby led to the Palace. Both of these reasons were sufficient in discouraging me from that direction.

Just as I exited the cottage, wrapped in a heavy coat I had managed to purchase the winter before, I spotted Jamie riding up on a dark horse. With a brief wave and an expression that I knew indicated he needed to speak with me, he dismounted next to my shed and quickly tied the reins to a hitching post he had installed there two years before.

I waited for him, stamping my booted feet in the cold. I was never as warmly dressed as Jamie; he was always well-outfitted in heavy durable coats, wool-lined boots and knitted hats and gloves. Last year

I had cut the fingers off of my gloves so I could keep them on while attending patients in Gran's old drafty bedroom; I stood in the shadow of the cottage now and blew heat on my exposed fingers.

Jamie walked over, smiling. "Red. Were you about to leave?"

He knew my daily habit of walking to Huntsville and back; he'd caught me more than once as he left the village on horseback or in his father's buckboard. "I could join you," he suggested. "Do you mind?"

I hesitated, briefly considered the fact that rumors would start if we were seen walking alone together, then dismissed this for today. I'd already been harassed endlessly in the past few years for remaining unmarried and un-pursued, just as Brewster had predicted. I was irresistible fodder for every parent within the Wood who had an eligible son. Nothing would change if they saw the two of us together.

"No, I don't mind," I answered him.

We set out side by side, Jamie setting his pace to mine. He was taller than I by over a foot and had a longer stride, forcing him to slow for my shorter steps. Tonight he asked a few conversational questions about my day and any interesting cases I had come across. We chatted about this for a few moments, then he moved onto the recent festivities he had attended. Jamie was a deeply social individual and had many friends from our school years that he remained close to, including several girls I knew he had taken various depths of interest in before he knew me. He remained popular with all of the older citizens of Huntsville as well, and never seemed to mind them as much as I privately did. It was clear he belonged here and was content with life in the Wood.

"I haven't seen you at any of the festivities," he commented.

"Have you ever seen me at them?" I asked him wryly.

Our feet were making tracks on the dirt-packed road in the small skiff of fresh snow that had fallen the night before. The dense trees around us were stripped bare of their greenery and stood stark and barren in the heavy gray light of late afternoon. Already we were losing light. Dusk would be upon us soon.

Jamie laughed at my comment. "No." He shrugged. "I was hoping maybe this year would be different."

I cast him a glance. "Why would this year be different?"

"No reason, Red. Nothing's changed, I know, but I was hoping maybe you'd change your mind for once."

"I don't see why," I responded. "I see all of those people frequently, sometimes more than frequently. There's nothing new to say to them I haven't already said. Chances are — and you know this is true — some of them would catch me *at the event* and ask me to treat them. If I truly want to have an enjoyable time, it's best that I stay home."

Jamie fell silent for a moment, considering my words. He couldn't deny all that I said was true. Clearly, I did not enjoy social activities as much as he did. "What if you came to keep me company?" he asked quietly. "Or I could keep you company, if that's the way you prefer to see it. The dance is this weekend —"

I cut him off quickly. "You know we'll be teased relentlessly. Rumors will abound afterward. I'll never hear the end of it from Gran when I see her."

Jamie was growing more thoughtful. His steps slowed unconsciously and I made the adjustment with him. "Do you really care? You never seem as though you care what any of them think."

"I don't, but if I can minimize the impact that my actions cause, I will. Most of them are quite persistent at wondering why I'm still unmarried. I've had plenty of sermons lately."

At last Jamie simply stopped in his tracks. He turned and fixed deep eyes on my face. "I know they give you a hard time, Red, and I know how much you dislike it. But I'd like to take you. I'm asking you. Will you let me escort you to the dance this weekend?"

This surprised me. I'd had no inkling of his desire to take me leading up to this query. Maybe he had handled it this way deliberately, I didn't know. But I could now see the earnest wish there in his expression... and perhaps more. Jamie was a man easy to read.

Uncomfortable, I turned back to the road, resuming our steps forward. "Why? Why do you want to take me?"

The bluntness of my question did not intimidate him. He moved ahead with me. "I like your company. You're fun. I'd like some of my friends to know you as I do. I also —" He clearly hesitated here, uncertain if he should vocalize his next thought. "I've also missed you at the last few gatherings. At the time I thought it would be more fun to have you there and hear your thoughts on everything. You're interesting, Red. You're not like anyone else around here."

I knew he was choosing lighter words to lessen the potential consequences for admitting these things. He was, in fact, inadvertently confessing to deeper feelings. I could suddenly sense them present, there in the space between us as we walked. It was possible, I realized, that he had fallen in love with me over the past two years and it had completely passed me by.

For a moment I found myself wishing I could return that love. I wished I could be content as he was to live here, wed, and live a simple life. Jamie was a good enough man for that life, and not such a bad match for me. But no feelings stirred towards him at the thought. My heart was dead, or nearly so. It had been crushed and I had never been able to repair it, no matter my best efforts to rest, move ahead, and embrace this life.

"Red?"

I had fallen silent, caught up in my thoughts. I looked up quickly. I was surprised when the next words fell from my lips. "Yes, I'll go with you. I can't guarantee I'll be the excellent company you claim I'll be, but yes... I'll go."

On the night of the dance I closed the clinic early and gave myself time to prepare. Not that I required an extreme amount of preparation. No one in Huntsville had the kind of money where new dresses and fanciful suits were planned and purchased for the event. In the Wood we pulled from our shelves and closets the nicest church-going outfit we still had in our possession, one that might have been seen dozens of times, and this is what we wore. No one expected very much — and you were most certainly considered vulgar if you did show up in a grand costume with your hair done and your face painted. A few had tried it over the years.

My dresses from White Palace were still the primary staple for my wardrobe after three years. Faded now, wearing thin, they were still of a nicer design and material than most of the clothing worn by the People of the Wood. Out of these I chose the darkest and heaviest cotton dress for the celebration that night. The weather continued to remain in freezing temperatures, I reasoned, and Samson's barn was certain to be drafty in places where dancing wasn't taking place.

There were neither thoughts of pleasure or of dread as I prepared; I was going for Jamie's sake, and because some part of me knew I had to try. I couldn't keep living like this. Some change had to take place, whether my heart was in agreement with it or not.

At the appropriate time, just at dusk, Jamie and I arrived at Old Man Samson's property in Brewster's buckboard. Other buckboards and rickety wagons were stationed up and down each side of the road alongside his little cabin. Citizens of Huntsville had already begun to arrive and were walking the pathways leading to it, in high spirits for the evening's activities.

Behind Samson's cabin by some yards was a large barn with the front doors thrown open wide, where the low rumble of chatter escaped. Hitching posts on one side of the barn were filled with horses who waited patiently next to their neighbors. The air was crisp and clear tonight, and there was an acute merriment in the atmosphere. The smell of warm food was borne on the wind and drifted to us as Jamie and I walked to the barn from where we had parked up the wooded road. I had never shared Huntsville's passion for each other's cooking, but tonight they were arriving with droves of it in hand, all of them heavy-laden with pots and pans.

"We will have fun tonight," Jamie reassured me. There was a happy enthusiasm about him that had been present since he helped me aboard his wagon this evening. He left no doubt that he was pleased I had come; his eyes often settled on me with pleasure as he drove the team and we carried on a light conversation.

I had no statement to offer in return to his. The only time I could remember having fun was at the White Palace; those summers had been a brilliant beacon in the persistent darkness.

But to my surprise, I did have fun that night. Perhaps not with the joy that I appreciated in every event with Desi — and even Jacobe at times — but I did enjoy myself. It was not the dancing, the food, or the conversation that proved to be any better. Jamie was the one who made the difference. He quickly showed himself to be the kind of partner I needed for the evening, both in leaving me alone in moments to avoid planting a firm idea in the eyes of our neighbors that we were a pair, and in attentiveness to me when we danced or stood aside talking. He introduced me to his friends, whom I already knew from childhood days, and these conversations flowed surprisingly well. Because of my escort and whatever words he'd already given them, the small group of young men and women were curious and willing to re-examine me with fresh eyes.

Of course Gran was in attendance, as well as Jamie's father. I had expected a brow-beating from Gran for my behavior, but it was Brewster who had words to say, clear and direct. He caught me during a moment Jamie was otherwise distracted.

I was at the serving tables filling my plate, heated and winded after a particularly robust turn on the dance floor. This reel had not required a partner, which was convenient for me; Jamie could see me, even laughingly pass me by on the dance floor, but we did not interact.

Suddenly I became aware that someone had stepped up next to me in line; in order to crowd close to my side, they cut off the person who was serving themselves just behind. Half-expecting one of my patients, I turned and recognized Jamie's father. He was dressed as his son was this evening in his best suit, comprised of a dark string tie, pale dress shirt and long jacket. This was common fare for all of the men in attendance, though admittedly Jamie and his father had a slightly higher income than most of their neighbors and this showed in the newness of their suits. Brewster stared down at me from a towering height, his eyes glittering with an expression somewhere between smug satisfaction and anger. We hadn't crossed paths much in the past three years and when we did he was always notably irritable.

"Good to see you out and about, Little Red," he declared. I noticed he held no plate in hand and did not seem the least bit interested in the long tableful of food before us.

"Thank you," I responded demurely. I continued to search through the food items spread out in buffet style, politely ignoring him.

"I knew you'd make a good match for Jamie," he insisted.

To this I said nothing.

He took a step with me when I moved forward. "I'd like to see the two of you together more often." This was not spoken as a request; I could hear the smug demand in his voice. "You're not going to find better, girl. Not around here. He's told me about how much you've avoided him over the years. You're still avoiding him. You ought not to take these things for granted. You're not getting any younger, you know."

I turned now, pausing to hear him out. I should have fled, but something about this moment froze me.

His tone transformed into a low whip, biting and bitter, hidden from those around us by the overarching volume of the instruments across the room and loud chatter in the barn. "I've told him to look elsewhere, but it's you he's stuck on. I have no idea what he sees in you after all this time. You got your nose in everything but where it needs to be. You need to be focused on a husband and children. You're just like his mother, that's what you are. I told him so."

For a moment I did not register his words, only their intent. I was too caught by the yellow flicker of eyes that seemed to glare at me from behind his. I swore I saw lashes blinking that were not his own, felt heavy monstrous breathing brush my face that was not escaping his lips. It was obvious that Brewster was as infected as countless others I had treated over the years, Gran included. Once again I wondered uneasily what it was I was seeing. This too was something I should have asked of Jacobe regarding the Wood.

Jamie must have perceived trouble from whatever distance he had been. He abruptly appeared before the two of us with a slightly nervous smile. "Pop! I see you've caught up with Red tonight."

This was enough to snap Brewster free of the spell that had possessed him temporarily. He was still angry, but it was controlled once more. His eyes were glittering at me again. "Yes, we were just catching up for a moment. I was telling her I was glad to see you two together."

Jamie boldly took my arm, pulling me away. "Thanks, Pop. If you don't mind, I'm going to snatch Red for a dance. Leave your plate, Red."

I obeyed him, allowing him to lead the way. Once we were safely outside of his father's hearing, he hovered close to speak to me, moving us through the dense crowd towards a safe place against the wall where we might have some privacy.

"You're very pale, Red. I'm sorry if he disturbed you any. Are you all right?"

I wanted to ask him right there about his mother, but was deeply hesitant to do so. I had only met her once or twice as a small child and remembered very little except that she was unusually beautiful for a woman of the Wood. Gran later told me she drowned herself. As a young girl, the most significant event that stood out to me at the time was Jamie's absence from school for most of that year. In the past three years of our close acquaintance, he had never spoken of her, never once.

Jamie did not release my arm even after we found a resting place and I was gratefully leaned against the wall. He was glancing down at me with concern.

"I'm — fine," I lied, trying to reassure him. I did not feel like telling him his father had so coldly lashed out. "I just need to catch my breath."

"What did he say to you? Was he unkind? I'll speak to him if he was."

I tried to smile and hoped it was successful. He wasn't going to be content unless I gave him something. "He seems very intent that we pair up. He made it clear he thinks I'm responsible for the delay."

Even this sparing description troubled him. His expression changed. "I'll speak to him, Red. I'm sorry. I've not complained to him. I've never spoken ill of you, I want you to know that."

My smile was genuine now. "I assumed as much. You're nearly the only person I trust around here, truth be told."

This brightened Jamie's mood at once and chased away any shadows threatening to ruin our night. Admittedly, it was rare that I complimented him, though my heart had been deeply thankful for his friendship and faithfulness over the years. He smiled down at me. "I'm glad to hear it."

That smile was a traitorous one, I thought, looking up at him. Everyone in this room would know he was in love with me, if they didn't already. Quickly, I pushed away from the wall and suggested impulsively, "We should dance."

His smile broadened into a slow grin. "*Yes.*"

It was later that night when I once again heard Jamie's mother mentioned. Tongues were loose at a celebration like this one, as I had often observed before I stopped attending them altogether. Information was not difficult to glean.

Jamie's closest friend, Geoffrey, also another classmate, was just leaving the dance floor, saw me standing against the wall waiting, and chose to join me. He was a young man of medium height and mischievous blue eyes. As a child, I'd had the same experience with him as Jamie. The two had been inseparable, always hatching some outrageous idea that inevitably infuriated our elderly school teacher and landed the two of them in frequent trouble. Both of the men had grown more sober with time, but there was an undeniable chemistry between them that had never faded. They brought out a restless energy in each other which still occasionally needed an outlet.

Geoffrey also had a loose tongue, much looser than Jamie's by far. He had never learned the simple wisdom that safety was found in discretion. This was proven tonight when he approached me with a sloppy smile and took up a place beside me with winded breath.

He heaved a sigh. "I've had enough for a bit. Need to catch my wind." He cast me a quick glance. "Unless you'd like to take a turn, Red? I'd take you."

I considered him for a moment. I did not trust him, but for more innocent reasons than my guardedness towards many others in this barn-room. That trust would take time to rebuild after the amount of pranks he had sprung on all of the girls over many years.

"I've just returned myself," I told him. "I need to catch my breath as well."

He nodded, accepting this falsehood without questioning.

His eyes drifted to the busy motion all around us, but his next words were addressed to me. "Jamie can't stop talking about you. He's crazy about you. Kind of took us all by surprise. I thought he'd stopped having eyes for you years ago." He grinned sidelong at me. *"But here you are..."*

Geoffrey was harmless compared to his seniors. He didn't expect a reaction from me; he simply enjoyed expressing every thought in his head to whomever would listen. Now that he was a man grown, I suspected many people used him for inside information, or to spread it. After all, he was son of one of the town fathers... and his tongue was a leaky spigot. He was a perfect target.

"Jamie says his father is really pressing you for the match," he continued; "It's a well-known fact that Brewster is bitter towards, well, *everything* because of his wife. I hope you don't pay him mind overly much."

Mention of Jamie's mother brought me to full attention. I stood upright against the rough-hewn wall. "He is persistent," I murmured, agreeing. "I don't know anything about Brewster's wife."

"That's because you aren't out much," Geoffrey assured me with another grin. "Jamie nigh hated his mother by the time she died. He still does. Brewster's the one who grew bitter and vocal about it."

His assessment of Jamie surprised me. Hatred was extremely uncharacteristic of the man I'd known the past few years. I told myself I could not fully take Geoffrey at his word. He was a simple man who probably did not understand the full scope of human reaction and behavior, even in his best friend.

"I'm sure you're mistaken," I told him. "Jamie has never mentioned her once."

Geoffrey was undaunted by my soft objection. He snorted laughingly. "That's only because you don't know the story. Of course he isn't going to talk about it." His eyes drifted out to the dance floor, where Jamie danced the reel with most of the rest of the townsfolk on the hard-wood barn floor, his handsome face alight with pleasure and happiness under the brilliant light of a thousand oil lanterns hung on drooping strings overhead. He hardly looked like a man who struggled with hatred within himself.

I didn't have to ask Geoffrey for any more; fortunately for me tonight, he volunteered it freely. I was beginning to suspect he liked telling a good story… and this one was particularly rich. "Everyone knows Ann was interested in a lot of things. She was smart, like you. Beautiful, too. She didn't like it here in the Wood much. Brewster says she felt she was meant for more. He doesn't say that kindly, either. As the years passed, she developed a wandering eye. That's what people in Huntsville call it. I don't remember her much myself; she was dead by the time I was old enough to really know her any. She started cheating on Brewster with a man who's long gone now. He moved up north to one of the villages, I think, after Brewster found out." He shrugged. "That's what led to the hatred. She drowned herself, you know. Life was miserable in their house."

This story, in spite of its effect on Jamie's life and the questions it answered for me tonight after Brewster's tongue-lashing, did not shock me any. How many tales had I heard from my patients about terrible events that led to such tragedies? How many had I witnessed myself over the past ten years as I started treating the People of the Wood? They could not resolve the many conflicts within them, or chose not to. One thing was certain, however. The People enjoyed repeating these woeful tales, delighted in discussing them as entertainment. By the time I heard them, the stories were so convoluted, most often filled with such high emotions, that they weren't even of any use as cautionary tales. There was nothing to take from it but grief and sorrow.

"I am sorry the situation ended so tragically," I sympathized. "It's a sad story for everyone."

Geoffrey shrugged. This was a favorite gesture of his. "You just look at it like a Healer. The story isn't that sad, I think. Afterward, Jamie felt he and his father were better off without her. He's always felt that way. Both of them do, I suppose."

I fell silent at this. Even aside from Geoffrey's appalling lack of empathy, his insistence that Jamie held his mother in such little regard left me uneasy. I didn't know what to make of it. Brewster had pointed out I was very like her, yet he was still determined that I should allow Jamie to pursue me. Apparently the older man did not consider me exactly like her and still approved of the match. Bitterness was a strange thing that flared up irrationally in moments; I'd observed that. So I didn't feel any undue concern over Jamie's interest, nor held any thought toward his potential for struggles with me because of his mother. However, I did wonder how he viewed the entire situation. It seemed strange that he had never mentioned Ann, when he had seemingly taken me into his confidence on every other situation in his life. Perhaps this delicate story simply needed more time between us before he spoke of it.

Just as quickly, Geoffrey was finished with the subject and ready for some other form of entertainment. He jumped to a full upright position and shuffled his feet charmingly in a robust dance step. "You ready for a turn on the floor, Red? The music is really starting to liven up now."

For now, I decided, I would set aside the news Geoffrey had given me. At least until I found an opening with Jamie to discuss it. There were some things even I did not want to bring up about my own past. He was entitled to his privacy.

I smiled at Geoffrey, more willing now. He was probably still capable of the same pranks he pulled as a child, but I had garnered enough from observing him in these past few moments to know that's not what he desired tonight. In his own way, he was trying to extend a friendly hand to the girl his best friend liked.

The music was roaring with the combined sound of hand drums and pipes; the crowd was surging with excitement. Even the air shimmered and sparkled in the old barn.

"Let's dance," I said.

Eventually the evening, borne on the wings of energy and community excitement, wound to a successful close. It was as Jamie asked me if I was ready to leave that I realized Gran had not spoken to me. She had remained at a distance throughout the long hours, busy with her friends, turning away deliberately when I caught her eye. Her message was loud and clear. She had nothing to say to me after hearing the chatter regarding Jamie and I and witnessing my behavior tonight encouraging it.

I didn't mind so much. A few days would pass and she would move on to some other piece of news that had replaced me. Then I'd catch her in town to say hello. This was a good procedure that had been working very effectively for three years now.

Jamie took me home under a clear sky, with stars so bright they broke through even the heavy canopy of trees on the roadways. We both chatted and laughed. Though the air was frigid in the coldest part of the night, there was an obvious warmth between us that was more comfortable than any fire or blanket. I had never felt safer in the Wood than I did then. Jamie was not a warrior as Jacobe was, empowered with whatever other supernatural skills were in his possession, nor was he a skilled fighter and able hunter as Desi had been. He could never defend me physically as they could. But he was steady and true. That was a defense in itself.

As the team of horses came to a halt before my little cottage, Jamie insisted that he help me down and came round to do so. When my feet touched the snow-covered ground, he did not move away. His strong hands were at my waist; he drew me close. By light of the little lanterns swinging from the sides of the buckboard behind us, I could see his deep eyes were sparking with a clear message.

I asked myself if I was prepared to kiss him. I wondered how he would react if I found I could not. Even then a large part of my heart wanted to turn away and close myself off from this kind of love.

He did not sense my hesitancy. *"Red — "*

What he would have said and how I might have responded would have to remain a mystery that night.

It was then we heard thundering horse hooves tearing down the road towards the cottage at a neck-breaking speed. The sound was disturbing and eerie in the quiet darkness.

Jamie murmured in surprise. I pulled away from him and turned towards the direction the rider was coming from. We didn't have to wait long. Within seconds he reined in behind the buckboard at the front of the tiny yard, his horse dancing on his hooves. I could see at once the dark figure in heavy coat and hat, now looking wind-blown and alarmed, was Geoffrey.

Before either of us could ask what was happening, he called out, "Red — there's been an accident. A few of the children snuck away from the party and were playing on the creek behind Samson's property. One of the girls broke through the ice. Some of the young men were able to pull her free, but we don't know — she doesn't appear to be breathing — I was told to come and get you — "

Before he had even finished, I was already dashing towards him. I was not properly dressed to climb up behind him; I was wearing my fullest petticoat for the dancing tonight. But no matter, improper or no, Geoffrey knew what to do and pulled me up on the horse. I'd grown quite good at this a few summers back; apparently the skill had not diminished with time.

As we wheeled away from the yard, Jamie shouted after us, "I'll follow in the buckboard!"

Then we tore down the road, back the way we had come.

5.

Upon arrival at Old Man Samson's, Geoffrey did not stop along the road. He swiftly turned the horse into the forested grounds behind the cabin, veering right of the barn, plunging into deeper snow here as we made our way. I clung to him in the freezing cold as the horse bucked and bounced through the heavy drifts. The darkness around us was frigid and still after the warmth and volume of only hours ago which had escaped the barn and swept over these grounds. I could see nothing, not even a glimmer of light, nor hear any movement or sound outside of the horse's struggle to master the snow, until we were nearly upon the wide creek that meandered and flowed through Samson's property.

Even in the darkness I could hear the gurgle and rush of the water beneath the snow-covered ice; in occasional places it broke through the surface. This creek-bed had been far too dangerous a surface for small children to be playing on. At the very least, they should have had guidance and proper light.

Geoffrey turned the horse so that we traveled parallel to the creek, still pressing us on. He was a good rider, even in the dark, and the horse responded well. The snow was thinner here along the banks, but the footing was more dangerous for an animal and made for difficult riding. We were in constant danger of slipping, possibly sliding into the edges of the creek only a few feet below. Ahead, at last, I caught sight of a little light, which grew more defined the more ground we gained. I realized it was comprised of several lanterns held in the hands of the people who had brought them; a small group of ten or fifteen individuals — dark shadows in this lighting — were standing in a loose circle facing the creek.

As Geoffrey slowed, the shadows turned towards us, eerie unrecognizable faces in the ghoulish light. In the center of the circle two figures huddled over a small dark form sprawled on the cold ground. The child.

Geoffrey had not quite halted before I barreled off the horse and hurried over to the quiet group, dragging my heavy skirts with me through the thick snow. Murmurs broke out around me.

"The Healer!"

Someone — a woman — released a broken sob.

Quickly, I crashed to my knees beside the two figures who surrounded the child. They drew back a little. I did not know them at once.

"She's not breathing," one explained tensely.

"For how long?" I asked. Then, "I need more light here!"

"Since we pulled her out of the water," the other man answered.

Someone scurried forward with a lantern, which immediately cast deep shadows upon the child's face and figure. Someone had swaddled her in their dry cloak, but even this was mostly soaked through. Her skin was freezing to the touch.

I saw at once she was blue-faced, particularly in the lips, and her body was horribly still, certainly more still than any child should be. Without further examination, I knew immediately that she was beyond my ability to save. I'd seen death now many times. She'd probably been dead for several minutes by the time Geoffrey and I arrived.

Nevertheless, I knelt closer and listened for breath from her nose, from her half-opened lips. This revealed nothing. Swiftly, my fingers tore away the cloak, peeled back the collar of her little dress, and I listened for a heartbeat with my ear bent to her bare chest. *Nothing*.

The people around me waited with held breath. I could sense the tension, the high-pitched fear in the little space where we were gathered. Many of them had stepped closer and were looking down with stricken faces. There was, I knew, nothing I could do.

I sat back up, eyes still fixed on the little girl's body. I put one gentle hand on her forehead, still pretending, still knowing nothing would come of it. This was for the people around me now. Then on impulse, I leaned down, parted her lips, and breathed.

Someone around me murmured, though the words were unclear. The child's small chest lifted from my exhalation of air, but she did not respond.

I bent and tried again, longer this time, slowing my breathing so the air maintained a strong steady flow. My thoughts were turning wildly. Jacobe had said that life was the power which Alameth used; Fumi's power, he said, was a creative power that gave life. If ever I needed access to this life and this power, it was now.

"Breathe," I heard myself telling her, sitting up again. *"Breathe."*

I bent once more and blew through her lips. Again her chest lifted from the force of my air.

And then, suddenly, before I'd even sat back up, the little body sprawled out lifelessly before me shuddered. She gasped.

I let out a sound of amazement. The girl lifted her head and violently coughed water, spitting over her front. Quickly, my hands reached out to support her; sat her up partially so she could rid herself of the rest of it.

I was aware several people around me began crying and sobbing loudly. Any sign of movement or breath from her was more than they'd seen since she was pulled from the creek. The little girl drew in a hoarse ragged breath and opened her eyes weakly. She was breathing again — shakily, feebly, but she was breathing.

I almost laughed in delight, but restrained myself. *Was it possible that my inner prayer had just been answered?* I had felt nothing, sensed nothing. I turned to the men around me quickly.

"She needs warmth, badly. We have to get her up to the cabin as quickly as we can."

Geoffrey suddenly stepped forward, breaking through the little circle. "I can take her on my horse."

In the intensity of the current circumstance, I had not remembered he was still present until he spoke. The others had a mix of reactions to this; most were simply hesitant, while several were still in tearful shock.

I assured them all, "He's a good rider. Safe." And to Geoffrey, "You must do your best not to jostle her. She's very weakened." Then, looking around, "Where are this child's parents?"

One of the men next to me identified himself. "I'm her father. John Blankenship. Her mother is behind you."

I thought, *The woman leaning on a few around her, no doubt.* She was sobbing hysterically.

"She will survive," I told the father, "But only if we take great care with her now. If you will allow Geoffrey and me, we will ride the horse with the girl back to the cabin." When the father nodded, his anxious eyes on his child, I added suddenly, "Where is Samson? Is he amenable to this arrangement?"

I searched the little group for the old man, trying to identify their faces in the shadowy darkness. I had learned over the years not to take Huntsville's compassion for granted. They did not always respond in a way you expected when it came to the sick or needy. There were many small feuds and unspoken resentments that they kept to themselves and acted upon irresponsibly in intense moments like this.

Thankfully, Samson was among those gathered and stepped forward in a gruff manner, a stocky, bearded figure draped in a warm cloak and heavy boots. "Of course you can bring her to the cabin. Where else would we take her?"

I knew him well enough to know he didn't like it, but he wasn't going to say so. At least not now, in the presence of the prevailing group of people who would have raised a bitter howl if he didn't respond rightly. We would all hear his honest thoughts later, however, circulated behind closed doors and in low-spoken conversations.

"Very well," I concluded, nodding at Geoffrey now, who stood by watching me with an attentive expression; "Let's ride back to the cabin."

I did not return to my little cottage until early the next afternoon, exhausted but triumphant. The little girl — Susan, her parents had informed me — was resting comfortably, with her family making happy plans to take her home shortly. I had stayed with her as long as I felt she needed care, and to ensure that no hidden dangers arose after such a terrible accident.

By this time everyone had departed who had witnessed the incident, even Geoffrey and Jamie; all had work to tend to and there was nothing more they could do. There was hardly room enough in Old Man Samson's cabin for more than a few people at a time without serious crowding.

Naturally this left me on foot when I decided to leave. Samson did not volunteer either his horse or a shared ride; he complained that the late night had left him weakened and sickly, and was unwilling to take any chances with his health.

"You're young and strong," he grunted, as I set out on foot; "You'll not suffer from it like I would."

He was right, of course. I was young and able-bodied. What he didn't see, or turned a blind eye to, was the simple fact that all the People of the Wood had been treated like this by their elders when they were young. Never spared a moment of the difficult life, Samson was weathered and spent now, with still so many years left to him. The people here did not have to be so withered if they were only willing to show each other more generosity and compassion, particularly in times of need.

I was nearly home, weary and cold, my heavy coat damp and a useless defense against the bitter wind, when Jamie came riding up the road on horseback. Too exhausted to notice or care who was on the little path, I only looked up when he slowed next to me. Grateful tears came to my eyes at the sight of him.

"Red!" He jumped from the horse at once, grabbing at the reins as he stepped in front of me with an anxious expression. "Samson wouldn't let you take one of his horses? He has *two*."

"He said he needed them for today's work," I answered, while making the discovery that my teeth were chattering. I was hugging myself for warmth. "They couldn't be spared."

"*Disgraceful...*" Jamie was muttering in disgust as he quickly led me to the horse and helped me mount. "You were the one who saved the child. None of them could do it."

"That's not how he will see it," I spoke up. I was almost too exhausted to explain.

Jamie mounted next, climbing aboard behind me, leading the horse from here. His warm arms encircled me as he kept hold of the reins and directed the animal forward. Immediately a sense of calm was restored to me. The weak desperation I had felt the last several minutes began to subside.

"Samson will say it was the child's fault for foolishly playing on a shifty creek bed," I continued. "You know he'll blame her parents for letting her out of their sight long enough to cause the accident. He's been thinking it since last night, I can guarantee it. There was no way he was going to loan me his horse."

From behind me, Jamie let out another snort of disgust. "You are not responsible for any of it. You certainly couldn't let the child die as payment for her foolishness. The least he could have done is offer you the loan of a horse for the afternoon. Why didn't you wait for me? I intended to come check on the situation before the day was done."

We were nearly to the cottage. I recognized the trees around us, the little bend in the road that hid the house. *Thank Fumi...* The overcast sky was dark, already threatening more snowfall.

I shrugged. "I didn't know you would return. I'm used to walking."

"You're exhausted," Jamie scolded. His tone was still disturbed, angered by the poor treatment of me. "Your coat is soaked. I wish you had waited..."

We were at my little yard now. I said nothing to him in return. I swung one leg over the horse and slid to the ground. My skirts, I observed, were nearly ruined by the work of the night before. Soiled, wrinkled, and filthy. No doubt they smelled of horse. The hems of the petticoats beneath were brown from mud on the roadways here and damp with moisture.

Jamie dismounted behind me and quickly said, "Please let me help you, Red. I could make you some tea, or see to the fire. I could keep watch over you while you sleep. It's clear that you are completely worn down."

I was already making my way to the front door, trying to shuffle through the fresh snow that had fallen today. The bitterly cold wind dragged at me even in these few steps. My stockings and feet were wet through my boots, which had not proven to be as waterproof as I had hoped. At Jamie's words I turned round and smiled at him.

"Thank you. I appreciate your kindness. The ride was enough. You dare not come in — you —" He would think I was going to add that such an action would create huge amounts of talk and trouble, but this was not the reason.

"*Red* — " His eyes were anxious for me, his voice showing agitation over the circumstances. "You should let me help you — I could hide the horse in the barn if the appearance of it troubles you —"

"I think not," I told him, still smiling. I was almost swaying on my feet. "These things always get out. Patients will come by, Gran will stop over, people will be curious to hear what happened with the Blankenships... *Someone* will inevitably discover you've been here with me all day, alone, after a night like last night where they saw us acting so friendly with one another. If they don't judge the facts rightly, they will certainly fill in the blanks with their own speculations. Neither one of us needs the trouble."

These truths still did nothing to calm Jamie's agitation. "Will you at least let me come by and check on you later today? At least for a few minutes?"

I nodded. By then, I thought, the emotion of the moment would have passed for both of us. And people would expect him to at least stop by for a quick confirmation that I was doing well. "Yes. Of course."

He didn't want to leave. This was evident in Jamie's bearing and stride as he returned to the horse and mounted. With a grieved face still turned towards me, he offered me a small wave goodbye before wheeling the animal around. Then he quickly disappeared down the road and out of sight.

I watched him go for a moment. His adoration of me startled me far more than anything else I'd faced in the past day. I didn't know what to do with it. As I turned back to the cottage and wearily made my way inside, I only knew that I was so emotionally vulnerable at the moment that I would have agreed to any future with him should he begin touching me with the warmth he so clearly held for me. I couldn't trust myself, and certainly couldn't trust that I would be able to examine the truth in my heart with an honest eye. I only knew I could not resist his kindness... and he deserved better.

Two days passed, two days in which I tried to quickly resume some sense of normalcy after the dramatic events of that evening. Patients returned, complaining of headaches and other kinds of small maladies after the long night of celebration. Many of them, I knew, were merely inventing convenient reasons to come by the little cottage and speak to me about Susan Blankenship. Her recovery was much more exciting than the other events that took place that night. I was grateful at least that any rumors surrounding Jamie and me seemed all but forgotten.

However, normalcy was not in my immediate future, nor was it likely to be for a very long time.

Gran was the one who brought me the news that terrible day. Gran who, soon after she heard it, rushed over in her rickety wagon, her face wind-blown and expression wild as she jumped from the seat and hurried across my front yard with the wind pulling at her skirts. I'd seen her through the kitchen windows and now opened the door for her just as she was prepared to throw it open and make her way inside without knocking.

"Gran!" I greeted her cheerfully, ignoring the obvious high emotion in her face. "What can I help you with today?"

She pushed past me, ignoring me just as equally. "I've got news, girl. You're going to want to hear it."

Immediately she shot for the fire, stripping herself of her coat and gloves and slinging them in the little wooden chair I kept there for guests. She extended cold fingers to the flames. Mincing no words, she declared flat out, "Susan Blankenship is dead."

Instantly I was stunned, mind whirling. Gran would not exaggerate this. "*What?* What's happened? Are they certain?"

"Oh, they're certain all right," she affirmed.

I stood in the center of the kitchen and stared at her. "Why wasn't I called? It's been two days since the accident. What's happened?"

Gran shrugged. Her words were simple and succinct, as if this wasn't the important news she had brought but merely an indirect part of the story. "She started breathing funny this morning, then stopped altogether. She's dead."

I could hardly believe her indifference towards this horrible news. "*Why wasn't I called?*" Thoughts running, heart racing, I announced suddenly, "I have to go see her. They could be wrong. They were wrong before. A Healer should confirm the death."

With this decided, I rushed for the door, reaching for my coat which was hung there on a simple hook. My mind was already running ahead towards the Blankenships and the roads leading to their cabin on the other side of town, just past Jamie's property. *Where were my gloves? My woolen hat?*

But Gran's crackly voice stopped me flat. "They don't want to see you, girl. Don't even bother."

I turned round quickly. She had already comfortably seated herself.

"*What?* What do you mean they don't want to see me?"

"That's what I came to tell you. Everyone sent me. Don't bother to go see the child. They'll only throw you out. No one wants to see you right now."

My voice took on a shocked edge. "There might still be a chance — she was fine when I saw her last — she could still survive — "

Gran insisted, "I'm telling you, the girl is dead. I saw her myself. The furniture maker — Jansen — is already preparing the casket. He's building it out front of his store, right there on Main Street. Everyone can see it."

I moved towards her restlessly, sickened to my stomach, stunned by the turn of events. "How would they know she was truly dead? What qualifies them to know it? I should go see for myself —"

Gran was getting irritated with my persistence. "You aren't listening to me. They don't want to see you. They sent me over to tell you not to come."

I stared at her, trying to grasp this. "Who did?" I demanded. "Who told you this?"

She shrugged indifferently. "Everyone. The Blankenships, the mayor, Danner, Old Man Samson, Brewster Morrison — do I have to run down the whole list? Everyone in Huntsville agrees you shouldn't try."

I was stupefied by this reaction. I scrambled for some reason to this. "Do they not want Susan to live? If there was a chance, any chance at all, for her survival — wouldn't they *want* me to take it? This is absurd!"

"I've never seen you so worked up before." Gran shook her head at me in dry disgust. Her indifference was as appalling as the news of Susan's death. "Truth be told, they don't want you to come because they hold you responsible for this. Haven't you figured it out yet, girl? It's your fault she died. You'd better just own it now and get it over with. You're going to have to live with that fact for the rest of your life, so you may as well just admit it now. You're fortunate they aren't all storming over here and closing your practice down."

Stunned as I was, it took me a moment to recognize the truth of the matter. Gran, I realized, blamed me as well. She was siding with the villagers and had been sent by them as their emissary. The truth was in her beady glimmering eyes as she looked up at me.

An icy hand wrapped itself around my heart in that instant. It was obvious to me she had no loyalty to me, nor had any interest in the truth. She, nor any of the community, held an ounce of gratitude for my many years of service to their family members.

For once in my life, I stood my ground, staring her down coldly. I no longer cared what consequences followed. *No more.*

"*What qualifies any of you to determine she's dead?*" I snapped. "You, of all of them, Gran, are the least qualified person I know to judge it. That little girl might be able to live if you'd get past your bitterness, your pessimism, and your need to find someone to blame."

She let out a sudden ferocious growl, one I dared say was inhuman, and jumped to her feet with a twisted expression. "You are no less guilty," she snarled in my face. "Don't you speak to me in this way. I can make you pay. Know your place!"

The tension in the cabin was nigh tangible. I had never so boldly spoken up to her before.

But today I only scoffed at her words, unafraid of her temper. She stood shorter and frailer than I was, looking up at me with fiery eyes. Let her do what she would, I was too shaken by the news to be sensible.

"*I am?* Did you say I am no less guilty? I think not. You are child killers, all of you. The guilt is upon *your* heads."

She didn't wait for me to finish these words. She was already shooting for the door, infuriated, running from the truth. As she flung it open and stormed out, I followed her out into the yard and cold air, calling after her angrily, "You *enjoy* finding someone to blame. It's a form of entertainment for all of you — and especially you, Gran. You should be ashamed of yourself!"

She jumped on the seat of her wagon and took up the reins, red-faced and angry, gray hair wild and stirring in the bitter wind. Surprisingly, she did not respond to me again, but put her fury into the horse, driving the poor creature down the road away from town, unwilling in her anger to take the time to turn the wagon around. She was soon out of sight.

Susan's burial service was that very day. I learned this from Jamie, who arrived shortly after Gran's departure, thundering into the side-yard on his horse with as much passion as she had. He was white-faced and tense, his dark eyes filled with sharp concern. Quickly, taking barely enough time to get in the door, he confirmed everything Gran had reported; she had not exaggerated. Huntsville was united in its belief that the death of Susan was my doing. Their feelings were very strong, he reported; everyone seemed to have forgotten the little girl was the one who had snuck away from the casual eye of her parents and had been playing on the creek bed.

For the most part, Jamie seemed stunned. Uneasy. His thoughts ran towards what had *not* been said by anyone yet in the little gatherings he had been present for on the streets of Huntsville. They were still angry and reeling from Susan's death. Yet what kind of long-term ramifications would an incident like this have upon the community, he wondered. Upon myself, the local Healer?

"I don't know what's going to happen," he murmured.

"Well, I know what's going to happen," I declared. I had not yet calmed from Gran's words, and Jamie's report only increased my irritation. I strode across the little kitchen to the front door, reaching for my coat. "I'm attending the funeral service."

Jamie jumped up from his seat before the fire. "Red, that's impossible —"

I pivoted to face him, daring him or anyone else to challenge me. "Susan deserved better. She still does, poor soul. She shouldn't have had to pay for the crimes of this community. I'm going to show my respects."

"They'll turn on you, Red," Jamie protested, low. "You have to remain unseen for awhile until they cool. *Please — listen to me —*"

This last plea was as I lifted the latch on the cottage door and opened it, my intentions clear.

He followed me to the outside. "At least let me take you. You'll be safer with me —"

I couldn't argue with this, it was probably true. I was also grateful to have a loyal friend — *any* loyal friend — just now. I stopped and turned towards him. "Very well. If you're offering, I'll take it."

Within a quarter hour we had passed Jamie and Brewster's property and were very soon upon the Blankenship's land. I knew immediately we had come to the right place; there were horse-drawn buggies and wagons lining the snow-covered road on either side. It seemed nearly everyone in Huntsville had already arrived. No one, I also took notice, was in sight. They had moved very quickly if Susan had died only this morning.

I did not anticipate the burial ceremony to last long. Those held in winter rarely did here in the Wood. Knowing this, Jamie and I quickly dismounted before the Blankenship's little cottage and walked around it through the snow. This snowfall was, I observed, hard-packed and well-trodden, making the earth slick and forcing our steps to slow out of carefulness. Clearly, a great deal of traffic had passed through here recently.

Behind the cottage were two crudely built out-buildings, one of which was being used at the moment as a shelter for several horses tethered inside its shadowy confines. Most of them were still saddled. This was indeed intended to be a quick ceremony. Behind these buildings was a recently cleared field; large tree stumps littered the landscape, peering eerily through the snowfall. Piles of brush had been left for later work. It was here, at last, we found the small crowd huddled together at its far end near the line of heavy trees.

The two of us set out side by side, saying nothing, hunched down against the wind. There was nothing to do but face what was before us. The group of attendees had already cleared a path in the snow and this made the distance easier and without struggle. As we approached the dark-clad crowd, I could hear the minister's quiet voice intoning a prayer over the bent heads of the people. They had not noticed us yet because of this.

Jamie veered us right, towards the front of the group, and stopped shy of the minister by a few yards. He was not quite comfortable actually mingling with those gathered, obviously. I could sense the nervous tension in him from the two feet we stood apart.

At the minister's feet I could see a patch of earth had been dug and the little wooden casket had already been lowered into the fresh soil. I knew the men would have worked all day to thaw the earth with fire and water. Their shovels, buckets and tools still lay aside, fresh spots of color in the disturbed snow. On the casket's other side were the Blankenships and their living three children, who all stood staring mournfully and with blank faces towards the raw patch of earth and the dark-robed minister before them.

Once again I was baffled and dismayed by the speed at which they had all been so willing to accept death and quickly move ahead. I found it devastating and shocking that none of them had come for me. Tomorrow, sadly, this patch of earth would be completely covered by snow and left forgotten until spring exposed it once more. The people of Huntsville seemed far more interested in celebrating death and finding someone to blame than fighting for life and reaching for peace.

When the prayer was ended, the crowd once again opened their eyes and turned their faces towards the minister. He tonelessly began reading from a small book in his hands. Their mood was grieved and expressions heavy. Most of these people had suffered loss of a treasured loved one in some form of tragedy or another. Among them I recognized Jamie's father, Gran, the mayor, many others that I'd had close interaction with over the past ten years.

In their grief and distraction, it took the citizens of Huntsville several minutes to notice us, and when they did a murmur broke out across the crowd. Heads turned, faces lifted.

Jamie had been right, I could see that at once. Anger washed over them. Expressions changed from sorrow to livid fury.

"What's *she* doing here?" someone whispered.

Then, when a feeling of agreement passed through the crowd, the same unknown voice repeated in a raised voice over all of their heads, "What's *SHE* doing here?"

The minister looked up in surprise, startled out of his reading. The elder Blankenships turned and stared at us with the same numb, troubled expression.

Quickly, Jamie took a step forward, raising his voice before I could. "Red is here to pay her respects, same as all of you."

Someone in the back instantly snarled, "She doesn't belong here. She's the one guilty —"

This caused a more violent ripple to run through the crowd. Many of them vocalized their agreement.

Even the ordinarily solemn-faced minister turned cold at the sight of me, shaking his head. "My daughter, you should not be here. You should have stayed home." His tone lashed out egregiously. "This is not an act of respect, this is an act of disrespect."

The crowd appreciated this; they were obviously primed for reaction and these words were clear incentive.

A male voice I did not recognize shouted, "She's no daughter of ours."

A woman joined him, snarking, "Never has been."

These words were like tinder for the flames. A deep broiling anger swept through them, stirring in their murmurs and their words, causing them to shuffle and move restlessly. Most had turned completely and were facing us instead of the casket, fists clinched and faces twisted with emotion. Even Gran had joined them, not hesitating to add her voice to the sounds of the crowd.

Jamie looked to me uneasily, wondering what my reaction was, uncertain as to how to respond.

In that moment I had every intention of boldly stepping forward and addressing them with all the volume I could muster in my voice. It was not me they had done the greatest injustice to, but Susan. She deserved justice, and she deserved that someone would speak the truth to these hard-hearted people on her behalf. Right now I could think of nothing else.

But just as I made the step forward and drew in air to give voice to my words, I saw something that stopped me short. Suddenly, all of their eyes turned feverishly yellow.

I would have thought this phenomenon was a figment of my imagination, a result of the current stressful events, but I'd had too much experience with the Wood to believe what I was seeing was not real. As I stood watching in horror, the little crowd before me began panting like dogs, seething out rough obscenities. *Surely these were words and expressions beyond their understanding*, I thought, stunned. Only the children among them seemed unaffected, looking around them in blind watchful interest.

In just seconds the faces before me began transforming, slowly at first, but then more quickly. Even before the change was clear, I knew what I would see next. Wolves were beginning to appear before me.

I stumbled back a step in shock. Turned towards Jamie and clutched at his arm. *"Do you see that? What's happening?"*

I could see from his expression that he was not the least aware of what was taking place right before us. "They're very angry, Red," he murmured, disturbed. "I will try and calm them, but I think you should leave."

I glanced back at the crowd. Nearly every face I knew was in that group of people. I'd known them all of my life.

They were growling now, still spitting out obscenities. A darkness had come over their faces, over their forms. I could no longer fully recognize the people I knew. I could only see the wolves standing with them, sometimes through the very body of their hosts. These were vicious, massive animals, an entire horde with glinted eyes and fanged teeth staring me down, glaring furiously. I felt at any moment they would charge towards me.

I shook my head in astonishment. *Was I seeing something in another dimension? Were they real and actually standing before me?* I could certainly hear them. They continued to hiss and growl out the most vile insults and threats imaginable.

Jamie's perturbed voice reached my ears. His mild reaction clearly revealed he knew nothing. "Red, *please.* Take the horse and ride home. They are only going to get angrier if you stay."

"Yes, Red, run," a deep hoarse voice mocked from among them.

I stumbled back another step, shaken, still not turning away. My breath caught in my throat. "Who — who are you?" I cried out.

Another one growled in a tone as black as midnight, *"Haven't you figured that out yet?"*

Then a third voice as sinister as his brothers explained, "We are here because they want us, Red. *We* are welcome here. *You* are the one they don't want."

These words left me sick. I nearly emptied the contents of my stomach right there. My breath was ragged now, my heart thundering.

"Yes, they do," I argued weakly. "They do want me. They are only in pain."

Jamie seemed to catch the meaning in my words, even if he wasn't aware of the intended recipient. He grabbed my arms and said low in his throat, "Red, I don't think they do want you. You need to *go. Please.*"

I was nearly weeping now. Turning swiftly, I ran without looking back.

I ran and ran. I didn't take Jamie's horse. My feet gave expression to the terror and heartbreak that was within me, driving me forward, face against the cold wind. My boots slipped more than once on the muddy roads, but still I pushed on. I didn't care if I fell. I would have fallen and simply clambered back to my feet and continued running.

I ran until I found myself at the cottage, gasping for air, stumbling through my front door with sweat running down my face and into my eyes. I didn't stop there, but quickly bolted the door behind me and stripped myself of my clothing. Too warm here in the cottage, I tore at the ungiving buttons, pulling at the lengthy skirt, the difficult shirtwaist, dragging my boots off and shoving them aside. Afterward I realized I was trembling uncontrollably. I was unable to fully comprehend what had just happened, what I had seen and the horror I felt. I was mostly aware of those terrible words: *"We* are welcome here. *You* are the one they don't want."

Over the course of the next two days I did not come out of the cottage, I huddled inside and I slept. When I ran out of firewood, I left the hearth dead and wrapped myself in my winter coat and heavy blankets. I didn't care, I wasn't leaving the house. Every time I considered it, the violent trembling began again. My heartbeat raced, my breath came short, my thoughts jumbled and collided. Until this passed, I decided, inside the cottage was where I would remain.

The only person who visited me was Jamie. Though I was accustomed to frequent interruption day and night, everyone else had mysteriously disappeared. I didn't answer when he came; I let him knock repeatedly and beg me to open the lock until he gave up and left. Then I slept again.

The second time he came he refused to relent. He pounded the door endlessly, determined to get a response. For a long while I let him do so, certain he would go away eventually. I didn't want to see him yet; I didn't want to consider what was happening beyond the walls of the cottage... or what would happen very soon. These thoughts would surface as soon as I saw his face. I wasn't prepared for the conversations that were sure to follow. I wanted to ignore the reality of my circumstances and my desperate future just as I was ignoring him.

But Jamie did not stop. His voice changed moods. He muttered through the door, "Red, don't make me break this door. *Please.* I'm not that kind of man, but I will." He grew desperate now. "I need to know you're all right. That's all I need. Nothing else."

When I said nothing, he smacked the door with the flat of his hand in frustration. *"Open the door!"*

Silence fell a long while after this. The sound of receding footsteps in the hard snow reached my ears. I assumed he was leaving now, returning to his horse or wagon.

With his departure, I realized darkness had fallen in the cabin. I hadn't lit any candles or oil lamps for two days.

I didn't want him to go, I thought suddenly. I just couldn't speak yet.

This contradictory thought was, at last, what drove me to my feet from before the dead hearth in the kitchen and caused me to move for the door. I unbolted and opened it. Cold night air rushed into my face; I shivered involuntarily. Brilliant moonlight lay across the pale snow in a broken pattern set by the extending branches of the trees on all sides of the cottage.

Jamie hadn't left quite yet. He was crossing the yard for the road in his heavy boots, a lantern swinging from his hand. The little light highlighted the snow at his feet with a warm yellow glow. His team and buckboard stood waiting.

I paused in the open doorway in my thin gown, blanket draped around me, and temporarily considered letting him leave. I couldn't speak yet. Not yet.

Ignoring this, I stepped out into the snow sock-footed and padded after him. He heard me come and turned in surprise.

"Red —" He rushed the few steps forward.

In another instant his arms enfolded me. So great was his relief that he lifted me off the ground for a moment, cheek to cheek, with his nose buried in my hair. "*Red* — you can't disappear like that. I can't handle it. Not after what they did —"

He was as emotional as Jamie ever became. He set me back down and stared into my face with hungry anxious eyes. "I was worried. If anything had happened —"

How grateful I was to him in that moment. He was the one true support that had refused to let me go through all of this. He didn't agree with them. Of them all, he still wanted me.

I raised one hand to his face. He hadn't shaved for two days, no doubt out of worry and alarm over me. "I'm fine." Even these words took considerable effort. "I'm — *fine.*"

It was then some desperate emotion overtook him. His relief drove him to drop the lantern impulsively in the blanket of snow at our feet and grab for me; he bent forward and kissed me deeply.

I could feel his need in his kisses, a great hunger that was more than relief and the emotion of the moment. He had a great need for me, I realized. To my surprise, his affection tasted good. I found comfort in his love; I responded to it. Standing there in his embrace, I experienced hope unlike I had been able to muster for months, possibly years. Maybe I *could* love him. Maybe some way forward was opening to me after all. If ever it was needed, the time was now.

At last he released me. Quickly, Jamie scanned my face for any sign of disapproval.

I was smiling at him, which he returned, pleased.

"We should go inside," I announced shyly. "My feet — as you can see —"

He glanced down, then took a quick step back in surprise. "*Red* —"

I laughed a little. "There was no time for shoes — I had to see you —"

These words stopped him. Made him smile down at me with a lovely light in his eye. "Let's go inside."

When I turned to go, however, my body refused to obey me. I found my head was light and my knees wobbly. It took me a moment to realize I was ill. I turned towards Jamie. "I think —"

I never finished the statement. I felt myself plunging forward, losing consciousness. The blanket dropped to the earth, leaving my arms exposed to the cold.

Jamie's strong hands shot out in time to catch me. Surprised, he said, "*Red* — you're burning up — are you sick? I thought your face was simply warm —"

I said nothing to this. Darkness was threatening to render me unconscious. The earth heaved and the air shimmered before my eyes.

I was vaguely aware in the next instant when Jamie stooped and lifted me into his arms with little effort, then gently carried me the few steps to the cottage and across the doorstep. After that was nothing; all thought was lost in the consuming darkness.

I woke hours, possibly days, later, and it was a slow awakening. I could feel how weak and exhausted I was long before my eyes finally opened and looked about me. Jamie had laid me in my own bed and covered me in blankets, leaving the door to the little room open so heat from the fire could waft in. The room was dark, but a warm light through the door spilled in from the kitchen. I could hear Jamie shuffling about, and the smell of cooked meat filled the air. My stomach growled a rough complaint. How long had it been since I ate?

I knew, at least, that I had not eaten over the two days I had locked myself in the cottage. Which begged the question — how long had I been asleep?

Aware I had been feverish and ill, I put one hand up to my forehead, then to my throat. My temperature was normal again, thankfully. Whatever Jamie had done, it had worked. Nevertheless, I did not feel any motivation to leave the safety of my bed. I had no strength.

I did not have to recall any memories as I lay there in the warm darkness. They were all immediately present as soon as I regained consciousness. I could still see Gran's yellow eyes, her enthusiastic condemnation of me as she joined the others in their vicious murmurs. I had never truly felt her love, I realized suddenly, but neither had I felt her hatred. Until now. I had always been aware that a rabid hostility was there and tip-toed around it, but there was no avoiding it now.

Then there was Jamie. Safe, dependable Jamie. He had returned to the cottage worried about my well-being, ready to beat down the door in his concern. He had kissed me. His kisses had said more than enough, his love so apparent.

Weak tears slid down my cheeks now. I did not know what to make of it all, I still didn't. I certainly didn't know what was going to happen. Surely I could never practice my healing arts here again. The People of Huntsville would never allow it, and even if they did eventually, I could not stay and look at their faces. What I had witnessed at Susan's burial service and their act of betrayal would likely haunt me for years. Yet Jamie belonged here. His home, his work, and his father were here. He was my only friend, and I had strong suspicions that he would not want to do without me now. I could not stay, and I could not go.

Thoughts of Alameth suddenly arose to my mind. I realized in that moment I had been holding out hope for years that somehow I might still have a future there. Fumi had rescued me, after all; Jacobe had assured me I carried a significant identity which would be revealed with time. The idea had clung to me even in moments when I was at my most lost and emotionally adrift. But I no longer believed it. The last of my hope for that future had died when the wolves made it clear they were welcomed and I was not. Nothing had emerged in the past three years, not even a sign. Even Susan, whom I considered a great victory, had died senselessly. It was time to move on completely.

I lifted a weak hand to my face and wiped away the tears with my palm. Slowly eased my way into a sitting position. I needed a third option and I was blind to it.

Jamie must have heard me move, or was simply driven by sharp instincts. He appeared in the doorway, blocking most of the light with his body. At the sight of me, he entered the room and came to stand by the side of the bed.

"Red? How do you feel?"

He was calmed now, confident again. I nodded. "Better. No longer feverish."

"That was the worst of it," he explained. "The fever. You've slept for nearly three days. I managed to get some broth down you several times, but you need to eat if you can. I can bring you some food if you think you're up for it."

I looked up at him, unable to see his face clearly. "Jamie —" To my dismay, tears began to spill again. I felt incredibly weak in many ways. "What's going to happen? What's happening in Huntsville at this moment? What will I do?"

At these soft desperate questions, Jamie sat on the edge of the bed at once and faced me. His expression, though deep in shadow, was clear enough to see his gentle concern. "Marry me."

He smiled sheepishly at my surprised expression. "Marry me and let's move to one of the Northern villages. I have enough money saved up to open a cobbler shop and find us a small home in town. You could be a Healer there. Wilsburg should be large enough to find an empty shop and a home fairly quickly. Your Gran has already sent word that she wants you to find other housing. So I say, let's leave them all behind and be married."

My mouth came open in surprise, trying to take it all in. His expression was in earnest, there was no joking there. "You — want to marry me? This quickly?"

"There's nothing quick about it," he said, laughing softly. "Not for me there isn't. Caring for you these past few days made me see how much I want to live with you, have a life with you. That desire has been there under the surface for months. *Marry me.*"

I shook my head at him. "What will your father say?"

But Jamie only shrugged, unconcerned. "I'm my own man. Pop has no real say in it. He's stubborn but I can handle him. He already knew I was considering a relocation to the North Wood, this won't come as a surprise. He also knew one of the main reasons I was holding back from leaving was you. My feelings for you haven't changed, he'll know that too. Obviously, I've spent the last three days here. I'll bet he will even help with labor if we find we should need it." One of his hands reached for mine, as if he anticipated hesitation from me.

He looked deeply into my eyes. "Red, I've spent a lot of time thinking about this in the past few days. You need a fresh start, we both do. Let me care for you. Will you?"

For a moment I sat there in the shadowy darkness and considered it. Life with Jamie would be a better life than I had ever known except those brief summers at the White Palace. I told myself the love of a few years ago was childish and this was the real thing. This love was practical and mature. It had been borne of a long-time, trusted acquaintance, which was the best foundation for a long-term relationship. Most of all, I needed him. I needed a shield between myself and this village, these People and this forest. Jamie would protect me. He would not abandon or betray me. The simple truth was, I needed his love... and I told myself I could return it.

After several more days, I was finally able to convince myself to leave the cottage. This took much persuasion from Jamie, who assured me we would take roads to Wilsburg less frequented by Huntsville citizens and safely away from the village. I still had not told him about the wolves, but I believed he would and could protect me, seeing as I understood now that the beasts were connected to the people. As I had always suspected, the citizens of Huntsville were the ones who gave power, agreement, and various degrees of control to the Evil that roamed here. Their choices over the years had obviously allowed for an entire horde to haunt this part of the Wood. No doubt these were the very packs that Jacobe often saw when he left the Palace. It stood to reason that if Jamie could keep the people calm, then the wolves were less empowered.

On the day of departure, we traveled through the Wood without incident and arrived safely in Wilsburg well before mid-morning.

Jamie had already visited twice earlier in the week, eager to secure housing and a small shop for the two of us. He had a few homes he wanted me to see and put my voice to before finalizing any arrangements. This day would also give us an opportunity to envision our lives here and the new future that awaited us.

Wilsburg was a larger town than Huntsville by far, with many dividing streets and a central road that led out of the Wood altogether. Very few ever followed it in or out; the Northern Road was mostly used for a coach that arrived every few weeks with mail and other deliveries. Enough of the Wood had been cut back in town and on its borders to actually allow for greater amounts of sunshine and open sky, though it was rare even here to see a great deal of sun or the beauty of the sky. A permanent cloud was almost always in effect in Wilsburg.

It was on its central streets that there were many stores and shops for various needs, a dining restaurant doubling as a small hotel, a government building made of brick where the mayor and marshal held business, and several large buildings with three floors or more which were used for multiple housing units. Jamie had decided we should avoid living in the latter as I would probably have regular visitors from patients and there were sure to be complaints. We needed private housing, he had decided, and focused his attention in the Housing District, located on the more outlying boundaries of town.

I was familiar with Wilsburg. They only had one Healer and I was often called for by its citizens when he was in high demand. I had become well-known here and was hopeful now, as Jamie and I roamed the streets on horseback, that my practice could continue uninterrupted. I would simply limit my services to the Northern villages, I decided.

By noon Jamie and I had chosen a home — a four-room cottage just on the edge of town not too unlike Gran's cottage, only larger, complete with a quaint little yard and storage shed. Jamie was full of excited plans and shared all of his ideas happily; I was the one who was quiet, still ponderous after the past two weeks. This was sudden change and I was slower to adapt to it. Still, Jamie never seemed to mind. I was attentive to all of his plans and that seemed to be enough support and agreement to satisfy him.

We also took part of the afternoon to see the empty shop he had discovered on Street B. This was just off Main Street; Jamie explained that all the rent on the main thoroughfare was much higher and this was just as nice. The little shop had a room over it, which meant he could eventually hire an assistant or train an apprentice. He had every expectation that he would be able to make good money here, as there was no shoemaker in Wilsburg at present. He had also been purchasing the various tools he needed over the past few years with this plan in mind, giving him a financial advantage now.

By the day's end my hope had been re-fueled and I was nearly as eager as Jamie to begin our life together. We both agreed the people here were a little less narrow than Huntsville, and more accustomed to outsiders and other ways aside from their own. Jamie was very certain that all the troubles we had faced recently could be put behind us and we would find happiness.

Upon our return to Huntsville, Jamie chose a different route than that morning. He explained that the earlier roads we had taken would now be more heavily traversed this late in the day. As we rode double over the winding roads and pathways, we chatted quietly. Jamie was not in a hurry and the ride was even-paced and relaxed.

Too distracted by the pleasant conversation, it wasn't until we came upon the pale-stone walls of the Palace that I recognized the road we were on. I knew it well. Not surprisingly, there was no sound from beyond its walls as we slowly journeyed past it, just that hushed quiet which made all passersby maddeningly curious.

I did not recognize my mood had changed and my voice dropped off altogether until Jamie said suddenly, "What happened here, Red? Something did."

This question took me some time to answer. The wall stretched on and on beside us; I had forgotten how large the property was. As if they had been threatening to burst free for years, memories flooded my mind, filling my heart with a hopeless longing. I was so terribly vulnerable after the recent events.

I could not look back, I told myself firmly, resisting emotion. That direction only led to sorrow and dead-ends. It was vitally important that I look ahead. Life was filled with hope now, and it was real and present. There was nothing about the White Palace that had been truly real.

"What leads you to believe something happened?" I asked Jamie eventually.

He shrugged. "Nothing I can zero in on exactly. You've always been private. It was just an impression I got after you worked here. You didn't seem well for awhile. You're the only person I know who's ever been inside the gates, you know," he added. "I asked my father as well and he wasn't aware of anyone either, in his time or his father's.

Some people have doubted whether the place is ever used by the Royals at all. Did they do something to you? Were you mis-treated?"

I didn't know how to respond to this temporarily. The words refused to come.

At last I answered, "No one mis-treated me. I was, in fact, very well treated. They were wonderful. It is a beautiful place, much more so than the Wood."

"Then what happened?" Jamie pressed.

I could see he was not going to be satisfied until he understood more. My sudden reaction to this place had confirmed everything he had already suspected. Finally, I confessed softly, "I fell in love."

This surprised him. Tightening his hands on the reins, Jamie slowed the horse even further until we were nearly at a crawling pace. "*What?*"

"I fell in love."

"What — what happened? Tell me." There was obvious discomfort in his tone.

"There isn't much to tell," I admitted quietly. "He didn't want me after all. He only said he did."

I expected Jamie to ask me who *he* was. I could sense the alert tension in him as I clung to him on the back of the horse. He was realizing there was an entire part of my life he did not know or was privy to.

For a moment I wondered how he would respond if I told him The Crown Prince of Alameth had stolen my heart. And consequently crushed it. Maybe, I thought to myself, it was wisest he did not know all of the facts.

"He left," I continued. "They all did. They've never needed my services since; I've never been asked back."

We were just coming upon the Palace Gates now. To my surprise, Jamie halted the horse suddenly before them. Without explanation, he swung one leg over the horse and dismounted, then turned and extended a hand up to me, sober-faced.

When I hesitated, his outstretched fingers signaled me to dismount. "I want to tell you something, Red," he said.

At these words, I obeyed, still wondering what the purpose for this was. I certainly would have preferred that we move on, even a little further. Standing in the shadow of these massive gates made me highly uncomfortable.

But I had nothing to fear from Jamie, I never did. As soon as my feet touched the ground, he took my hands and looked down at me solemnly. These were words he wanted to exchange face-to-face.

"You know I want you, don't you, Red?" he asked me. "You understand I'm not just offering you empty words?"

I was grateful to him at once. "Yes. Of course. There has never been any question of that."

"Good. That's settled then." He broke into a grin. "I say we get married next week after we haul everything from Huntsville in the next few days. Would that suit you all right? It could be just you and me if you like for the ceremony. We could use the minister in Wilsburg. I already asked him if he would and he agreed to it."

I realized then that Jamie was not going to pursue any further detail about my history with Desi. He simply accepted what I gave him and this was enough.

"Yes," I told him then, ready to leave this place behind as quickly as he had; "I say yes to all of it."

The next day found me organizing the little cottage in a way that its contents could be moved. Most of my larger belongings would stay, since Jamie had so much and the house in Wilsburg was already fashioned with many shelves and storage spaces. Even my bed was not necessary, as Jamie assured me he owned one large enough for the two of us. Apparently he had been planning for marriage for some time, unlike myself, who had never planned for anything.

In the early afternoon I heard the creak of a wagon and the heavy clod of a horse's hooves outside the house and moved for the front windows to investigate. I was not expecting Jamie, who was still doing some small work for Danner until we departed. It also seemed unlikely that any of my patients would return during this time, as it appeared that the entire town had come into agreement that I was not to be consulted for healing services.

So it was with great surprise that I identified Gran's rickety cart and weary gray horse at the edge of my yard. She was slowly dismounting; I could not accurately determine her mood from her noncommittal expression.

This would probably have to do with the cottage, I thought. Jamie had assured me he had told her I would be vacating the premises within the week, but perhaps she wanted to drive her point home with me personally. I braced myself and reached for my coat, determined not to let her in the house.

Before she had even crossed the yard, I opened the door and faced her. Today held no wind and the snow had melted down to uneven patches, but the air was still cold. Though she was warmly bundled in a heavy coat and woolen knit hat, I could see Gran's cheeks and nose were a bright shade of pink. She paused where she stood at the sight of me.

"What do you want, Gran?" I demanded.

I had no patience with her today; she should have known she would not be welcomed here until after I left.

Expecting reprimand, criticism, any of the usual responses I received from her, I was surprised when she said, "The news is all over town that you and Jamie are getting married and moving North."

This statement held no emotion in it; I couldn't say what she was thinking. She just stood there and waited.

I shuffled in the doorway. "You could have sought Jamie out if you wanted confirmation of that news. Danner's shop is two doors down from you in town, in the case you've forgotten."

With this, I intended to shut the door and bolt it, but she raised her voice quickly, "You don't want to marry him."

I couldn't help myself. Wisdom dictated that I should not engage her in conversation; one of us was sure to walk away angry. There was also no forgetting the venom that she was capable of, nor the Evil that often drove her. Foolish though it was, I opened the door fully again and stared her down. "And why not, Gran? Why would it matter to you?"

She didn't answer this second question. "I know you're angry, and you have good cause to be." Her tone was almost a mutter. "He's been tainted same as the rest of them. Same as all of us. Don't marry him."

This was as close to apologetic and humble as I thought Gran had ever been, but it was still not enough, not nearly enough.

"He's no more tainted than I am, Gran. We've both suffered losses."

She shook her head, her tone still low. "He's not worthy of you," she insisted. "He's not."

"That isn't what I see." I narrowed my eyes at her. "And I hardly judge you to be the person qualified to make that call."

She took me in for a moment, studying my reaction. Then she shrugged. "I didn't figure I could convince you."

She turned away, back towards the wagon, but then seemed to make a decision and turned back once more. "I stayed at the White Palace as a girl," she announced.

This stunned me into silence. I stared at her.

She continued, "They invited me. I met King Fumi. He was an old man by then — in Alameth they live longer, you know. So I do know a thing or two," she added, as if this sparing admission proved it. "I know enough to know you aren't normal. What you *want* isn't normal. Jamie is normal," she insisted. "You should wait."

These last words irritated me at once. "Wait for what, exactly? Are you suggesting that I stay among all of you, cast off and alone? I'd starve, and you all would let me starve."

Gran was too subdued to roll her eyes, though she wanted to. Her quiet tone was dry. "You won't starve. They'll get desperate enough for a Healer that they'll come. Trust me, they'll come."

I wondered suddenly how much she did know. "And the wolves, Gran? What if they stir you all up and you come for me? It could grow worse. I'm not entirely stupid."

"That you're not," she agreed dryly. Again she chose not to address my words. "I'm telling you, Red, you should wait. You have a destiny. Don't miss it."

"Is that what happened to Jamie's mother?" I asked, ignoring her persistence. "Did the wolves come for her because she made everyone angry?"

Gran's tone went flat. "Ann drowned. There's Evil in some of the waters around here —"

This made me fall quiet. That same Evil had nearly taken me like-wise. For once, Gran seemed to be offering me full disclosure.

At my silence, she added, "You don't need Jamie. Not even to protect you. You don't need him."

Instantly I went cold. Stared her down icily. "You don't know what I need."

She shook her head. "Oh, I think I do. Your grandfather was just like Jamie... and look where it got me."

I had never heard about my grandfather. She'd been close-mouthed regarding anything to do with my family for the entirety of my life. I studied her closely now. "Where *did* it get you, Gran? What are you alluding to?"

But this was, at last, too much for her. She couldn't face it, whatever her troubled history was. She spun back towards the wagon. "Do what you like. At least I told you. My conscience is clear."

I let her go. I wasn't willing to exercise patience with her anymore. She was dangerous and shifty. If she truly wanted to make amends, or to protect me from making a poor decision as she claimed, she would need to provide more context than she had.

She didn't actually admit to anything, I thought, watching her board the rickety cart and take up the reins. She was master at two things, Gran was — giving opinions and guarding her secrets.

6.

Jamie and I were married nearly a week later, just after the new year began. We stood in the minister's living room and took our vows in front of his wife, who stood aside with an enthusiastic expression. Neither one questioned our story; as an orphan I had no family, we told them, and Jamie's father had been too ailing to come all the way from Huntsville though he blessed the proceeding.

There was nothing significant about the ceremony, which was perhaps why I began to doubt. Jamie meant every word he vowed to me, his eyes aglow and spirits bright. He had worked hard to win me, and this moment was important to him. But as I spoke the words of eternal love after the minister delivered them to me, I felt nothing. The moment, the ceremony, the words, Jamie's joy at being able to slip a simple silver band on my finger — all lacked the sparkle within me I thought should have been present. I should have been thrilled, at the very least *happy*. Instead, I found myself tired almost to the point of tears.

We returned to the cottage after a quiet supper at the local hotel. Jamie had made several trips in the past few days to prepare the house and make it habitable. He wanted everything to be perfect.

When night fell, I was more weary than I desired to be. The rush of the past week... the illness before that... the difficult emotions of the past month... All demanded a toll tonight. I found myself sitting on the edge of our bed in the quiet little room that just now looked so unfamiliar to me, staring into empty space. I had come in here on the pretense of preparing for bed, while Jamie, who was fostering an unspoken excitement since the ceremony, chose to remain in the kitchen just outside while I readied myself.

What was wrong with me? I asked myself. Why was this so difficult? This life with Jamie was what I wanted; *he* was who I wanted.

After what he considered a sufficient amount of time, Jamie knocked and entered. He had already lit several lanterns hanging on hooks at the walls and could see me clearly, though the heavy curtains were drawn at the windows behind me and the lighting was a mix of deep shadow and flickering light.

"Red?" he asked. "Is everything all right?" In his excitement, this was the first time he'd noticed a lag within me in the past two weeks.

He came and sat on the edge of the bed next to me. It was a large feather-tick mattress set low to the floor on a box frame which he had built, just now covered in heavy blankets from both of our respective homes. Everything in the room — the large bureau, the chair in the corner — had all been hand-built by him. Knowing how hard he had worked and prepared for this only added guilt and confusion to the moment for me.

"What is it?" he asked.

I answered him honestly. "I don't know. I can't make sense of it."

He put an arm around me. I could sense a nervous tension in him even now as he tried to offer comfort. "Your feelings are no doubt perfectly normal, or so I've heard. Just kiss me, Red. You'll relax into it."

He initiated this, beginning to kiss me heavily. His breathing quickly intensified. Jamie had always been a good kisser, but tonight it was obvious his kisses were filled with the need for pleasure; I could not sense love in his affection. Within only moments his fingers were clawing at the collar of my dress, fumbling for the buttons. The other hand pawed hungrily for my breast.

This was when I sat back, leaning away from him, reaching up with one hand to stop his fingers from success. "Jamie —"

He stopped at once, confused. At his expression, I stood to my feet and moved away from him entirely. I turned and looked down upon him. He was frowning now.

"What are you doing?" he asked.

I shook my head, riddled with guilt. "I don't know. I thought I wanted this —"

His expression changed to incredulity. "You *thought* you wanted this? You aren't certain?"

"Something isn't right," I murmured. "I can't explain it — Possibly I'm just tired — Tiredness can alter your perception —"

"Maybe you should *try* explaining it." For the first time in my history with him, impatience surfaced in Jamie's voice. He had not appreciated being turned away. "I was under the impression that you wanted a life with me — and all that goes with it — as much as I did."

"Of course I did," I assured him. "*Do*. Of course I *do*. We're just moving very fast — this past week has been a whirlwind, Jamie —"

"A whirlwind I thought you enjoyed because it meant a life together." He was pressing his point, surprising me with his persistence. "What else could you possibly have on your mind?"

"Nothing is on my mind. Nothing. But I didn't picture it like this," I confessed. "I didn't imagine this —"

"What did you picture?" His tone was turning surprisingly cold. I was accustomed to such a sweet tenderness from him. "What else could you have possibly imagined, Red?"

"I don't know — I have no answer to that, only —"

"Only what?" He stood to his feet, staring me down. He was almost scoffing at me now, the flickering light dancing across his stony features. "What else could you possibly have pictured? This is all I have to offer. I've given you everything —"

"Yes." This was very true, only adding further to my guilt and confusion. "Yes, you have. I'm most grateful to you, Jamie. You have not held back. I just need some time — some rest, possibly —"

He was still uncomprehending, glaring down at me. Every word he said created an intensity and increased the pressure I already felt. *"Time?* How much time do you need? I've waited years for you. I've done everything your way from beginning to end. I would have taken you to my bed years ago if you had let me — other women have, and were glad to — but I knew it wasn't possible, so I waited. I waited for you. Do you understand that?"

When did this situation start to get out of hand? I asked myself suddenly. What was happening?

"Jamie —" I tried to reason with him. After all, he was *Jamie*. He had always shown me such grace and loving kindness. "I'm most grateful for your patience. Many things have been difficult in my life and you have made them better by doing what you've done.... *all* that you have done. Where would I be without you? I'm not deliberately trying to reject you or your advances, I only —"

He cut me off. "*Good*. Then climb into the bed." He motioned to the low mattress behind him. "I'm not going to hurt you, just climb into the bed —"

This demand was reasonable, I told myself. His frustration made sense. I'd given him very little in return for the constant faithfulness he had shown me. Only shy of a couple of weeks ago I had told him I wanted a life with him and he had placed every confidence in me. Now here I was, after all of his efforts and unwavering loyalty, expressing uncertainty, unable to explain myself.

I found myself climbing into the bed that night, hopeful that I could soothe his disappointment and somehow rally from my own disinterest. My clothing was still on, but this did nothing to dissuade my young husband. He lay down next to me, turned my face towards his, and resumed kissing me without word. Soon, his fingers moved for the collar of my dress and I allowed him to unbutton this now, exposing the chemise beneath. An excitement began to build in him again; he wanted this with a need I did not share. I wondered briefly if I was capable of sharing it with him at all, not just tonight. My heart simply refused to function.

As he began to peel off my clothes layer by layer, I grew quieter and quieter. My body grew still. At last he looked up at me, saw something in my face that irritated him, and he growled, "Are you even attempting to participate?"

At these words I sat up and reached for my clothing, which he had tossed aside. "I'm sorry, Jamie," I told him, decided now. I moved away from him on the bed and began re-dressing myself. "There's no sense in trying. I have nothing to offer."

He let out a strangled sound of aggravation and jumped off the mattress. He stood at the foot of the bed, nearly naked now, and glared at me with eyes I did not recognize. He was quickly becoming a man I did not know. "Is this what life is going to be like with you for the next twenty years? I'm not sure I can cope with that."

These words were a blow. I wanted to please him. I wanted to re-pay the love and generosity he had given me. I wanted this to work, badly. He was my one friend, my only support. Without him, where else could I go? I bowed my head and could not look at him.

"I'm sorry, Jamie," was all I could murmur. "I'm sorry."

Angry now, he wordlessly stormed from the room. In another second I heard the front door slam. Apparently neither one of us had enough strength of person to give any more to the situation. He had left me behind.

That night, alone and in a strange place, my sleep was fitful and anxious. When I did finally sleep, I dreamt. And in the dream someone called my name from out of the darkness, as if trying to summon me.

Strangely, he called for *Isobel*. I had no idea who it was. The tone and timbre in his voice was not one I knew or had known. But he was persistent. By the time I woke early and pulled back the drapes from the bedroom windows to let in the cold winter light, I felt as though the man had been calling my name all night long.

Jamie returned the next morning, but his mood was sullen and he had little to say. He gave no explanation for where he had been. His clothing was rumpled and untidy; I suspected he had slept in an alley somewhere. I prepared us a small breakfast and he ate it eagerly, but this did not seem to assuage him. Shortly after, he emerged from the bedroom well-groomed and in clean clothing, pulled on his heavy coat, and muttered something nearly indiscernible about the shop. With these brief unhappy words, he was gone.

The following week followed a similar pattern. Jamie arose early, disappeared for the day to the shop, and did not return until well after dark, when I was safely asleep and out of his way. During these days I could not help but think of Gran's words and felt uneasy, but I still had hope that we could reconcile. There was every reason to believe that, with time and rest for both of us, we could resume the happy contentment that had been prevalent in our relationship thus far.

This point seemed proven several days later when Jamie returned home early just at the supper hour. After shedding himself of several winter layers of clothing, he immediately sat down at our table in the main room and watched me with an interested eye as I rustled about the little kitchen preparing the evening meal. His countenance was not dark or brooding as it had been and I took encouragement from this. As I examined the single portion of food I had prepared upon completion, I concluded I was happy to divide my meal with him if it meant we could reunite.

As I joined him at the table and we began eating, Jamie was the one who broke the silence. He casually spoke of the customers who had placed orders this week and all that his work had required of him. Everyone thus far had been pleased with his craftsmanship, had paid him and promised to return. It was clear from the amount of human traffic that word was quickly getting out to Wilsburg of a quality cobbler who was available for service.

As we talked, a ray of hope seemed to part the overcast sky that had ruled over us the past several days. Jamie brightened and relaxed. I told him I had been preparing our second room for receiving patients and hoped to begin this soon after a brief visit to the other Healer in town. I did not want to begin a new practice without respectfully communicating it with him. Jamie could see my enthusiasm and seemed to take heart. My recent efforts gave us cause to look ahead together and recall our plans; this could be a good life if we both applied ourselves to it.

We pointedly did not discuss the struggle of our first night, nor did Jamie offer assurances of more patient behavior. We simply moved ahead.

That night, lying in the dark side by side, Jamie's hands reached out for me. I could sense his craving in his touch, in his restless actions, but this did little to awaken my heart or my desire for him. He wanted my body, strangely, but did not seem in these moments to want me. For a short while I allowed for it, hoping my feelings would change, hoping to please him, hoping I was wrong about him. A tremendous amount of guilt and obligation towards him battled within my soul.

I tried to convince myself that I was simply inexperienced and all men became lost in the need for physical gratification, but I knew better. Something was driving him I did not understand and could not explain...

After a while, as Jamie's passion increased into a fire, I realized I could not meet his need and pushed him away. He did not at first respond to this, until I used the force of my hands to shove him entirely away from me. I had nursed many strong and heavy patients over the years and my body did not lack for muscular strength.

This action, which caught him by surprise, nearly threw him off the bed. He immediately came to his feet, cursing. I quickly grappled in the darkness for my gown and discovered it on the bed, trembling as I pulled it on.

For a moment I heard Jamie fumble in the dark for matches on the bureau, then light broke as he put the small torch to the oil lanterns on the opposite wall. His foul curses did not stop even during this action. He was more furious than I knew him to be capable of.

At last he spun around, eyes burning in the eerie shadows of the little room, jaw agape with fury. "I see I will have to lower my expectations exceedingly if I want to keep you," he snarled.

Again his words were a powerful blow. My love and appreciation for him had been birthed in the revelation that he wanted me when no one else did, had loved me when everyone else had abandoned me. His steadfast love for me defied the idea that I was unlovable, un-keepable and undesirable.

"Maybe everyone was right about you," he lashed out mercilessly.

I recoiled. His harsh words implied that I was the reason he was angry and disappointed. I was the cause and the failure. This entire situation I found myself in was my doing.

The transformation occurred for Jamie instantly, unlike the people from where he had come. The wolves had taken many years to gain the level of influence and control they had over the citizens of Huntsville. Tonight it happened for him at once as he gave way to it. In a single heartbeat his eyes burned an intense yellow, gleaming at me with evil intent. His breathing became hoarse and ragged. His lips parted, panting. I watched in horror as he disappeared altogether and a venomous creature took his place, standing taller on all fours than the height of the bed, a shocking incongruity in the domestic safety of the little cottage. He was a hairy beast black as night, dangerously muscular, pale fangs bared.

The creature spoke to me in a low raspy snarl from the foot of the bed. "You are useless. A failure as a woman. We cannot stand you."

He knew he held the power in this situation; it was there in his tone, in his smug expression, in the proud slow way he turned his body and moved for the side of the bed which faced the door, blocking my only exit.

Trembling violently, in shock, I peered at him over the hem of the blankets, which I realized I had grabbed to hide myself beneath. There was no possible way I could fight myself free of this room. His teeth alone could tear me limb to limb.

"Speak!" he commanded. "Speak your mewly little words. I enjoy playing with tiny kittens."

Odd shadows danced and swayed on the edges of the room from the flickering lanterns as they caught the wolf's image and distorted it. I could hardly breathe.

"I have nothing to say to you," I told him, but the words were small and unshed tears were heavy in my throat. Fear felt like a crushing force resisting my entire being.

"Every kitten has a cry," he assured me, yellow eyes narrowing.

"Return Jamie," I murmured. "Let him go."

He thought this was amusing. He sat down comfortably on the round braided rug next to the bed, certain he held the controlling power. "I wouldn't be here unless he wanted it. I made the invitation and he accepted."

"He doesn't want it," I insisted. "You deceived him."

"How would you know what he wants? You have never truly known him."

Was this true? Had I never known him? I had seen his goodness, felt his heart. This could not be true.

"Jamie has been holding conversations with me long before you ever showed up in his world," the wolf bragged. "Why do you think I encouraged him to pursue and marry you? You are just like his mother. The perfect candidate for the snare which I set. He hasn't forgotten her or what she did. I've made sure to keep the memory of her betrayal fresh and alive. Thanks to you, he has chosen me at last."

"Get out," I murmured compulsively at these terrifying words. "Get out of my house."

This command roused him to anger instantly. With terrific speed, he lunged forward with a growl, teeth bared. Terrified, I shuffled back on the bed, cowering away from him, but I was too slow. He let out a low roar in his throat as he swung one massive paw, bringing it across my face.

My head reeled back from the blow. I screamed as his claws tore through my flesh.

I had never known such searing pain. Blood splattered onto the blankets, running down my face from cheekbone to chin, spilling over my hands as they immediately reached for the source of pain. I slumped to the bed in a huddle, powerless, weeping.

Expecting further punishment, I did not stay there long. I opened my eyes weakly, still cowering, whimpering uncontrollably. To my surprise, the wolf was gone. My glance moved to the door, but it still remained closed. The cottage was quiet and still. He and Jamie had seemingly disappeared.

I was gasping for air, I realized, and told myself to breathe. The pain was almost too much to bear. For a short while I lay on the rumple of blankets and focused on simply drawing in air and exhaling it in slow even breaths, slowing my heart rate, attempting to calm my nerves. *He was gone now,* I told myself, trying to ease the fear.

After an indeterminate amount of time, I told myself I needed to doctor my face. I could feel the wound was still seeping blood, though I had pressed it into the blankets to stymie some of the flow. But unsurprisingly, I couldn't move from the bed. In spite of my best efforts, I could not control the violent trembling in my body, nor the horrific images in my head as the wolf's evil words returned to me again and again. Pain continued to come in waves, though I could not discern between the physical pain of my injuries nor the emotional pain brought on by what the wolf and Jamie had said. Both were equal in strength and torment.

I had no idea how long I remained there on the bed. Wilsburg was a quiet place here in the Housing District. There was no sound or disturbance outside the walls of the cottage, not even a winter wind stirred in the darkness. I was more alone than I had ever been.

Eventually, the oil in the lanterns burned out entirely. At last, at long last, I slept.

I dreamt again that night. This time the voice had a face and I recognized him. King Fumi manifested in the darkness, real and tangible. He stood before me in a velvet blue jacket and ascot tie, looking impressive in his long boots and dress sword, wearing an expression of gentle kindness. *How like Desi he looked*, I thought longingly, even within the realm of the dream. Along with him came the same enchanting light and presence that had arrived with him last time.

"You must call me and I will come," Fumi said. "I will come, Isobel. *Call me.*"

I awoke the next morning on the floor of the bedroom, stiff and uncomfortable. I realized I had tumbled from the bed at some point in the night, perhaps in my efforts to leave it. Stretching, drowsily making my way to the curtains, I threw them back and allowed the harsh light of a winter day to pour in. It was mid-day already. Snow had fallen in the night, covering our yard in a white undisturbed blanket. The little cottage directly across from ours reflected snow on its roof; small icicles hung at the windows and door frame. Such a picturesque image was deceptive, I thought. The snow looked inviting, when such cold temperatures would inevitably drive everyone back inside.

It was then memory flooded back. Shocking, disturbing. My hands reached for my face immediately. I felt nothing there.

My mind whirled for a moment. I rushed for a little hand- mirror I kept on the bureau and raised it to my face, heart racing. What I saw there stunned me. There was no trace of the wolf's strike; my face was completely whole.

I turned away from the bureau, confounded and confused. My eyes caught sight of the bed and I quickly rushed for the blankets now, searching them for stains of blood. Again there was nothing, not even a trace. It was as though the night before had never happened.

Standing there in the little bedroom, half-afraid to explore other parts of the house for fear of finding Jamie or the wolf, I had no doubt that what I had experienced was real. For a moment I was tempted to doubt my sanity, but quickly resisted this. I didn't know how the Evil had managed this illusion, but the pain I had felt, the trauma I had experienced, was entirely authentic and still present within me. I was shaken and trembling even now. I determined that I didn't care if the wolf had taken all proof that he had come and torn away at my body and my soul; I knew it was tangible and my suffering was not an illusion.

I wanted to leave right then and there. This was not negotiable. I could not stay in this house. However, I realized desperately, a single challenge worked against me — I had nowhere to go. I knew no life outside of this Wood, no people but my own. All of them were equally dangerous. I would probably starve by the time I found another town or village outside of the forests, and even then I wasn't certain what to expect. There were many conflicting reports describing Hadithi and other parts of the land.

Memories of the dream came wafting back to me now. Briefly, I considered this. I found it difficult to grab hold of King Fumi's assurance that he would come for me. The White Palace seemed ages ago now and nothing had come of it. In my despair, it was easier to believe I could find my own way out of this trap rather than rely on an invisible spirit or persons from another dimension to save me. That had not worked so well for me last time.

I *will* try and get out, I promised myself that morning. I would not stay. But it would take time and financial planning.

With this vow made, I moved for the other parts of the cottage and began my day.

This season of my life played out with great difficulty. The wolf returned again and again, always appearing after Jamie flew into a rage, which grew frequent and his words stronger. More than just unrequited physical desire enraged my young husband; with time, a great deal of my overall behavior miscellaneously triggered his intense frustration and fury. Each time the wolf would come as a result, consuming Jamie until he disappeared entirely, delighting in the slow kill of my spirit and my person. The beast often struck me again and again with his forepaws, tearing through my flesh. Our house was filled with the sounds of my screams. And each morning afterward I awakened physically whole, with my mind reeling and my inner person damaged outside of my control.

At times I grew desperate to escape, but did not know how. No one would believe me, I was certain of that. Even Wilsburg, who was deeply committed in their relationships no matter what state they as individuals were in, would have no understanding or toleration for my claims. I obviously lacked any proof of Jamie's abuse or the difficult situation I was in; he was, to the people of Wilsburg, charming, at times entertaining, and a sound businessman. Additionally, my healing services did not often receive cash payment for the treatment I delivered and saving was a slow long process.

To my shock, I looked up one day and realized years were passing. How adaptable I had become, I thought. How clever I was at holding myself together in public with my patients, with various members of the community, at church when we attended, and with Jamie when we went out together. In its twisted obscene way, life had taken on a normalcy and a routine.

For a long while I didn't know what Jamie wanted. He was after something in every conversation we held, but what? Over time he had decided he needed to convince and persuade me of his beliefs and thoughts. I knew the wolf only desired to take my soul in any way he could, perhaps even eventually control me as he had everyone else I knew — but it was not clear what the man wanted.

Jamie never demanded, commanded or insisted. Somehow he knew this wouldn't work. Instead, he used implication. He used anger to force his will. When he was calm, he used extreme intelligence and calculating rationale to persuade and convince, even when I was uncertain or doubtful, *especially* then. The words "come let us reason together" did not exist for him. He verbally forced his way. There was a consistent, marked lack of encouragement and validation for what I had done right.

Over time, as I examined it closely and examined him, I realized he was trying to shape me into the woman that was pleasing to him. I became convinced he really did want me, but I did not meet his criteria. So he resorted to manipulation and pressure to gain control. This was different than giving voice to frustration, hurt or disappointment. There was a difference. This had motivation.

At the same time, I was equally convinced he didn't know he was manipulating me. The man himself only thought he was passionately expressing what he felt. He had not been made aware yet of his own behavior. The truth was, Jamie had probably been manipulating in his relationships since he was very young, especially with women. High chances were he had learned this skill from watching his father, I guessed.

In later years, when I heard people talking about controlling individuals, I knew when they were wrong or falsely accusing. I knew from experience.

Control was not being bossy or the act of requiring something of you. It was not standing in a place of authority, or even presuming authority over you inappropriately as sometimes people did. Its way was not blunt or direct speech alone, and its indicators were not just because I felt pressure from the conversation. Just because I felt pressure did not mean someone was applying it. This was more clever than that; it was both wheedle-some and forceful. Inadvertently, Jamie was attempting to bend me to his will and shape me into his ideal by training me to avoid his temper and displeasure.

By age twenty-four, I had grown in success as a Healer in the Northern communities. Wilsburg's second Healer, Nodden, often shared his patients with me when he was away or tending to personal matters, increasing my name even more. Jamie too had done well and was already training an apprentice as an assistant with the hopes that he would not have to work so hard and for such long hours in the near future. There were many days and nights we did not see each other, such was the nature of our work. I was often called away to other parts of the Northern Wood and was glad for it.

I never returned to Huntsville during these years, nor did I see Gran. Occasionally one of its citizens would arrive in Wilsburg on some errand or other, but I avoided them in the streets if I saw them. When it suited him, Jamie would make small trips to see his father and would bring back news of the community. This alone was satisfactory enough for me. As much as I needed free of the situation I found myself in, I was also determined to leave my first twenty years behind me and remain looking forward.

In late spring of that year, I was visited by a patient I had not seen in some years. This was an older woman who lived in downtown Wilsburg with her son and his family and proudly preferred Nodden as her Healer over myself for reasons she never fully disclosed. Like all People of the Wood, even the Northern population, she enjoyed a good story about her neighbors. That day she arrived complaining of pain in her knee joints, but I knew immediately from her expression that she had much more to tell.

She waited until I had already examined her knees and encouraged her, as I had years ago, to make small adjustments in her diet and to exercise regularly. She was clearly overweight and was not in the least active. Unsurprisingly, today she allowed this counsel to wash right over her and then fixed me with a clever eye. I knew that expression; Gran had worn it so much and so often I could have identified it a half-mile away.

Standing in my little examination room with her, I asked, "Is there something else, Mrs. Bansburry?"

She nodded primly. "Yes, I'm afraid there is. But I'm not quite sure how to broach the subject."

She enjoyed appearing fragile and frail, but carried a mighty verbal bat to swing with when she wanted it. This I knew well. "Well, just say it out then, I guess," I told her. "Healers hear and see all kinds of absurd things, it's unlikely that I will be surprised."

"Oh, I don't know about this one, dearie," she assured me. "I imagine it would be difficult for any young bride to hear."

Hinting was a classic trademark among the lovers of gossip. That I knew well too. Unmoved by her implications, I moved away from her to the door and threw it open, indicating that she could go. I doubted there was anything she could say to hurt me that had not already been expressed in my short life-time. "I will leave the decision to you then. You can tell me or not, it is entirely up to you."

She didn't move from her place next to the examination table, she decided to speak. "There's been rumors going around for awhile now. I ignored them until I saw it for myself four days past right there on Main Street. Do you know what I'm talking about at all, Mrs. Morrison? It involves your husband. I'm sure you've heard the rumors."

I forcibly held back a sigh. "Wilsburg is filled with rumors, Mrs. Bansburry, even rumors about my husband. I would have to know more details before I could confirm or deny."

She shook her head. "I just don't know if it's my place to say. But I'd feel like a poor neighbor and a poor friend if you weren't made aware. Your husband has been seeing another woman, Mrs. Morrison. I saw it myself. He was walking with her on Main Street, and shortly after they entered the hotel together. Mind you, I waited around in case it was something else entirely. I took a seat right there in the hotel lobby, and lo and behold, they both came down from the upstairs together *an hour later.*" Her expression was pure vixen at this point; she was enjoying her moment tremendously. "I don't suppose he was going up to her room to see about her shoes, do you?"

Now it was my turn to shake my head at her. She was a true professional in her craft. But I'd grown even more skilled in the past few years at keeping an unmoved expression in the midst of fire. "Did you know the woman?" I asked.

"No, not at all," she assured me. "I've never seen her before."

I smiled at her with perfect composure. "That was Mr. Morrison's sister, my dear Mrs. Bansburry. She was visiting from out of town and we have no room here in the cottage to host her. She comes from time to time to visit. So you see, the situation was entirely harmless."

Mrs. Bansburry was not at first entirely convinced. I could see it in her narrowed eyes and shrewd expression. Eventually, however, when I gave her nothing else and seemed so unconcerned, she was forced to abandon her hope that she had discovered the story of the century.

She hobbled to the door where I still stood waiting and said as she passed me, "As long as you feel certain, I guess... Sounds like Mr. Morrison is on the up and up..."

"Yes," I agreed, "It certainly does."

Shortly after, once I'd shown her to the door and was persuaded that she was safely on her way down the street, I drew a heavy breath and leaned against the back of the door. Somehow I had no doubt that her story was true. Jamie hadn't attempted to touch me in ages. We hadn't had a romantic interaction more than half a dozen times in the past few years. I had never grown fond of anything physical much beyond kissing and suspected he knew this fully. Physical contact for me required intimacy and love, and there was precious little of that between us. It stood to sound reason that Jamie had been seeking pleasure elsewhere.

That night he came home at the supper hour and joined me for the evening meal. His talk was filled with recent customers and challenges at the shop; he did not notice that I was unusually quiet, listening.

Earlier in the day I had briefly considered not saying anything at all about what I had heard, but this eventually passed. I could not sleep in the same bed with him without both of us acknowledging his indiscretions. Even if I risked his temper and a foul evening afterward, the truth had to be brought up. We could not pretend.

After Jamie had completed his meal and was preparing to leave the table, I said to him, "Mrs. Bansburry came by today. She had the same complaint she did a few years ago."

"She pays well, at least," Jamie inserted. "There's that."

"Yes." I pondered this temporarily. I decided the best approach was the direct one. "She says she's recently heard a lot of rumors that you were seeing other women. She followed you and an unfamiliar woman into the hotel the other day and observed you both come from upstairs together about an hour later. I told her the woman she saw was your sister visiting from out of town."

Silence fell. A dark cloud came over Jamie's face as we took each other in across the little round table. He had aged in looks in the past five years, but the change had only served to compliment him. He was handsome and distinguished for the People of the Wood.

He glowered at me now. "I wouldn't have to find other women if you were a more willing lover. Don't make this out to be my fault; I'm not the one to blame."

When he said these things in the early days, I was devastated, but the blunt lack of love in his words did not affect me as deeply any longer. I had grown numb and callous to it. Instead I asked him, "Why do you stay then? You could leave. You aren't obligated to be here, at least not by me."

Jamie's eyes glittered. I'd never asked him this question before. Somehow, I could see at once, this was a point of pride and self-respect for him. "Oh, I'm not leaving," he muttered. "If anyone leaves, it will be you."

Once he had allowed this statement time to sink in, he suddenly shifted in his chair, leaning back with a belying casual air. His voice raised to a normal level. "Besides, I'm not the only one who is protecting secrets."

I raised my brows at this accusation, caught by surprise. "I have no secrets from you."

"What about the letter under the loose floorboard in your examination room?" He was glowering again. "Did you think I wouldn't find it?"

I was unmoved by his discovery of Desi's letter and responded instantly, without concern. "That letter is over eight years old. I kept it purely for sentimental reasons. The only reason it is under the floorboard is out of respect for you. I didn't want to upset you."

Jamie scoffed and stood to his feet. "The source of *that letter* is the root of all our problems. The fact that you kept it at all says something, and it says it loud and clear. Now if you'll excuse me — " He glared down at me, daring me to defy him. "I'm going to head back to the shop for the evening. I have some rush orders to complete."

I said nothing further and he was gone within seconds, slamming the door shut as he went. I jumped with the sound. Over the past several years I had grown increasingly sensitive to abrupt noises. After his departure, I sat in the silence that fell over the cottage and allowed myself time to breathe. Our confrontation hadn't gone as badly as I thought it would; I was grateful for that. I did wonder, however, if Jamie had destroyed the letter.

Curious, I went in search of it. I lit a lantern and found my way into the examination room. The floorboard in question was located in a corner next to a long wooden counter space I had paid workmen in Wilsburg to install years ago. I hadn't visited this little space since days after we moved here; I wondered when Jamie had discovered it.

Soon enough, I found he had left the note in its tiny forgotten hole just above the foundation of the house. This surprised me; I had fully expected him to have destroyed it. The little note was aged now and well-creased, but largely unaffected.

Tonight I took it out and opened it; I discovered the words were legible and clear. I had not read it in many years, long before Jamie and I had ever become serious. Desi's thoughts jumped out at me boldly from the written page.

"Dearest Red..."

I don't know why or how the thought came to me as I read it this time. Maybe I came to a new suspicion because I was older now and understood more than I once did, I wasn't certain. But it did suddenly occur to me that this letter was not written in Desi's voice. I had known him well. I spent two summers listening to every expression he used, including his many admissions of love and ardor. He didn't speak like this; the words were not his.

This was Jacobe's voice, I thought suddenly. Of the two, he was the avid correspondent. Didn't Desi say the Huntsman often wrote letters to the King and Queen? How many times had I caught Jacobe in the library penning out his thoughts?

Surprised by this revelation, I read through the note once again, this time imagining Jacobe crafting the words. *Of course he had authored it.* He had been deeply grieved by Desi's behavior and his own inability to change my circumstances; he had given me the words, the *idea* of a goodbye from Desi, in an effort to offer me comfort and hope in my final moments. How utterly like him.

I was grateful to him for it. This did make Desi even more of a coward than I had thought, sadly, but Jacobe had tried to salvage the situation with love. For a moment I held the note to my chest and smiled in quiet thanks. I had not felt love of any kind or in any form for many years.

Then I folded the slip of paper neatly and returned it to its nesting place in the ground.

It was the letter — Jacobe's letter — that gave me the courage to throw caution to the wind and leave Jamie in spite of the risks. Somehow knowing the words had not been a weak attempt to pacify me, written by a naive boy, gave me strength. This had truly been a considerate act of love and kindness. Love, I had begun to learn, gave me strength. It gave me the faith to believe I could walk free.

I began to make my plans, privately, intending to take little with me. I would take the horse and enough food provisions to survive a journey out of the Wood, following the Northern Road from Wilsburg into the unknown lands of Hadithi. I had no maps or sense of which direction to take should the road divide ways, nor could I risk making quiet inquiries beforehand in Wilsburg where Jamie was so loved and respected; I would have to rely on my own instincts and good fortune. Faith was required for this part.

Summer weather would begin in only a few weeks, leaving me several months to find a remote town or village, adequate housing, even work, before the bitterly cold months of winter settled in and survival would be difficult to impossible. The finances I had managed to save in the past five years would make this practicable. I had no form of protection, not even a dagger or boot knife, but I was willing to take the risk. Whatever dangers came, I determined, they could not be worse than living with a wolf.

I chose a day when I had no patients scheduled; Nodden, I felt confident, would ensure that the People were well cared for after my departure. He had a Healer's nature and would keep the People's best interests at heart. Two days before, I had visited the local emporium and purchased canned goods and a little pack which I would carry on my back. The rest of my provisions would be stored in the horse's saddlebags, which we already owned for the purpose of my Healing visits in the Wood. Jamie had little use for the animal, I reasoned, and the loss would not be outstanding. He had enough financial stability by now that he could easily purchase another horse after I had gone. He would be bitter about it and he would consider the act a theft, but that was all.

That day dawned with the usual heavy clouds settled over the width and breadth of town, but I woke feeling an inner excitement I had not experienced since all those years ago when Jacobe told me they would need my services a second summer. This was a momentous day.

I rose at once and prepared myself breakfast, calmly following my regular routine until Jamie was out the door and gone. We had not spoken much since the discussion about his mistresses; he was sullen and simmering with resentment when in my presence.

After his departure, I changed quickly into my riding habit. I had hired the local seamstress to create this for me three years ago, to be used for my regular jaunts into the Wood on house calls. I had deliberately requested that she make it with durable cloth, even at the expense of beauty and design if necessary, and this she did. Her efforts had created a modest, plain brown suit with split skirt and mid-sleeved shirt of the same material, well-designed for riding astride a horse and capable of enduring repeated washings after rough travel through difficult weather or when handling sickly patients. The little habit came with a jacket for cooler weather, and I owned a pair of brown leather boots that would suit my purposes as well.

I pulled my pack out of where I had stored it in the examination room and moved to the bedroom to retrieve additional clothing. There were changes of underclothing, scarves for protecting the ears and head during windy weather, stockings, weather-proofing oil for my boots, and a single skirt should I need it for regular use once I settled into my new life. This would have to be enough.

Before I left the little bedroom for the last time, I slipped my ring off and placed it on the bureau. This would serve as my goodbye and make my message clear. I didn't feel any other form of communication was necessary. I also didn't bother to consider how Jamie would respond or what he would do. He would always do what he willed, he had proven that. He had had plenty of time to work for this marriage, plenty of opportunity to learn to trust and love me. Instead, he had chosen a way filled with hurt, self-pity and hatred. He had chosen to keep the wolf... and his ways.

The last item I wanted with me, I decided, was the note from Jacobe. I would carry it into my future. I certainly wasn't leaving it here to deteriorate under the house.

Moving away from the bedroom and into my examination room, I looked around the space one final time, saying my goodbyes. Once again I was leaving the safety and continuity of this life and beginning anew somewhere else. I took quiet courage. Even without Jamie's help, I would find my way and build again.

I moved for the little corner where the note was held, lifted the floorboard and peered inside using the help of an oil lantern I had brought with me for this purpose. But to my surprise, it was no longer there.

"And what would you be looking for? This?"

I turned quickly. Jamie stood towering in the doorway, eyes burning, the folded note held aloft in one hand. *Of all mornings for him to return home*, I thought. How could he have known? The coincidence was bizarre but not unexpected, considering the amount of strange things I had witnessed about his People and this Wood.

"Yes," I answered directly, "I was. I wanted to see if you had destroyed it. I thought possibly you had."

His voice held rancor as he smiled a wry little smile at me. "I thought it was only for sentimental reasons that you kept it."

"It was. It still is," I told him. "I have no interest in the young man who wrote it. But the note still holds some value to me. It reminds me of a time of happiness."

"And where would you be going?" Jamie asked in that same acerbic tone, glancing at the pack which I now carried on my back.

Slowly, as if I was facing down a difficult patient, I stood to my feet and confronted him across the room. There was something about his manner and his tone that was sending alarming signals to my body and my emotions. "I'm going to see a patient," I told him. "I intended to leave you word. The summons came just a few moments ago and sounds urgent. I'll be gone for the remainder of the day, maybe more."

His eyes narrowed. He was unconvinced. "That's interesting. What exactly is this then?"

He reached inside the front pocket of his breeches and pulled out my ring, which he held up clearly for me to see.

My heart began to beat a quick rhythm. It would be difficult to lie my way out of this situation now. He was too intelligent for that.

When I said nothing, he held both the ring and the note up in his respective hands and smiled again. He knew he had caught me. His voice was cold and sardonic. "Hmmm... A note, a ring, and a full pack. What does all this add up to?"

I did not deny it. "You tell me, Jamie. What does it say to you?"

The tension in the little room was palpable. I could feel myself beginning to tremble. The wolf and his influence on Jamie held a strong power over me. I was weakened and intimidated in these moments, fearing punishment, terrorized by the thought of abuse. They held the power — they had always held the power. Their words were as deadly and as piercing as arrows; the wolf's claws were as torturous as a long slow death.

In that moment a great wave of fury came upon Jamie. He reared back with a low growl and threw the ring at me across the room, viciously. But when he spoke, his voice was the gravelly snarl of the wolf's voice, and Jamie was instantly transformed into the beast. The ring clattered to the floor beside me.

"And where do you think you will run? Where do you think you will hide?" Yellow slanted eyes glared at me from the black face of the wolf.

Instinctively I took a step back, pressed against the far wall of the little room, trembling violently now.

His massive body stepped fully into the dark and windowless room, moving slowly, like an animal of prey who has zeroed in on his next target. He spoke with teeth bared. *"Tell me.* Tell me, Red. Where do you think you can go where the wolves will not hunt you? Where Evil will not find you? There is nowhere for you to go. We dominate."

It took courage, but I said it. Weakly, and with little left in me to resist him with, but I said it. "I will find my freedom. I will find my way."

The wolf thought this was amusing. "What a plain, ordinary woman you've turned out to be, Red. There's nothing impressive about you at all. I thought you were someone great." He paused almost indifferently. "Surely if you were someone great it would have shown up by now. And yet, sadly, here you are. *Nothing. Less* than nothing."

He was nearly to me now, taking his time with his words and his steps. He enjoyed this part of the torment, the wolf did. Often the physical strikes were delivered only when he was finally driven to impatience by my responses. I refused to yield to him.

"I will find my freedom," I repeated. "I will find my way."

Once he was before me, he sat down at my feet casually. Even sitting his muscular body stood nearly as tall as I did. I cowered away from him, pressing myself even more tightly against the wall.

"Now, now, Red," he snarked, eyes glimmering with Evil. "You will never find your way. We will make sure of it. We will tell everyone who you *really* are, what you are *really* like." As if this threat was not clear enough, he proceeded to list the reputation he would give me. "You are difficult. Impossible to live with. An unfaithful wife. A quitter. A runner. We have lived with you and have seen it for ourselves. You are controlling. You are dominating. You are strong-minded and willful. You are a non-conformist. You are disingenuous and cannot be trusted. You are wounded, and you are proud." He blinked at me benignly. "You will never be strong, Red. Not truly. You will never be healthy, and you will never be whole."

These last words, finally, broke me. I found myself releasing a little sob. *Resist him,* I told myself. *Resist him.* This was not the truth. He twisted the truth. He validated the lies others had spoken. He mixed just enough truth in with his lies to add persuasion and cause confusion.

The wolf loved uncertainty, and he could sense it in me now. "Am I getting anywhere with you, Red? You've been such a slow learner. Look at all the mistakes you've made. You could be so much farther along in life, you know, if only you had been a quicker study. Are you getting this now, at last?"

Something in me could never verbally agree with him. Even if I battled and wrestled with these words and these lies... even if all of his horrible thoughts caused me restless nights and distracted days... I could not, *would* not, come into agreement with them. He was trying to break me with his lies... and I refused to be broken.

Frightened, terrified, cowering, I raised my eyes to his and said simply, "I will find my freedom. I will find my way."

This at last infuriated him. He let out a furious growl and jumped up with his forepaws heavy on my chest, pushing against me with his weight, staring into my eyes with a malicious expression. His hot foul breath was in my face.

I was weeping by now, sobbing softly in terror. I knew what was coming next.

"*We* determine your destiny," he snarled. "*We* decide your fate!"

With these terrible words, the wolf raised one paw and swiped at my forehead. I screamed. The force of the blow knocked me away from him and to the floor.

Bleeding profusely now and filled with pain, I had no defense against him. He struck again, this time at my legs, my hips, across my chest. Again and again he struck, tearing through my clothing, searing my flesh. Blood flowed everywhere, in such great amounts I did not think I would survive. I screamed again and again in response. When he grew tired of swiping at me, he sank his teeth into my arms, my hands. He gripped my hair with his jaws and tore away at it, snarling, growling, delirious with a feverish rage.

I was powerless against him, unable to defend myself. Even my screams faded away eventually; they used too much strength. Without resistance he was free to exact the revenge he wanted, the punishment he felt was deserved. There was no way to survive this attack, I thought.

Then at last, mercifully, as it always did, darkness enfolded me... and I remembered nothing more.

Someone called my name.

The sound at first seemed as though it came from the end of a long dark tunnel. They called me again. This time it seemed closer, more tangible, echoing against the walls of my darkened mind.

They called me a third time, even closer still.

At last I stirred. I was unable to open my eyes, unable to move, but somehow I knew they were in the cottage. Curiously, I knew nothing else, remembered nothing else, but my self-preservation instincts understood someone had entered the house and was searching room to room for me.

They called my name again.

No strength returned to me, so I could make no response. They would simply have to find me, *here.*

A light broke through the darkness. This light was not glaring or difficult to look into. I opened my eyes very slowly. They had found me now and stood in the doorway of the room, on the other side of the examination table.

I realized the light belonged to a body, and the body swept into the room until he stood looking down on me. I could barely peer up at him. *Did I know this man?* I wasn't certain.

"She's in here!" he called to someone else.

In another instant he was kneeling beside me, looking into my face. "Can you hear me? Do you understand who I am, Isobel?"

This was Fumi, I realized. *Fumi was here.* He was dressed just as I'd seen him in the dream those many years ago, a refined and distinguished nobleman with that inviting manner and warm spirit. Since then he had grown a full beard and heavy mustache, both well-groomed. But it was his eyes that struck me. Large brown pools of compassion and tenderness stared into my face.

My voice was but a croak when I attempted to speak. "*Fu — mi —* "

He understood this. His voice was thick with kindness. "Yes, my dear. You would not come to me, so I broke the rules and came to you."

Weak tears slipped down my face. I was too frail, too numb, too broken to say anything in response. My body would not move.

He smiled tenderly hunched there next to me, glowing like the warm silver light of the moon. "You've been very badly wounded, but with your permission I would like to take you somewhere safe. Will you let me care for you awhile? I will protect you as no one else can." There was a vow in these words as well as an assurance.

"Yes," I murmured, and then lost consciousness again.

The second time when I woke another light had entered the room, this time as a large, brightly lit lantern held in the hands of a massive man in a sweeping red cloak and heavy boots. Something told me I should know him, but I could not recall who he was. The blazing light made me wince and I closed my eyes. Randomly, I wished somehow that sleep would take me once more; there was relief in sleep. It was in that darkened state that I didn't feel anything whatever.

"Red?"

I knew that voice, I told myself.

"Red, can you hear me?"

I didn't answer him, but I did open my eyes again and stare at him. He was kneeling on one knee before me, studying my body and the state I was in. In a quick motion that was too dizzying for me to follow, he untied his cloak and swept it free.

He intended to throw this over me, but as his hands moved closer I recoiled suddenly, violently, then shuddered from the immediate pain this caused. "Don't touch me," I gasped out hoarsely. "*Don't* — touch me."

The man stopped instantly. He leaned back, away from me, his hands raised palm up as a sign of surrender. In a low hushed voice, he said, "It's just me, Red. Jacobe." His wild eyes, I noticed, were deeply grieved. "I'm not here to hurt you. I'm going to take you to Fumi. He's outside waiting."

"Fumi?"

He was very patient. "Yes. King Fumi. He was just here, remember? He asked me to take you to him. I'm here aiding him in your rescue." He gave me a moment to digest this.

Now that he had given the explanation, I could recall, faintly, that King Fumi had been here and spoken with me. *That seemed ages ago,* I thought, surprised. Along with this understanding also came the acceptance that this was *Jacobe. He was here in the cottage...*

"Jacobe," I murmured.

This made him break into a small pitying smile. *"Yes.* Will you allow me to take you outside? We have a litter for you. It's very comfortable and you will be safe the entire way there, I promise you."

I nodded weakly.

This time when he brought the cloak forward he kept his actions slow and his motions paced. He dropped it over me carefully.

Immediately I was bathed in a holy warmth from head to toe. I marveled within myself. *What was this?* A small amount of strength entered my limbs and fed me life, and I felt myself gaining a little more lucidity.

With exceeding gentleness for my broken body, Jacobe maneuvered me so that I was entirely wrapped in the cloak. Nimbly, he brought the giant hood down over my brow. Then, with great tenderness, he slid his arms beneath my form, lifted me, and stood to his feet.

This action alone was almost too much motion, too soon. I tensed and murmured. Jacobe halted his progress instantly, peering down at me beneath the hood.

"Red? That's the worst of it, I promise. All right?"

I nodded feebly.

With this confirmation given, he tucked me into his massive chest and walked me from the cottage.

Upon exiting the house, I realized it was night and wondered how long I had been lying on the floor before the two of them arrived. I couldn't remember much still, but I knew it had been daylight hours when I was last awake. Something terrible had happened.

Jacobe took me to a colossal red horse, lit just now by the brightness of the moon, which shone with a rare brilliance down upon us. This was *Thunder*, I realized. Along with Jacobe's horse, another one stood waiting nearby, its rider mounted and quiet. The enormous hood prevented me from seeing little more than that, but I understood, with a slow careful understanding, that the second rider was Fumi, we were in Wilsburg, and the two of them were escorting me to safety.

Behind *Thunder* an empty litter had been towed in anticipation of a need for it, covered in a small mattress and several blankets. Jacobe took me to this, swept aside the blankets, and laid me gently down upon it. There were wide belts attached to the litter, which he buckled around me, explaining quietly as he did so.

"These are for your safety only, Red. I don't want you to slip out during the journey, you understand? In a few moments you will not feel or know a thing. I'm going to put the sleep on you. Do you remember what that is? It simply means you are going to sleep during this journey very peacefully. This will be easiest for you."

I nodded again, acknowledging his words. I fully understood who he was now and knew I would be safe in his care.

"Everything is going to be all right now, Red. Everything —" Even the mighty Huntsman could not finish his words. Grieved, he shifted back to his feet, intending to leave me.

But I stopped him. "Jacobe —"

As small as the sound was, he halted and turned back. One of his hands reached out and lifted the hood so my face was fully exposed to the moonlight. He waited.

I could see his face clearly, lit now by the moonlight that seemed to illuminate the world tonight in a wondrous pale-stone color. The rare, midnight-blue skies behind his bent head were cloudless and sparkling with the glow of a thousand stars, adding to the deep sense of mystery and beauty. Like Fumi, Jacobe too was bearded and had cropped his long, wild hair. His facial hair now hid a great deal of the scarring on the left side of his face and brought less focus to his colored markings, but those powerful eyes were still his, glancing down at me. I was in awe that he was actually *here*.

I had to work a moment to find the physical strength to say the words, but he waited patiently until they came.

"You — you wrote the letter. Didn't you?" I prompted him.

A look of surprise came over his face, quickly whisked away. His answer was simple. "Yes. I was hoping to give you something, since Desi left you with nothing. I'm sorry, Red."

I attempted a smile. A weak tear slipped from one of my eyes, burning painfully as it streaked downward over open wounds and fell to my ear. "Don't be," I whispered. "It was beautiful."

Jacobe's voice dropped to a low tone, moved by my words, almost unable to speak. "Sleep now, Red. The journey won't take long."

Part 2

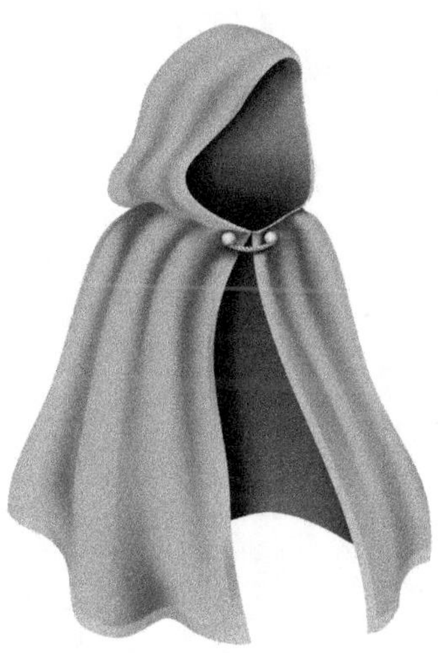

7.

I woke peacefully in a beautiful place, though I had no idea where. The vaulted ceiling above me, as tall and as arched as the sanctuary in a grand cathedral, was fashioned of framed clear glass. Through this I could see a bright cloudless sky of azure blue. Certainly no sky I had ever witnessed shined so bright or appeared so limpid.

As I slowly became aware of the happy sound of gurgling water and the slight rustle of wind in leaves, my gaze drifted from the ceiling to the walls around me made of white stone brick. These were decorated with hand-woven tapestries at eye level, which revealed peaceful images of bright-colored flowers and treeless rolling countryside. I had never seen pictures like them; even the White Palace had been decorated with strange weapons and other masculine items that represented a different taste. The images themselves, I took especial note, were of places and plants I had never seen in the Wood.

The room was long and wide — again, like the sanctuary of a cathedral — and caught me momentarily. It was difficult to believe this was a bedroom. Filled with light, airy, the size of it alone was as large as the central room in the Palace. Slowly, I scrambled to a sitting position, taking it in.

I lay in a white-painted, wooden poster bed as large as Gran's kitchen room in Huntsville, outfitted with a sea of silk coverlets and soft woven sheets. This enormity became a natural divider for the room. On one side a sitting area was piled high with deep cushions and pillows. Leather chests and other carved boxes served as low stands and end tables, upon which dozens of strange lanterns and brass fixtures had been placed. It was in this direction, at the end of the long room, that I saw two arched doors shut just now and also white, as nearly everything seemed to be here.

To my right was the source of the water and leaves. Here the brick floor ended eventually and became a small patch of dirt, grass and soil. Amazingly, a full-grown oak tree spread its limbs and grew in the natural sunshine of the room, its root system trailing over the ground at its feet until it reached the banks of a tiny creek that gurgled and chirped happily on a low bedrock, running through that side of the room. On the opposite side of the creek was a tiny plot of grass and beautiful flowers, just now bathed in morning sunshine, which streamed in through a glass wall of windows built in a half-circle from floor to ceiling.

Unable to resist this, I swept back the blankets and moved from the bed, making the discovery as I did so that I was pain-free and scar-free. My hands moved quickly for my face; my eyes roamed over my hands and arms where the wolf had bitten me. There was nothing there. Whether this was a result of the natural phenomenon that occurred every time he came, or whether I had been miraculously healed, I did not know. I did know I could move freely, as I took my first waking steps around the room. There was no sign of the terrible damage the wolf had done to my body.

I could also remember almost everything before this present reality with clarity. As I roamed over the room, investigating the oak tree first, stepping over the creek barefoot and burying my toes in the downy grass of the other side, I remembered the final events that had brought me here. With every memory that surfaced now, I felt safe. Safe in this warm sunshine, in this quiet air, in this hushed room... wherever it was they had brought me.

Thoughts of Jacobe and Fumi made me curious. Outside the walls of this room, through the glass wall, there did not seem to be any markings or fences to mark boundaries. Instead I saw thin belts of trees and bare rolling hills, an empty countryside that glowed with natural greens and browns in the morning sunlight. *Where had they brought me? Alameth?* Whatever this place was, I had a great sudden longing to explore every inch of its countryside. Outside of the White Palace, I'd never walked anywhere that I was not buried in shadow from the dense, impenetrable trees around me, haunted by the Evil that resided there.

Even more curious now, I moved soft-footed for the other end of the room, intending to leave and find my rescuers. My eyes caught sight of Jacobe's cloak, a bright red splash among the muted colors in this room. Someone had draped it over the back of an exquisite dressing chair. I was dressed in a loose thin gown, I realized, and quickly reached for the cloak. As I draped it around me, the bulk of it was obviously twice my size; the hem trailed behind me by a few feet and the shoulders dragged heavily. The hood was impossible to see through if I used it. But I could not deny the warmth the cloak instantly brought to my entire body, an additional security that came at once which had nothing to do with the fact that it belonged to Jacobe and what he represented. Not surprisingly, the cloak was as gifted as he was.

Wrapping it around me as securely as I could, I left the room, quickly discovering that the entire Palace — for surely this was a Palace, as large and as grand as each room was — was built and designed in a curious mixture of glass, simple white-painted woods, and pale stone brick. High vaulted glass-ceilings were a prevalent fixture here, allowing for warm sunshine and bright skies to shower down upon its inhabitants within.

As I padded bare-foot through the spacious rooms, strangely without a fear of becoming lost nor worry about my destination, I found it was also filled with a hushed quiet, reminiscent of a holy or sacred place... somewhere one could easily sleep or freely laugh without retribution for either one. I walked through living rooms and common rooms, surely enough space and accommodations for a large number of guests and house parties. Yet there were no other people here, I observed. Not even the faintest sound of activity stirred within its walls and spacious passageways.

Eventually I did find my host. He was seated at the end of a long stone table, at the end of an even longer, narrow hall built with many arched doors and exits. Behind him a massive hearth burned with open flame, putting off a warm heat that reached me clear at the end of the table where I found him. Fumi looked up and smiled warmly at once when I entered; before him was an array of beautiful silver dishes filled with food.

"Isobel, do come in. I was waiting for you to find your way. Please, come sit and eat. You must be hungry by now." His voice was warm and inviting, rather like I imagined a good father would be. I had known precious few of those in the Wood.

I moved for his end of the table; he came swiftly to his feet and pulled away a high-backed chair on his left. Not even its heavy feet scraped the stone floor with a harsh sound as I was accustomed to; everything here was muted, its volume soothing and relaxed. Fumi seated me, then resumed his own place, motioning towards the spread of food before him. A setting of silver plates and cutlery had been placed for me in advance.

"Please, eat," he said. "You should eat as much as you are able while you are here. It will bring you life and health."

I could not reach for the food at once; I was too struck by the majestic man seated casually next to me. The crown upon his curly-mopped head, nestled comfortably at his brow, was a different one than I'd seen him wearing before. This diadem was notably magnificent, created in white-gold and designed with several sharp points, each imbedded with tiny blood-red jewels that burned and glowed in the sunshine streaming in from the glass overhead as he moved. He wore a pale velvet robe cinched at the waist by a matching belt, from the ends of which dangled loose tassels, also blood-red. His clothing rippled and shimmered slightly as he moved.

His form, I noticed, was strong, but not a warrior's like Jacobe, nor a manual laborer like the men I had known. He was a king, and there was no forgetting in Fumi's presence that he was a king. He had a dignity, a stature, a confidence. He was a man among men. There was no sign of the broken, abused boy of Hadithi I had read about in the White Palace books.

Yet I was not afraid of him, nor did I feel small in his presence; rather, I was drawn to him. He was the greatest being I had ever been near. Just as before, a light emanated from his person. Though muted now in this place that already shone with so much freedom and light, it was present still and part of him.

Immediately I was filled with questions. Unable to contain myself, they quickly overflowed. "Can I ask what this place is, your Highness? It is beautiful. Glorious. Are you real, alive before me? You look young, yet my Gran told me the last she saw you, you were an elderly man." I looked down at my hands and arms in wonder. "Where are the injuries? I had many. Have I been healed? How long have I been asleep? You call me Isobel. You have a reason for it," I guessed. "I — I have no sense of time. Have I already been here long, or did I just wake from our journey?"

Fumi, as I had safely assumed, was not troubled or harassed by my many queries. He paused between bites of the soft bread he was eating, smiled in amusement, and swallowed. He looked over at me. "Questions are a good sign of recovery; I'm glad for it. I promise you, my dear, I will eventually answer them all. But for now, you must eat." He motioned towards the abundance of silver bowls and plates before him filled with foods I did not recognize. "The fruit here is especially full of life that will restore you. Your body has recovered, but the injuries are still there beneath the surface, within your soul. This will take time. There are also many things I want to teach you, to help prepare you for the future. These lessons will grow you, and make you strong and able. Will you allow me to do this?"

His words quieted me, held me in awe. I nodded humbly.

As I reached obediently for the food before me and began eating, Fumi's eye fell to my garments. "I recognize that cloak," he announced conversationally. "I gave it to Jacobe many years ago, when I first met him as a very young man."

I glanced up, thoughts running elsewhere now. "Is he here? I should return it to him."

The King shook his head. "He left for other tasks he must fulfill. Jacobe has found himself in great demand lately in Alameth." He offered no further explanation regarding this. He added, "I'm sure he would have wanted you to keep the cloak or he wouldn't have left it. Consider it a gift."

These thoughts gave me pause for a moment. I considered how often I'd seen Jacobe wearing it in the time I knew him. The cloak had been a primary staple of his wardrobe, surely as notably as his broad-handled axe was always strapped to his back.

Fumi continued, "The cloak has special properties that will protect and keep you safe. I'm quite certain he left it deliberately. If you like, I can have it re-sized for you."

I nodded, still pondering, agreeing to this. I still had not returned to my food.

Fumi seemed to read my thoughts then. He reached comfortably for his goblet, speaking gently just as he lifted it to his mouth, his compassionate eyes still on me. "Be at ease, my dear. You'll see him again. You can thank him in person, I promise you."

Instantly I looked over at him with quiet gratitude. There was such a kind grace about him, especially poignant after the harsh experience of the past many years. "Thank you. *Thank you.*"

With time I discovered many facts about this place I had been brought to. The Palace was called the Qasr of Peace, and was aptly named. Even the immediate grounds around it were wrapped in a blanket of quiet and undisturbed rest. As for the land, I learned it was another dimension similar to Alameth, unoccupied by anyone but Fumi and his guests; this land he called Shamayim. No one came here without express invitation from Fumi and had to be escorted by a Dimensioner, such as Jacobe or the King himself.

Though I could touch and feel him, Fumi was an immortal spirit, I learned eventually; his physical body had died two generations ago. From Shamayim he lived and guided his people, and aided in the growth of Alameth and its citizens. Many people called him Father; others called him King. He was considered the greatest ruler Alameth had ever known.

The Qasr was filled with many delightful inventions from Alameth, scattered throughout the palace in various locations. Some were operated by Fumi's power, I learned; others ran on science and natural resources. He introduced me to many of them as I lived there with him. There were machines for cooking, for heating food, for cleaning, and for building. All of them obeyed verbal commands and worked at incredible speed. I'd seen a few of these at the White Palace, but never to this degree or this ability. There were also other devices which I could not operate as Fumi could — these brought healing and truth and enlightenment. They changed time and altered the future; they saw through dimensions and observed individual lives.

Many weeks and months passed. I had no real sense of time; Shamayim was outside of time, and life with Fumi was abundant and always at ease. The sun never completely died here; there were no moon or stars by which to count the days, and no changes of season to mark the differences in the land outside the Qasr. When I slept, I was unable to tell if it was for a moment, or for days on end.

My only confirmation that time was passing was as my hair began to grow. It had never done so; just as I had told Desi so long ago, it had been unable to. The long strands grew thick and glossy here in Shamayim, with such length that I was forced to seek Fumi out with a request for different brushes and tools to care for it than the simple-toothed combs I had always used and had been left for me in my room upon arrival.

As I always found when requesting something of him, the King's generosity was extravagant. Not only did he provide me with a myriad of hand tools and clever inventions to care for my ever-lengthening hair, but along with this came an entire wardrobe of new clothing that filled the closet in my room. Up till now I had lived with him bare-foot in simple, loose night-gowns that were left for me each morning and evening for changing, always cleaned and pressed. Over these I wore the red cloak, now re-sized, everywhere I went. These new clothes, however, were not of my people or recognizable to me in any way.

This clothing required a skill which Fumi taught me — the draping of long scarves around the neck and shoulders, the swathing of shirts and sleeves. Even the sandals, soft-hide boots, and cloth sashes required an understanding of twisting and tying the materials they were made with, sometimes over-laced by leather string and colorful ribbons, oftentimes decorated with colored beads. I learned eventually to put matching beads in my hair, and created beaded rings for my fingers and bracelets for the wrists and ankles, made with the leather pieces of string. All of these materials were designed of muted colors, autumn reds and oranges, forest greens and browns, both beautiful and yet, uniquely, not attention-seeking. Split skirts of the same colors became part of my primary wardrobe, which provided unrestricted freedom of movement.

I once asked Fumi if this was how Alamethen women dressed, but he told me it was not. His country dressed as Desi and his friends had at the White Palace, he explained. He gave me no further explanation as to why he had chosen this style of clothing for me; I simply accepted it, and enjoyed it. Wearing Fumi's wardrobe, I felt more myself, set apart from the Wood and the places I had known, free in a new life and a new way.

There were other reasons for feeling freer and in a new way. Fumi spent long hours walking with me through the open countryside, speaking truths to replace many lies I had heard my life long. There was no subject he did not eventually touch on, no statement ever made to me rooted in half-truth that he did not correct. Often I became so moved we were forced to halt our steps, and he would enfold me in his loving arms, allowing the tears to freely fall.

As freedom in my soul came, so did life and health. The entire experience with Jamie and the wolf had taken something from me, if not just strength of person. I was, at first, shockingly weak, a withered and broken spirit. Now that I was safe and did not require such an unbending strength, I lived for days trembling quickly, often at the merest disturbance. I walked slowly. My responses were quiet. I was grateful my surroundings were hushed, the sunshine warm, the blankets soft. Eventually, I grew strong, even able to run through the open fields outside the Qasr. Through the looking glass in my room, I could see my skin gleamed now with color, and my dark eyes, so shadowed and heavy before, were sharp and bright.

Fumi was, I learned, often cryptic. He did not reveal everything at once, and many times wanted me to reach my own conclusions which we would then discuss. Yet even in his mystery I always felt he was trust-worthy. There was no truth he wouldn't eventually give me; he was not a ruler who withheld.

At one point I asked him again, "Why do you call me Isobel?"

This time he answered promptly. "Because it is your destiny. Destiny is often found within the name."

"And what is my destiny?" We were walking again, and I paused to ask this of him. "I suspect it must be of some importance or I would not be here, in Shamayim, and you would not have gone to so much work to rescue me."

Fumi stopped with me. He was squinting at the darkening sky, reading the weather which had been threatening rainfall since we set out from the Qasr. He wasn't truly concerned; rainfall here was never difficult and did not last long. Aside from that, Fumi carried the power to change the weather if he wanted.

"I would have rescued you anyway," he said then, and turned powerful eyes upon me. They were filled with a love that could make a strong man weep. "I have rescued many with far lesser callings than yours. Greatness in a person does not motivate me alone. But yes, my dear, your destiny is of great importance. *You* are of great importance. Haven't you sensed that within yourself? Haven't those around you seen it, even those, like your Gran, who are difficult and unloving? Isn't this truly what drew Jamie to you in the beginning and for many years afterward? The wolf did not influence Jamie towards you; he is a master deceiver. Jamie himself saw your uniqueness and desired you. Hasn't Jacobe mentioned it, he being a man who has known many men and women with great destinies and even serves many of them? You must fulfill your destiny, Isobel; I *need* you to fulfill it. You will know it soon enough."

I was crying now, moved by his words.

He read my thoughts then, as he so often did. He smiled gently. "Don't be concerned. You won't fail. *You* won't let you fail, and I won't let you either."

To this, I could only weep all the more.

Our conversations covered a broad range of topics over time. We discussed the wolf, and Jamie, and my life in Wilsburg. He knew everything, every conversation I had endured; he was aware, with intimate understanding, of every moment of difficulty. He had been watching my life, he said, for some time.

"I should have listened to Gran," I told him. "She warned me about Jamie. Even his friend, Geoffrey, alluded to Jamie's propensity for hatred. I should have read the signs."

But Fumi merely shook his head. "You are too critical of yourself, my dear. Your grandmother should have given you love far sooner and was capable of it. I know this to be true. It was impossible for you to listen to her. She had never been a voice of truth, but rather a voice you were forced to guard yourself against. If a man or woman speaks out of both sides of their mouths, how can any word they say be trusted?

"Jamie was the one who showed kindness and love when others sorely rejected and mistreated you. He had not yet chosen the wolf or his ways and very possibly could have chosen another way. He did love you; you were not fooled. Sadly, he had ample opportunity to use your introduction to his life as a chance to love and live, and win your love, but did not. This could have had another ending for him and for you. No —" Fumi smiled at me without criticism. "The only way this could have gone differently is if you had called me sooner. I could have spared you a great deal of pain. But no matter, you are healed now, you have learned, and we will move forward."

After I had been in Shamayim for some time, Fumi brought up a topic we had never before discussed, almost as if he were waiting until many other questions and past wounds were resolved and settled for me. This subject was also mentioned during a walk, where most of our lengthier discussions took place. We never determined a specific direction when we set out on these long hikes, but they took us for miles in all directions around the Qasr.

"About the subject of love, Isobel," Fumi said that day, and then stopped.

I turned to him, curious what he would say. He was dressed as he always was, in a loose robe and sandals, with the sparkling diadem on the crown of his head. He was handsome, regal, and walked alongside me with great dignity. I once thought Fumi had a face that held many secrets, unlike Desi's, who was like him in resemblance only. But Fumi's face held no secrets for me anymore. He was open and transparent.

"Do you still want love, my dear?"

I couldn't answer him right away, struck as I was by the question. I had not reached this point just yet in my own heart. It seemed enough to recover from Jamie and the wrenching disaster that the relationship had been.

Fumi asked another question. "What do you want, Isobel?"

I shook my head at him, answering frankly. "I do not know how to recognize love. I've been deceived now twice. Both nearly destroyed me. Even if you say Jamie could have made a different choice, I don't think I can survive another man like him. I must have someone who is steady, true and enduring from beginning to end."

"I quite agree." Fumi paused. "And if you could recognize it? Would you want love then?"

We walked some distance further. I pondered the answer to this question.

"What do you want for me, Fumi?" I asked quietly. "Do you want love for me?"

He liked these questions; I could sense his pleasure in the small space between us as we took our steps. They revealed how much I had come to trust him, how much I desired his leadership in my life. He truly had become a Father to me.

"Yes," he answered gravely. "I do. But you deserve something extraordinary, my dear. Something not common, not typical. Someone who will never take you or your destiny for granted. I could teach you to recognize the love I send you if you like."

"Am I capable of love after Desi?" I asked him then. This was the real question that had always hindered me from exploring any further thought of romantic love in the amount of time spent here with Fumi. *"Real, abiding love?* I found myself unable to love Jamie fully and he knew it."

Fumi was dry. "You could have eventually if he had not felt he was entitled to you because of the down payment he had made in the relationship. His love was never for free. But I do see your point. Yes, I do believe your heart is very capable of love, now more than ever. You've been healed. Jamie feared you still held love for Desi, but it was the state of your heart that was the issue. Your eyes have always been opened — about yourself, about Desi. You understand love more fully than you ever have... because you've been loved now."

It was true, Fumi's love had somehow healed me. My heart seemed alive and strong again, made whole by his devotion and his ability to speak truth into my darkest areas. He knew all of my secrets, all of my desires; there was nothing hid between us. I had never experienced such a relationship in all my twenty-four years.

I paused in my walking again and turned to him with a watery smile. "If you can teach me to recognize it, Father, I will take love. I will receive it gladly. But he has to be like you. Chiefest of ten thousand."

Fumi's brown eyes were shining at these words, almost to a point of laughter. I had delighted him. "That *is* the secret you seek, my dear. You will know I sent him and know he is true because he is like me. He will sound like me, and have my love for you. He will be a man among men. Does this please you?"

I laughed softly. "I've been ruined on your love. Are you certain this is possible? Can anyone possibly measure up to your love for me?"

It was then Fumi's sparkling eyes narrowed playfully, taking me in. He was the best and closest friend I had ever had. "Don't under-estimate my ability, my dear Isobel. Even a mortal man can be full of my great love for you. I'll make sure of it."

Eventually the day came when Fumi said it was time to return to the Wood. It was a difficult idea and not one I wanted to consider, but I knew he was right. As he often told me in my final weeks there, I had a destiny and must return to follow it. I could not remain in Shamayim forever.

On the day I was destined to leave, I met with Fumi in the dining hall one final time for our evening meal. I had already roamed the Qasr, saying my goodbyes to all the nooks and corners that had been a sanctuary to me for the past several weeks and months. I would miss this place terribly; it had become my refuge and my home unlike any other. Fumi gave me final instructions and answered any lingering questions I had during the meal. There was a quiet awareness between us as we spoke; the hours before my departure were growing shorter with every moment.

"I will always be available should you need me," he told me. "For any reason at all, mind you."

I nodded, acknowledging this. I knew, without being told, that he was returning me to Huntsville. It was there I must take up my life again and proceed forward.

"You will find the atmosphere in the village much changed since you were there," Fumi assured me. "Your reception will be a different one than when you left. You will have victory in every area, I promise you, Red. All of the things I have taught you and told you will aid you in the days to come."

Towards the end of the meal I began to grow drowsy, unusually so. I could barely keep my eyes open as Fumi continued speaking, and scolded myself. I had wanted to savor our last moments together and tell him all that was in my heart. He had saved my life twice, and in the time spent here he had saved my soul; I owed him deeply for that.

"You will have tremendous success in your life, by and by," he promised, as I fought sleep. "You will one day look back on your days in the Wood and smile to yourself because of how great your life has become, how enriched and prosperous your surroundings. You needn't work or strive for it; I will bring it to you. Be brave, my dear Isobel. All will be made clear soon enough."

Finally, I couldn't resist it anymore. I slumped down in the velvet-covered dining chair and fell asleep with Fumi's soothing voice in my head.

When I woke, I did not at first recognize my surroundings. Life at the Qasr had seemed like an eternity and any life before it had grown dim and distant. I opened my eyes and looked around me. I could see I was lying on a bed in a tiny room with a solitary window, which just now reflected sunlight streaming through the thin glass panes. Across the way I recognized a doorless closet full of colored scarves, shawls, and linen materials from my time in Shamayim. That I did understand.

Fumi had transported all of the belongings he had given me, together with me, to this place.

When I crept from the room, I recognized it at once. I was in Gran's cottage in Huntsville. The house did not look as though it had been occupied since the last I was here many years ago, though I couldn't be certain of this. Certainly none of my furniture had moved, and cob-webs hung heavy in the corners of the ceiling. Dust lay across the counters and chairs in thick layers. It certainly needed a good cleaning.

I threw open the front door and found the little yard was grown over and unkempt. The road was damp and muddy from recent rain. The weather, however, was late spring and a warm breeze greeted me invitingly. *So this was where he brought me*, I thought. I had neglected to ask Fumi what his exact plan was; I simply trusted him to work out the details.

To my surprise, I was not oppressed by the sight of the heavy dense trees around me, nor the familiar gray sky above where sunlight battled to break through the cloud coverage. Thoughts of Gran and Huntsville did not discourage me, nor the idea that wolves were here aplenty and had last hated me before I left. I was ready to find this great destiny Fumi had spoken so much about, and to see where my path would lead me. He felt confident before my departure that I was prepared to face the difficulties that had once defeated me, and I felt ready, shockingly, for the challenge. Love was rich in my heart and could not be stolen from me by anything these people had to say. I was returning from a place that had changed me, and I would bring that change into my future.

I immediately worked out a plan. I would need food supplies, firewood for cooking, and herbs and bandages for Healing. I had no idea if the village would receive me as a Healer, but I was intent on finding out. Long before Fumi took me to Shamayim, Jamie told me that the village never replaced me as a Healer in the handful of years I was with him, so this meant many of its citizens either did without or consulted the animal healer far north of the village. There was a high possibility Fumi had known this when he brought me here.

Fumi, I discovered, had left me a sachet of gold pieces on the night stand by the bed; this would give me a good start. He had thought of everything, I thought warmly, and sent out a message of thanks to him in my heart. Somehow, I knew he was here with me, watching my life unfold, as eager as I was to see the events commence.

I set out for the village that very afternoon, observing the budding forest around me as if I hadn't seen it in a lifetime. I would need a horse, I told myself. There were surely enough gold pieces to purchase one, and possibly even a little cart like the one Gran once owned. This would be helpful for hauling supplies and firewood, or simply for saving my strength during difficult weather. It was important to be able to function here among these people as independently as possible. I also purposed to require more coin payment from my customers; they were not so poor as they had always led me to believe and I understood my value better now as a Healer to this tiny little village.

With my ideas well in hand, I entered Huntsville that day with a curious eye. Unsurprisingly, the village itself had not changed much. If it had grown or shrunk, I did not recognize it. Fortunately, the emporium was well-stocked and carried the basic supplies I needed; the owner, I observed, stared at me as though he was seeing a spirit, but I attributed this mostly to Jacobe's cloak and the foreign clothing I wore beneath it. I told him to tell others that a Healer was taking up residence in Gran's old cottage, to which he nodded mutely, unable to say anything more.

When I was completed with this transaction, I walked the breadth of Main Street, curious to find what shops were still in business. Gran's little store, now adorned with a fanciful, hand-painted sign outside, indicated she was well and prospering. A light shone brightly in the front windows, but I did not enter. She would know I was here soon enough. Other stores were still in operation as well, mostly quiet today.

At the end of the street, I entered the Herbalist's shop, a low-ceilinged solitary room with a scuffed wood floor and a brass bell that rang noisily when opening the door. The room smelled like rose water and cinnamon, the proprietor's favorite aroma; this covered for the harsh smell of medicine and dried herbs.

Gloria was behind the counter. She had not been present at Susan's burial service, I remembered; I had no idea how she felt about me during that time of Evil. But always before we had had a reasonable relationship. I was her most devoted customer for many years.

Today her back was turned to me, reaching for shelves behind the counter which held dozens of bottles, mixtures, and brews. "One moment," she called.

I did not respond, but instead turned my attention to my right, where another set of shelves consuming the entire wall revealed a wide variety of wraps, bindings, straps and bandages. There were hammers and vices and all manner of tools a person of medicine might require, such as needles and empty vials. There were rows of useless pills and bottles of elixir, labeled with promises of eternal beauty and cures for countless diseases and discomforts. There were even hair dyes and perfumes. Now that I had been to Shamayim and witnessed the machines and inventions Alameth was capable of, this shop seemed archaic and laughable. These people were simple, and I, in my humble knowledge, was nearly as simple as they. I was surprised the White Palace had ever hired me to act as their Healer those two summers; surely this was *only* because Jacobe knew Fumi's gifts resided within me.

I became aware that Gloria had turned around and was staring openly. To this I moved towards her and smiled in a friendly manner.

"I have need of bandages and many healing supplies," I told her. "Would it be possible to order them now and come back for them when I have a wagon to do so in a day or two?"

She was still staring. She was a woman only ten or more years older than myself, with dark hair and plain features. I had known her on a closer basis since I was ten when I first began trekking through the forest with my little healing basket. She had been unmarried then.

Her eyes roved over my head piece — which served me as a cowl and multi-layered neck scarf today — then dropped to the red cloak. The sight of this seemed to truly startle her.

"Of — of course," she answered nervously. "I can also order supplies from the Northern Wood if I don't have it here. They should have anything you might need."

At her reaction I did not think she knew me. I stepped closer to the counter, so the light of her lanterns on this side of the shop could rest on my face.

"How are you, Gloria?"

Her mouth dropped open. "Red? That's you, isn't it?"

I smiled. "It is."

She looked stunned for a moment. "Rumor had it that you were dead — had died in a fire in Wilsburg over a year ago. They said Jamie died in the fire too, but I'm not sure I believe that now either, seeing you standing here as you are." She seemed bewildered. "I didn't recognize you. You look — *changed*." She was still uncomfortable; her eyes kept shifting to the cloak. "Are you — are you here to visit?"

"I'm here to practice Healing," I told her, smiling at her reaction. "At least for the time being. How are you? How are the children?"

Gloria had had her challenges, I remembered. She was a woman who consistently lacked transparency because she had to appear as though she was a busy, wonderful mother. She was never able to admit to stress or the deep-rooted feelings of inadequacy I knew she felt as a mother. It was vitally important to her to foster the image of a happy energetic home instead of a place where she struggled to maintain order to the point of terrible duress. In truth her young children were at times so out of control that they physically abused her. Her husband had called on me more than once to come to their home and treat her for deep bruises and small wounds inflicted from their tantrums. These clandestine trips to their house were always conveniently forgotten by her next time we saw each other; she pretended they never happened.

Today Gloria brightened considerably at the mention of her children. "Everyone is doing well. They're nearly teens now, you know. My little people are growing up." A frown returned then; her eyes shifted uneasily to the cloak. "How — how are you, Red? You look — well."

"I *am* well," I said, suddenly feeling a surge of joy. How far I had come since the last she had seen me. "How is Huntsville? It looks the same."

"We've needed a Healer, that's certain," she answered frankly. "How long has it been since you left? Six years? At least that. They'll be glad you're here. Everyone will. Probably even Brewster. He's been sickly for some time now, you know. So has Danner. There should be plenty of business for you. I'll be happy to get word out, if you like."

I thanked her for this. Then, after she had filled my order, I bid her goodbye, assuring her I would be back in the following day or two for the supplies.

As I stepped out into the street, I considered all that I had learned in this short interaction. Gloria had given me a great deal of information I needed and had hoped for when I entered her store. Clearly, Fumi had been right. The village had suffered without a local healer and their attitudes would be different now once I quietly resumed business. The wolf had threatened to smear my reputation by spreading lies about me through the Wood if I left Jamie, but thus far I didn't see any sign of this. It truly seemed as though I had nothing to fear here.

Gloria had also inadvertently confirmed how long I had been in Shamayim, a burning question I had had for many of the days and weeks I spent with the King. I had been married to Jamie five years before I decided to take my leave and the wolf attacked.

I walked home that day in ponderous thought from one other comment she had made. I wondered what had become of Jamie after I left? Because it certainly seemed he was no longer in Wilsburg.

The next several weeks fell into a quiet routine. Though I had once thought I could never be content in this Wood and with these People, I found for the time being this was no longer true. I was happy applying myself to my work again. Customers soon began drifting in after word circulated of my return, and I was as busy as I wanted to be. As I suspected, Fumi's coin enabled me to live comfortably until patients began to pay with consistency. I purchased a dependable horse and new cart and hitch, and settled into a new life entirely.

Once, early-on, I saw Gran in Huntsville. She was at the opposite end of the street walking towards her little shop and caught my eye boldly. I noted that her gait was still strong, her weathered skin a healthy color and her head lifted proudly. She said nothing, however, and did not seem surprised to see me. She had obviously heard the news that I had returned. Still, even from this distance I could tell there was none of the previous animosity I had always sensed from her. Her steps and her nature reflected an unusual quiet, and she lived her life quietly. She did not disturb me.

Indeed, I found this to be true of many of the people of Huntsville. They seemed subdued, silently thankful I could assist them with their physical troubles and woes. They paid well, and went about their lives without the strife and contention that had always existed here. I no longer sensed the presence of the wolves and wondered where they had gone and why.

Even Danner and Brewster, who were once so mealy-mouthed and brunt, kept their thoughts to themselves, or seemed to lack them altogether. No one asked me where I had been, and did not circulate speculations on what I might have done. Their eyes often roved over my clothing, more frequently dropped to the red cloak nervously, but they said nothing and stirred no trouble. The mayor, the minister, and even the Blankenships appeared to have moved on from the horrific troubles that had inspired my departure; they made no mention of it and simply accepted my presence.

Seeing Gran again did stir some curiosity about her. Fumi had mentioned her several times as if he remembered her well; he had called her to the Palace to stay for a period of time as a girl, though I never knew under what circumstances or why. He had wanted to help her, of course. He had given her opportunity to make different choices than she had. I wondered what her story was, and what my grandfather had done to her that seemed to her so like Jamie.

As if in answer to this unspoken curiosity, Old Man Samson called on me shortly after I began to ask myself these things. He was aging now and his back had driven him to such a point of discomfort that he had sought me out. It was he who brought up Gran during this first visit. He was seated on my examination table shirtless, his boots still on, which he refused to remove; he absently peered around the room while I probed his back for trouble.

"I helped build this house for your Gran and Gramps, you know," he stated. "I see it's endured well. That was back right before they married. Your Gran kept an eye on all of us the entire time we worked on it; she wasn't having any mistakes made or any slacking on the job." His blue eyes were sparkling surprisingly, as if the memory did not irritate him, but rather, amused him.

"Sounds like Gran," I commented, smiling at him.

"There are some things that have changed about her," he reflected, "but not all." He lifted his arms in various ways as I directed him, his thoughts still running. "She was an unusually happy girl, but after she married Pascall, she grew sharp and bitter. She was tough — but I supposed you'd have to be living with a man like him. He wasn't a kind man, your grandfather."

Uncharacteristically, Samson stopped here and seemed to have no interest in continuing. I wondered to what degree Pascall had been unkind. Samson himself was a gruff man, and it was difficult to picture the level of roughness that would cause even him to make comment.

I asked him to step down from the table and prompted him to bend, stretch, reach in various ways, observing his flexibility and mobility as he did so, asking further questions about his complaints. When the moment seemed right, I asked idly, "Did he strike her?"

He didn't seem bothered by this query. He grunted, remembering. "Ruby was always showing up in town with bruises, some of them pretty ugly. She'd cover them as best she could, you know, but for those of us who knew her, the truth was plain. Pascall was bigger than her by a lot. It was real bad for awhile. He was always sunshine and cheerfulness with the rest of us, but there was a fierce anger in him. I saw him wrestle a wild boar to the ground once without harm to himself. She must not have talked about him much to you, eh?"

His words had revealed the truth at last. I answered him thoughtfully, thankful I knew it now. "No, she hasn't spoken about him at all," I answered.

"Well, I'm not surprised," Samson commented, with another grunt. "If I were her, I'd leave it behind too. That man was as Evil as they come."

Shortly after this I saw Gran again in town. We always exchanged glances from a distance, but never pursued any interaction beyond that. Today, I noticed, she was limping. Immediately I strode across the dusty street to where she was hobbling towards her storefront with a determined expression.

"Gran, why are you limping?"

She batted away my hand, which had reached out instinctively to offer assistance. "Girl, don't fuss over me. I'm fine."

These were the first words we had exchanged in well over six years. "What happened?" I asked her.

"I fell off a ladder yesterday. Hurt my ankle. I'm fine."

I motioned towards her front door, which was now only a few feet away. "Let's go inside and let me look at it. At the very least, I have some salts you can soak it in. It will heal faster."

She muttered and shook her head, but was obliging. She swung her door open and we entered together, both of us squinting for a moment as our eyes adjusted to the dim lighting. The little store, like Gloria's, was filled with large shelves overflowing with her wares and a tall counter against the back wall for taking orders. Gran's front lobby held wooden chairs for her waiting customers, and I aimed for one of these, moving it into the gray light which streamed in through the front windows.

"Sit down and I'll examine it," I told her.

She shuffled over to this obediently and reached for her boot, wincing as she slowly untied the laces and pulled her foot free. As I peeled back her stocking and examined the ankle, her eye dropped to my basket on the floor next to us.

"You been over to Brewster's then?" she asked, calculating the direction she had seen me coming from. "I heard he was ailing."

"I was," I confirmed. I asked her a few questions regarding the source of pain and quickly determined she had no serious damage. "You twisted it, but it's not broken, bruised or overly swollen, which would indicate a more serious fall. I'll give you the salts to soak it in for a few days. You should be just fine."

Gran's eye settled on me as I pulled a little glass jar from my basket. "You do me proud, girl. He doesn't deserve your kindness, he never will. But you still help him—"

I looked up at her from my position on the floor at her feet, surprised. She was talking about herself, not Brewster, though she couldn't admit this. The truth was there in her quiet expression and muttered words.

A silence fell between us. Fumi had been right; many things had changed since my departure. I had never expected to hear Gran come even this close to humility. I also understood now what had made her who she was.

I extended the jar, along with a few additional instructions. "Hot water only. These salts come all the way from Northern Hadithi, so they'll have a certain fragrance. Don't let that stop you from using them. They work well for sores and bruises."

Gran nodded and took the jar. As I replaced her stocking and laced her boot, her eye fell on me once more.

"You look well," she said suddenly. "As if you'd come here from some island or desert place with sun, like in the storybooks."

I paused and smiled up at her. "Something like that, yes."

Her thoughts were turning at these words. We understood each other perfectly well. "Brewster says Jamie disappeared," she added then. "Everyone else thinks he burned up in that fire that swept through Wilsburg, but that's just a tale. I knew it was a tale and Brewster was telling the truth the minute I saw you. I'm glad he's gone."

I stood to my feet and reached for my basket, my task completed now. My voice was solemn when I answered her. "So am I."

Unlike previous times, Gran said nothing more. She did not gloat; there was no retaliation. She understood the unspoken things in this conversation and pursued it no further.

After that there was a quiet understanding between us when we saw each other in the streets. I was grateful for it. Perhaps we would never be close; Gran had made her choices and did not seek to change them. But the past was behind us now, and could be quietly left there.

8.

In late-summer, after I'd been in Huntsville for several months, a knock came to my front door early one afternoon. Sickness and calls for healing assistance had been less frequent as the season progressed, but I rarely ever had any other kinds of visitors. Huntsville, as content as they seemed to be to pursue peace now, did not socialize with me. Expecting someone laden with an injury or burden, I opened the door and greeted my visitor. My breath stopped.

There on my doorstep was a man of short height dressed in a livery costume in blue fringed with gold. I instantly knew that costume and those colors. He was from the White Palace.

I couldn't find my words, but he spared me the effort. "I was told there was a Healer in residence here. Are you the one I seek?"

I nodded mutely, staring at him, heart pounding.

"We have need of your services, mum." His brown eyes were calm beneath his blue-colored beret, but there was a sense of urgency in his tone. "There's been an injury. A hunting accident. Can you come quickly?"

For a moment I was too stunned to respond. I had anticipated many things because of the words Fumi had given me, but not this one. Then, nodding wordlessly, I turned away, thoughts churning wildly.

The man did not cross my threshold, though I left the door open for him to take his liberty. He was too well-trained to presume, naturally. "I'll wait for you here, mum," he explained.

Within moments I had collected my basket and cloak, exited the house, and was hurrying to the stables for my horse. The livery man's horse was tied to the hitching post, a grand animal that could have only come from the Palace stables. I had no intention of riding double; if I should need to return home at any point, my own mount would give me the freedom to do so. Even in this I would not depend on others for my liberty.

The man did not protest as I saddled my horse quickly, cinched and adjusted the girth strap, and fixed his bit. I'd become rather proficient at this procedure in the past several weeks. In another few moments I swung myself up and sat astride the animal. I realized my hands were trembling.

I nodded at the Palace servant, who was already mounted and waiting. "I'm capable of riding fast, if you want to make time. I'll follow your lead."

I was a very different woman who rode through the ornate Palace gates some fifteen minutes later. Though my heart was pounding profusely and my breath came short at the sight of the magnificent edifice, I was no longer the young girl of eight years before who had loved so quickly and been left forsaken and heart-broken. I told myself this as the livery man dismounted near the stables and another servant exited to take the animals. And I told myself this again as we walked past the familiar statue of Fumi and rounded the back of the Palace.

The grounds were in all their glory. Flowers bloomed, birds sang, the gardens radiated beauty. Someone — no doubt an entire fleet of servants — had worked hard over the past many years to keep this place flourishing and the ever-encroaching forests at bay. The waters of the lake were still and quiet, as they always were. How I had loved this place. Every corner and edge of the property within sight held some memory that tugged at my sleeve now.

As the livery man made his way through the gardens and to a back door of the Palace, I could not help but glance down at the water's edge on this side of the property. The half-circle stone bench was still settled there, facing the lake under the shade of the cottonwood. It was almost as if I could hear the sharp echo of happy voices rising up from that secluded corner… Low laughter reverberated in the air… Whispers and murmurs called mysteriously from the base of the tree.

My hands were trembling suddenly. I clasped my cloak closer to me as an excuse to do something with one of them. Re-adjusted my grip on my small basket and found it sweaty.

The livery man took me to one of five doors on this side of the Royal residence. This was a lovely set of glass doors that opened straight into a private bedroom. I estimated that it was next door to the library where Desi's private quarters were hidden. No one greeted us as we entered the room, and the livery man motioned immediately to a bed on the left. I did not know this room and had never been in it.

The room itself, like all rooms within the Palace, was warm and beautiful, a mix of dark colors cast by heavy rugs, oil paintings, and oak furniture. The light allowed in by a hundred windows in each of the rooms and floors fed the building a natural light that kept the mansion cozy and inviting no matter how shadowed the furniture or how empty it stood. The sweeping red cloak encompassing me blazed like a crimson stain here.

I realized at once I had been brought directly to the patient's room. Who-ever the injured party was, he was lying soundlessly upon the massive bed, his face hidden from my sight by the angle of the drapes and bed-curtains around him. *Who could it possibly be?* I thought; my breath was growing more and more shallow with every step I took.

As I approached the bed, I also realized there was a second party in the room, seated in a low armchair. She was a tiny blonde woman close to me in age, exquisitely dressed in a silk bodice and long skirts I could only imagine were fashioned specifically for her. The skill required to make her clothing was far beyond Gran's, I knew. The young woman better belonged in a portrait as an art piece than as a live being living an actual life. Compared to Desi's other friends years ago, who had certainly not lacked for beauty, she was stunningly beautiful. She looked up at once and took me in, scanning me from top to bottom before her blue eyes narrowed.

"Who's this?" she demanded. "Where are the Healers?"

"We sent for the local Healer," the livery man explained. He had already made his way to my side at the foot of the bed. "It will take some time before the Royal Healers can arrive."

"Well, I hardly approve," the young woman huffed. She was still eyeing me with deep suspicion. "We have no idea what this woman's qualifications are — "

"We dare not take the risk otherwise, your Highness," the servant cut her off. In spite of the title he addressed her with, he did not seem under her authority and was entirely unmoved by her demands. "If you will please move aside..."

The young woman only took a moment to decide to cooperate, and this was done with an impatient *hmmph* that clearly expressed her feelings on the matter. She stood to her feet with offended elegance, and swept past me and out of the room with obvious irritation.

I was far too distracted by what was going to happen next to give her much attention. My heart was thundering loudly enough by now I was certain it could be heard clearly in the quiet silence of the room.

"You may examine him now, Healer," the servant instructed, motioning again towards the bed.

He hadn't asked for my name in our short acquaintance. That was fair, I supposed. I didn't know his either.

I stepped closer to the bed, brushed aside the sheer drapes that hung in my way, and bent closer to the figure on this side of the canopied mattress. My breath came out uncontrollably in an exhale, hissing through my teeth slightly.

Its one occupant was a young man, tow-headed, with a chiseled jaw and a full mouth. A set of bare strong shoulders peeked out from beneath a sea of blankets. His expression was one of intense pain, his eyes closed and coloring dangerously pale. He was beautiful, almost as perfect as the woman who had just stormed out.

I bent closer to him. The livery man was at my elbow now, ready to answer questions, take instructions. I could feel the urgency of his concern more intensely than ever. The accident must have been severe, though I could not at once see evidence of it. *Why, oh why had they sent for me?* I asked myself. I would have gladly doctored anyone but him.

I knew the man's eyes would be soft blue before he ever opened them. When he did, I couldn't speak.

He caught sight of me. I didn't know if he had the strength to address me.

But he did. Desi smiled a little smile, entirely conscious in spite of the pain that left his words breathless and weak.

"Red," he murmured with relief. "I told them to find you."

The next thing I remembered I was by the water's edge of the lake. I hardly recalled the anxious steps from the Palace here. I'd found a spot just past the mansion, where the grounds and lake were undivided by the stone railing and bled straight into the calm waters. I knew the place well; Desi and I had often picnicked on the edges of it.

Heavy oak trees with massive root systems grew in abundance here, stretching their feet out over a bed of round flagstones in the low waters. I found myself leaving the shore completely, still in my soft-hide boots, slipping across the rocks, clinging to the trunk of the nearest oak for balance.

Originally I had intended to dip my hands and face in the cold water and somehow felt this needed to happen just off-shore, in the lake itself; but then one foot slipped, and I found myself crumpling suddenly, falling to my knees on the rocks. My cloak dragged in the shallow water behind me. Shaken, disturbed, I retched, trying to empty the contents of my stomach. Nothing would come, however, only that helpless exhausting outburst from my insides pushing its way to the surface.

I lay there shivering in the cool shallow water, gasping for air, knees burning from their recent impact. *How long had it been since I'd been this disturbed by anything?* I had truly been caught by surprise.

A low strong voice spoke to me from the shore only a few feet away. "Are you disturbed by the gravity of his injuries, Red?"

I knew that voice; I looked up. I had not assumed Jacobe would be here if Desi was; he was no longer the Prince's bodyguard as I recalled, and Fumi had said his responsibilities in Alameth were keeping him very busy. But there he stood, bright as day, outfitted in his blue cape and gentleman's attire, tri-corn hat in place. He was staring at me with that fixed intense gaze.

"Jacobe," I breathed, and felt a rush of relief. Surely this experience would not be so difficult if he was present. He immediately offered a bedrock of stability.

"Desi will survive his injuries," I answered him, as a roundabout way of not having to directly answer the question. I struggled to my knees, shivering.

Without pause, Jacobe calmly stepped into the lake-waters, made the two or three steps to my side on the rocky foot-bed, and helped pull me to my feet.

"I could carry you," he suggested, as I paused a moment to gain my balance. His voice was notably low.

I shook my head, *no*, and smiled up at him briefly. "I'm fine, actually. I just needed a moment."

He didn't release me entirely, but chose to aid me back to shore. As we took the careful steps through the shallow water, I said lightheartedly, "Why is it you are always appearing when I am in my weakest state? You never see me at my best."

This disturbed him slightly. I could feel it from his person, though there was no other indication.

"You are always at your best, Red," he responded, gently depositing me onto the dry ground and stepping away. He did not seem affected by the cold water, or a wet cloak, but I was trembling now, trying to collect my composure. I stood to my feet shakily before him.

"What disturbed you, if not his injuries?" he asked, dark eyes still on me.

He was wearing the beard I'd last seen him in, and his hair was cropped. Many things about that night were vague and unclear, but this was not. I remembered how moved he had been by the condition in which he had found me, how gentle his actions as he carried me from the cottage.

"You have to ask that question?" I told him.

He was still studying me. "No."

There was a pause between us. His eyes flicked to the wet cloak I was currently swaddled in, then back to my face. The brown scarf-cowl I had been wearing had slipped off at some point since arriving here and was settled around my shoulders, exposing my long hair, the ends of which were now sopping wet.

"Fumi did a remarkable job," he said then, quietly. Apparently his thoughts were running back to that night, too. "You look —" He paused to find words, his expression surprisingly haunted for the Huntsman. I could only imagine what his thoughts had been when he found me in the state he did.

"The last time you saw me I was horribly broken," I supplied for him gently. "And though I can't prove it at the moment given what you just witnessed, I'm whole now. I owe Fumi my life. And you. I owe you, too."

Jacobe merely shook his head, denying this last part. He quickly changed the subject, his voice quiet. "You don't have to treat him if you don't want, Red." We both knew who he was referring to. "He asked for you, and I had heard from Fumi that you were back in Huntsville, so I took the initiative. But I know enough about healing to keep Desi safely alive until the Healers arrive. I've spent enough time on the battlefield to understand the rudiments of caring for an injury, even as bad as his is. They should be here within the next hour or two. You don't have to stay."

I pulled myself upright. I had fled Desi's side as soon as I took one look at the terrible injury his accident had caused. Word had probably circulated through the Palace very quickly at my reaction, sending Jacobe in search of me.

"I can help him, Jacobe; I can do it," I answered, teeth chattering traitorously. Whether this was from cold or nerves, I could not have said. I pulled the cloak closer, though this was a futile effort. Even the powers of the cloak had abandoned me for the moment.

The Huntsman still wasn't moving for the Palace. His dark eyes were studying me again, closely. "Red, if you do plan to do this, I should prepare you — Desi is set to be married soon."

I stopped, jolted. I was not expecting him to say that. "Yes — yes, that stands to reason. There was a young woman in his room when I arrived."

"Princess Delophinie," he confirmed. "The entire kingdom is preparing for the wedding as we speak."

"I am not disturbed by this, Jacobe," I assured him. "Fumi healed me of Desi's past actions and my heart has been made whole. Coming back here, though, that was the difficult part. I promise, I will not be a distraction. I will doctor the Prince and will quickly be on my way."

"It wasn't the Prince I was concerned about, Red."

I had to smile at this. Eight years seemed like no time at all. Or perhaps because Jacobe had witnessed the conclusion to that terrible night over a year ago, resulting in my devastating brokenness, we had a closer connection than ever. He knew my secret of the past several years, the secret no one knew but Fumi.

"I'm strong," I told him softly, looking up into his face. "I'm strong enough."

He did not dispute my resolve. Jacobe merely inclined his head, accepting this. "And I'm here if you should need me."

He turned suddenly, ready to take the little hill that would lead back to the gardens and the Palace. "I *am* going to ask you to take my arm, however," he announced. "Your clothes will be heavy from the damp and you are trembling."

It was true, I was shaking. Worse than ever.

I stepped forward obediently and took his arm. He was as solid as a pillar. At once I could feel myself calm and my breathing steady. As I leaned on him up the hill, I felt grateful. Yes, Jacobe knew my secret... and held it sacredly to himself, determined to spare me as much struggle as he could.

Jacobe escorted me back into the Palace to the Prince's side. Two female servants were close at hand, trying to make Desi as comfortable as possible. He was too weak to resist their fussing at the blankets and dabbing a damp cloth at his brow, though I knew he must hate it. The Prince had always resented anyone fretting over him. Unfortunately this attention naturally came with his position in life.

"Red is here," Jacobe announced, which caused the women to curtsy quickly and scatter at once.

Desi looked up weakly from the bed and caught my eye in relief. He was very pale and feeble from his injury. He did not have the strength to speak immediately.

"Will you need anything?" Jacobe asked me. "Bandages? Water? Assistance of any kind?" He stood at the foot of the bed waiting. I could feel his concern even from this small distance and understood that it was not for Desi.

"For the moment I have everything I need," I told him. I was already reaching for my basket, which I'd abandoned on the bed-table next to Desi. My strength of person had returned in just the few moments walking to the Palace. "That will change, though, I'm sure."

The Huntsman's almond-shaped eyes fell to the Prince. I knew he was considering whether to go or stay.

"Very well. I'll be back in a few moments." He turned swiftly and strode from the room.

Desi's blue eyes were on my face as I sat on the edge of the bed next to him, a roll of bandages in hand, and gently pulled back the blankets around him. He had been gored by a wild boar in the stomach and trampled badly. Given the violence of the animal and the strength of its attack, he was fortunate to have escaped its teeth and any other more vicious wounds that would normally occur in a fighting match with a raging pig. His bruising was not life-threatening either from what I had determined in the brief few moments I'd examined him before running out of the room. Even more importantly, the boar's tusk had merely made a clean incision across the muscle wall of his stomach, missing his organs by mere centimeters. All that he was in need of, shockingly, was a series of ligatures across the flesh of his stomach where the slice had occurred, a relatively light procedure considering.

He had suffered quite a bit of blood loss, which had weakened him, though this had decreased by now. Jacobe or who-ever else had been with him when the accident occurred had been quick-thinking and bound the wound up well and with pressure. After a second examination, I felt certain the Prince would survive even if I did nothing and simply waited until his own Healers arrived to sew the wound themselves. He would need rest, and be forced to take great care for several weeks and months, but he would be fine.

I meant to tell him this at once to give him peace of mind, but Desi was swifter than I at finding words after all this time. "I thought you'd gone," he murmured.

My eyes were carefully on his left side, at the source of the wound, while his were still on me.

"You should save your strength," I responded at once. "You're very weakened."

"*Red* —"

He did not seem aware of how awkward and uncomfortable I felt at the moment. I looked up at him. "I didn't leave... Of course not. You're wounded. I'd never run out on that, feel assured. I just needed some air."

He was more handsome than ever, there was no sense in denying it. Eight years had given him strength and muscle. More than that, experience had given him stature. He was a man grown now.

Surprisingly, he found the stamina to address my words. "That statement implies you would run out on me, but would not run out on an injury."

I felt nausea climb my esophagus and threaten to choke my throat again. *Fumi, help me...* I coughed a little, breaking his gaze to return to his stomach and the bloodied bandages. I kept my voice quietly focused. "Desi — perhaps now is not the time — those sound like fighting words — I really should turn my attention to your wounds — "

He sighed. Winced. His voice still wasn't any louder than a murmur. "I'm not fighting with you, I'm fighting with myself. I abandoned you."

My hands were trembling, but I was grateful he could not see it. I had hoped this conversation wouldn't take place so soon, if at all. "That was a very long time ago."

"Eight years is not so long." He shot me a wretched glance from the deep pile of satin-covered pillows his head was sunk in. "Eight years is forever, Red," he amended. "It's been forever."

I was beginning to wish Jacobe had not left after all. "Possibly not in Alameth. In Hadithi — "

"That makes it even worse."

I looked back at the injury, anywhere but him. Distress was not what he needed right now. "I can see this has troubled you. Please, Desi, release yourself from it. As you see, I'm alive, well, and have done well. There's no need to hold onto it."

With his next words I caught that he was in desperate need of reprieve. "I'm sorry, Red. I can only say I'm sorry. Obviously I hurt you. You just ran outside at first sight of me. I've had to live with guilt over my actions every day since I left."

I sighed. Deeply. There were many words I once would have liked to say to him, but they had faded away in Shamayim, gone forever. Certainly if I did still have them to say, or anything on the matter, now was not the time or place.

On an impulse I reached for one of his hands, borrowing on familiarity from long ago. I could only hope his future bride did not walk into the room at this moment. "Desi — *please.* Let it go. I forgive you. Let's put it behind us. I already have, long ago. Please move ahead. *This very moment.* Can you do that?"

This quieted him. "Yes."

I sighed again and released his hand. "Good."

"Excellent," he returned, looking contrite and feeble with his head sunk in the deep pillows.

"Wonderful," I responded, returning to his wounds.

"Tremendous."

This could go on for hours, I thought, and stopped.

The Healers arrived within the half hour, a small group of four men in brown robes with tonsured hair. Somehow I had always imagined Alameth's Healers to look similar to this. Jacobe brought them into the room, introduced us, and I gave them my assessment of Desi's wounds. Quickly, they examined him themselves and determined, as I did, that only simple sutures were needed and plenty of rest to restore his blood loss.

For a moment there was some discussion on who would give the stitches, but I quickly conceded from my place at the foot of the bed next to Jacobe, who also stood waiting.

"I think the four of you should oversee the Prince's care entirely from here, obviously. I was only brought in until you arrived."

It was Desi who objected from the bed. "I want you to do it, Red."

His word clearly had clout; the deeply amenable expressions on the faces of his Healers reflected that. I shook my head at him. "Your Highness, these men are far more experienced than I am. It is in your best interest that they perform the procedure. Do you agree, Jacobe?"

He was the only person present whom I thought would give the Prince his mind and could settle the matter. However, at my question, a strange tension came into the room I was not expecting. The Healers looked to the Huntsman in sudden reverence, as if prepared to tremble at his words. Desi instantly looked stormy-faced and sullen.

From his place next to me, Jacobe took his time answering. When he did at last, his tone was thoughtful. "Desi, let the Healers do it. It's what Red wants."

This response mollified the Prince somewhat. The tension, at least, eased for him, though the others almost looked stricken at Jacobe's words. Desi gave as much of a shrug as his strength would allow. "Very well. Let it be the Healers. But Red —"

I raised my brows at him, already preparing to exit the room now that the matter was settled.

"Please return. I want to speak to you."

I might have protested under any other circumstances. I certainly had no curiosity in knowing what he might possibly have to say; in fact, I dreaded it. But to save face in front of the men present, I said, "That's fine, your Highness."

Jacobe and I exited together. As we stepped out into the passageway beyond the bedroom, I had no idea where to go or what to do next. My thoughts were still wind-blown and scattered in the aftermath of the past half hour. I found myself following Jacobe wordlessly, who, I soon discovered, strolled quietly to another exit, held the glass door open for me, and we went outside into the gardens together.

With few words between us, he led the way down through the garden paths until we reached the lake terrace. The sun was high, but not hot. This summer had been an unusual one, bereft of its usual intense temperatures. I did not choose the bench under the tree; there were too many memories there. Desi and I had often hidden beneath the cottonwood's low branches where we could not be seen from the windows of the Palace. Instead, I chose a bench squarely facing the lake in broad sunlight.

Also a departure from days of old, Jacobe seated himself next to me and we sat quietly for some little time gazing at the lake, a red-cloaked figure and a blue one side by side. He was always a calming presence, now more than ever.

Jacobe was the one, at last, who broke the silence. "He is going to ask you to stay and nurse him back to health," he guessed. "Someone will have to do it and he'll want it to be you."

I sighed at this, not knowing how to respond.

Jacobe continued, "He trusts you. I can't say I blame him. Our Healers might have more experience, but you have more of Fumi's power. Anyone from Alameth who has experience with his power does not have to look very hard to see it. You could have easily sewn the sutures, Red."

I fell quiet at these words.

Jacobe wasn't done yet, however, his voice thoughtful. "Having worked with many people who have large and note-worthy destinies, I've seen many times that people recognize greatness and need the gifts these people provide, but will not honor or acknowledge the greatness and rarity of their destiny itself. So the person of destiny only ends up used, never —"

"Validated?" I finished.

"Yes. We fear pride. Or we are filled with pride ourselves and have a difficult time believing in the greatness of others. We fear our own smallness. But a great person, particularly if we make use of their gifts, should be affirmed as much as a man who is low needs affirmation. We should show honor where honor is due."

These words were profound and exhibited a wisdom in Jacobe I had always admired. This brought back conversations with Fumi, who often spoke in this manner and had ruled his kingdom with a reputation of having been very loved. He had said Jacobe could recognize greatness in a person from having worked with so many individuals of importance.

Finally, Jacobe drew his point to a conclusion. He pressed quietly, "You don't have to say yes, Red."

"I know." Both of our eyes were still on the water. "I hear what you are *not* saying as well. I won't agree to Desi's request if I don't desire to."

"Good."

More time passed. A dry breeze rustled the trees around us and stirred the water slightly, blowing down from the gardens. A sweet fragrance carried with it and swept over me. In my younger years, I remembered, I always wished Jacobe would speak more, but I found now I appreciated the companionable silence as much as his wisdom.

He broke the silence again eventually. His mood had grown even more thoughtful, if this was possible. Had the wind been any stronger, it would have whisked his soft words away. "Since finding you that night, Red, I have deeply regretted discouraging Desi away from continuing to pursue you. Surely if I had not interfered, a life in Alameth — even lonely and foreign to you, even a life of obligation as a Royal bride — would have still been a better one than what you endured. It has bothered me so deeply I went to Shamayim after you left there and spoke to Fumi personally about it."

For the second time today I was jolted in surprise. After all that he had done, I found Jacobe's grief too much to bear. It was his note, after all, that had given me the courage to leave Jamie and seek out a life of freedom. I hadn't forgotten this small act of love and never would.

I answered quickly, "I do not consider the series of events that happened to be any of your doing. Desi was weak and I was young and foolish. I loved too quickly, too deeply. He was not proven. You were the one straightforward and direct with him; you responded out of love and concern for both of us. As for the events that took place afterward, in the Wood, those were my doing too. And the wolves' doing. I didn't call for Fumi as I should have. Before you left, you said yourself you were not in a position to help me," I added. "You have always been honest with me. You should have no regrets over this."

He was silent for a time after this, but nodded eventually, as if settling it in his heart and mind. "Very well then. I will let it go. Fumi restored you, and that is the most important thing to take from this. He assured me you were well when I saw him and now I've seen the proof of it."

I smiled, nodding, eager to leave this behind us. "I was hoping to see you again, to thank you for the cloak. It was a tremendous gift."

"Of course."

His brevity of words amused me. I turned to him. Even sitting, Jacobe was a good foot-and-a-half taller than I, and I was forced to look up to catch his gaze. "Of course what?"

His eyes flicked to mine; he answered directly. "Of course meaning it was my privilege to give it to you. I was hoping it would give you comfort, and additional safety, and a small reminder of me."

I smiled at him. "It has given me all of that and more, especially after returning to the Wood. So I thank you." I frowned now. "What finds you here this summer, if I may ask? Are you body-guarding for Desi again? In Shamayim last year Fumi said you have been in high demand in Alameth."

Surprisingly, Jacobe paused abruptly, as if he was making a decision before answering. His words were slow. "You may always ask me anything, Red. I have been busy, it's true. I came this summer, frankly, in hopes of seeing you. I caught word that Desi was vacationing here while his wedding preparations heat up in Alameth and I chose to join him. We only just arrived a few days ago. I was not expecting to greet you under these circumstances, of course. It was my intention to seek you out at your cottage."

"That would have been a shock," I told him, laughing at the image this brought. "But every time I've met you has been a shock, I suppose."

"You always take it well," he asserted. "I have always been impressed by your reaction to me."

This made me laugh again. "Once a person looks past the fact that you are outright intimidating and more fierce than any being in the known lands, then yes, it is not too difficult to take you well."

This made him break into a quick smile. He glanced off at the waters again. He probably would have laughed... if the mighty Huntsman ever laughed.

Suddenly, in the lightness of the moment, a question rose that I had wanted to ask him for ages now. "How *old* are you, anyway, Huntsman? No one has ever said and I've always wondered." At his expression, I added with coy humor, "You said I could ask you anything."

He glanced down at me sidelong. "You've grown bolder, Red."

"You're avoiding the question," I insisted, laughing.

He shook his head at me, smiling. "I am thirty-five, almost thirty-six."

I was surprised by this. I had been correct those many years ago in my guesses.

"So young to have done all the things you have!" I exclaimed. I could voice freely now what I could not before. Somehow the discovery that he had authored the letter had forever altered my perspective of him.

Jacobe's expression changed. His gaze was on the lake-waters again. "*Yes*. My life has taken many surprising turns. I can't say I have found all of them entirely what I would have chosen, but Fumi has helped me to find my way and I continue to press forward."

Immediately after this we were interrupted by a female servant, who arrived to tell us Desi's procedure was complete and he was resting comfortably. Jacobe stood to his feet quickly, sobered and focused again.

"I should speak to the Healers once more and travel back to Alameth," he announced. "The King and Queen will want to know. They were already aware he had been injured and will be waiting anxiously; I want to deliver the news myself. This will take me the rest of the day, but I'll be back on the morrow." His eyes settled on me with a question in them. "Can you return then, Red? Desi will be awake by then. Also, I — I have something to tell you. A piece of news."

This last part struck me momentarily. He sounded hesitant; his eyes were unusually dark. What news could possibly leave Jacobe even close to this state? He hadn't even seemed this uneasy earlier today when he had given me the news that Desi was marrying. Concerned for me, yes, but not uncomfortable.

I answered him at once. "Yes, of course I can return."

"Do you need a ride home? I could take you first before I leave."

I shook my head. "I have my own horse, no need."

I was still puzzling over his reaction even as he nodded absently, gave me a brief distracted smile, and left with a firm strong stride to return to the Palace.

I returned the next day at mid-morning, assuming this was a good time, after breakfast would be well finished and Desi would be better prepared to receive visitors. As I rode up to the gates, I thought it felt strange to be returning here after all these years; I also had no idea how to open the gates. Always before Jacobe had been with me.

Sitting there astride the horse, I tried not to think about the last time I sat here in the shadow of these gates. The memory was acute in my mind today. Then, Jamie had halted us here to assure me he would not treat me as Desi had and expressed how deeply he wanted me. Bad memories no longer had any hold on me, not after my year with Fumi, but my preference was still not to dwell on them and I resisted the memory today. Both men, I determined, were better kept in the past.

My wait didn't take long. Soon, the gates opened without prompting, and on the other side I found a livery man waiting, as if he knew, somehow, that I had approached. His skill, whatever it could be called, was a clever one indeed.

Today no one accompanied me as I made my way around the Palace on foot and to the room where Desi had been yesterday. The grounds were, once again, peaceful and empty of people. I knocked on the glass doors and entered when a feminine voice answered. This would be Delophinie, I thought, as I turned towards the bed and found her sitting in the same chair as yesterday, looking equally flawless in a blue sea of silken skirts. She rose at the sight of me and approached.

"Hello," she said, in a much friendlier manner today; "I'm Princess Delophinie. Desi tells me you are Red and will be watching over him for the next several days. I'm afraid I didn't realize who you were yesterday. He speaks very highly of you and your abilities. Please excuse my unfriendliness."

Surprised by this, I said, "Of course, your Highness. And congratulations on your upcoming marriage. I hope you'll both be very happy in your new life."

She beamed, clearly excited. "Thank you. It's very soon. That's why I want the Prince to have the best of care. He has to be well as quickly as possible." She turned back to the bed then and called, "I'll return later, Desi. The Healer *Red* is here."

As she exited, I made my way over to the side of the bed. Desi lay in the same position as the day before, shirtless, covered in heavy blankets. He was pale but awake and smiling handsomely as he caught sight of me. "*Red.*"

I nodded at him and set my basket on the bed-table again today. "*Desi.* What's this I hear from your future bride about me caring for you in your convalescence?"

The smile broke into a charming grin. His voice was still weak, but the words were clear. "I was hoping you would."

"I'm sure you have plenty of Healers who would be honored to fill that role," I told him, sitting on the edge of the bed.

"Yes, but none of them whose name is Red," he responded.

Unheeding, I peeled back his blankets and examined the bandages over his wound. There was no blood stain, which was an initial positive sign. It would take removing the bandages to examine closer. I sat upright and faced him. "Actually, from what I observed, I think your Healers are so devoted to their Prince that they would allow you to call them Red if that would satisfy you. Then you would have everything you are hoping for."

He thought this was witty, I could see. Desi was always easy to read. His eyes sparked a little. "Will you stay, Red? For my sake? We could house you here so you wouldn't have to leave every night."

"And so I would be on call to you, no doubt," I told him wryly.

Just then someone entered the room behind us and I turned to greet them as they approached the foot of the bed. This was Jacobe, dressed as he had been yesterday, sans his hat and cloak. Now he looked extremely like a distinguished gentleman, save for the facial hair that spoke of a rugged outdoorsman. I was glad to see him and smiled.

"Who is it?" Desi asked me.

Jacobe answered for himself as he came into view. "*Jacobe.* I heard you had just arrived, Red. How is our patient today?"

I glanced at Desi dryly. "He appears very well. I have yet to check the stitches."

"Red has agreed to stay and watch over my recovery," Desi announced, grinning without shame. "I've told her she can stay here at the Palace. Do you have any qualms with that?"

Jacobe's glance swept to me. His face was expressionless. "None. As long as Red is comfortable with the idea."

I said nothing to this, merely shot Desi a dry glance and stood to my feet, returning to my basket for a small pocket knife and fresh bandages. "We will see, Desi," I told him primly, "We will see."

I turned my back to the two of them and swept off the red cloak, laying it aside on the chair which the Princess had so recently occupied. "Let's first check the wound and see how it is doing."

When I turned back around, however, and reached for Desi, I found both men had gone strangely silent. Something had changed in the environment I could not identify.

Desi's brows raised. *"Red."* To this, he could not seem to add anything further.

I looked over at Jacobe, searching his reaction. Unlike Desi, whose eyes betrayed him, the Huntsman was observing me thoughtfully, saying nothing. I could guess their reactions had something to do with my clothing and appearance. Yesterday I had never removed my cloak in either man's presence.

Today I was wearing a muted orange split-skirt, set off by a red shirt the color of autumn leaves, which was essentially several scarves twisted around me decoratively. My attire was by far more form-fitting than anything I had worn in their presence in the past. I had foregone any head covering today and tied a dozen colored beads in my hair, which hung in two long swaths at my front. From what I had observed, this loose style was never practiced by the women of Alameth; Delophinie's hair was bound in tight buns on the top of her head, same as all of the female servants of the Palace. They also did not exercise the practice of jewelry; my hands and wrists were covered in beaded leather rings and bracelets just now. This morning I had given no thought to my choice in clothing; I dressed this way every day. I was, I also acknowledged, much changed physically after my time at Shamayim. This was probably contributing to the sudden quiet as well.

Glancing away from both of them, I determined to ignore the awkward silence. It was particularly important where Desi was concerned; he could hardly keep the admiration out of his eyes.

"Let's check these stitches, shall we?" I asked him, and quickly put my little knife to work cutting away his bandages.

I did choose to stay at the Palace. I knew I would be paid well; that was my primary motivation. I also knew they would all leave and return to their world eventually, probably within a few weeks at the close of the summer, so I wanted to enjoy as much of Alameth as I could and enjoy the two men as well. That first day I returned home and hung a painted sign on my front door communicating that I was gone; I had begun to use this for my visitors when I left on patient calls. I then transported some of my clothing over to the Palace in my little cart, settled into a small luxurious room they gave me two doors down from Desi's, and began life there temporarily.

Most of my time over the next several days was spent with Desi in Delophinie's presence. She attended to him faithfully until she grew bored or tired, and then wandered out, always faithful to thank me for my service to him as she left us. From what I could gather, she was good-hearted towards Desi and genuinely cared for him. At times her behavior towards the household staff was lofty and condescending, but I supposed this was common for the land she was from. Desi told me she was not Alamethen; he had met her when his father sent him as an emissary to a neighboring country where she was Princess. The resulting union was welcome news to both sets of parents.

As for Desi's feelings, I knew him too well to be fooled. He did not love her, and in fact held a dangerous attraction for me which I constantly ignored when in his presence. Fortunately, Delophinie did not seem aware of the natural chemistry between her Prince and me, a chemistry which I could not deny any more than I could deny the rich history we shared together. The Princess was obliviously excited about their upcoming nuptials. But Jacobe, I knew, was always aware. He was aware of everything.

The remainder of my time at the Palace was spent in the gardens. This was usually during the evenings, just as the sun set on the opposite side of the mansion and I could enjoy the cool fragrant breezes that blew in from the lake as dusk fell. Aside from Shamayim, this was the most glorious place I had ever seen thus far in life and knew I would always be appreciative of the beauty I found here after a life in the Wood. It would not last now anymore than it had before, but I determined to hold it to me, this time with better memories when I left at the end of the summer.

It was here, while gazing at the lake just as twilight fell, that Jacobe found me a few days after my arrival. He had never discussed with me the news he had wanted to; we had had little opportunity to be alone now that I was attending to Desi. Though deeply curious, I had been unconcerned. Jacobe was an intentional man and would not forget.

"Red," he said in surprise, as he came upon me; "I was just coming out here for some fresh air myself. Do you mind if I join you?"

I smiled, always glad to see him. "Of course."

This evening he claimed the stone bench under the cottonwood to my right. He was a small giant seated there, leaned against the tree trunk with a quiet expression; he was dressed in the familiar gladiator's costume tonight. This brought up special memories for me and I was privately glad to see it. For a long while we said nothing, each of us wrapped in our own thoughts, watching the skyline above the end of the lake in respectful silence as it turned from pink to gold to a deepening blue. Stars began to appear slowly, studding the sky overhead in a canopy of tiny sparkling jewels as the world lost the light of the sun.

When we were sitting in near darkness, Jacobe suddenly asked, idly, "Who taught you to dress as you do, Red? It takes a special skill."

I looked over at him. His face was still clear in spite of the shadows. Tonight my head was buried in a scarfed hood and I took this down now so he could see my face while we conversed.

I didn't have to answer him; he guessed, looking at me. "Fumi?"

I nodded.

To this, his dark eyes settled on me thoughtfully, saying nothing, just as he had done a few days ago when I first discarded the cloak.

"Do you recognize this style of dressing?" I asked, as one of my hands toyed with the beads on my rings. "He did not tell me which land it is from. I've been curious since."

"Yes, I know it. It's from my own. *Bergl*. All the women there dress as you do." He looked away, back to the horizon. "They are, in my opinion, the most beautiful."

I knew, without having to be told directly, that the Huntsman was offering me a compliment. He had made it easier and less awkward for both of us by turning away.

"What does Bergl mean?" I asked, aware suddenly of the silence that had fallen.

"'Hills,'" Jacobe answered. "It is a land of many hills, thus the name. I was raised there by my mother before I became a soldier."

To my dismay, I could think of no more questions to ask him. I was certain I had more — and this was certainly the time to ask them of him since he seemed in a willing mood to answer — but my thoughts dried up like a fountain that had lost its water source. I was becoming aware of the first signs of something new between us and it left me mystified and speechless. Surely Fumi had not dressed me this way with intentionality, I thought to myself. *That's not what Jacobe was thinking too, was it?*

My thoughts fell back to the note Jacobe had written in Desi's proxy so long ago. *Was it possible,* I dared to ask myself, sitting in the darkness across from him, *that the words were true?* My heart was suddenly beating a quick rhythm; these wild conjectures were more uncomfortable than Desi's subtle advances in the past few days.

But I had nothing to fear of Jacobe. Later I scolded myself for my apprehension. When I asked no further questions, he began speaking that night, calmly and with no hidden motivations, of his homeland and the many foreign customs they followed. He had not been there in many years due to the demands on his time; his mother had relocated to Alameth years ago, giving him further cause not to return. He spoke of her as well for a short while. No longer able to see his expressions now, I could hear in his low voice the deep love and admiration he held for her. He was, he explained, his mother's only son and she had raised him bravely, through many hardships, by herself.

Soon after this, his voice dropped away. A comfortable silence fell between us. Night beetles had begun singing and filled the air gently with their song. A sweet-smelling breeze blew through the terrace with frequent percussion. Behind us, the Palace was quiet, all the windows dark by now.

Jacobe announced, "It's late. I'm afraid I've kept you, Red. You're probably tired." He stood to his feet, preparing to go.

"I enjoyed it," I assured him, and meant it.

He paused. "There's more — I have more to say — but I took the long route in telling you. We'll speak again, I promise."

This was as rife with mystery as the rest of this evening had been, I thought.

"Let me walk you up to the Palace if you would," Jacobe said then. "I don't like the idea of leaving you out here alone in the night, not even as safe as the White Palace property is."

He had taken the few steps over to me and now waited for my agreement. There was just enough light cast by the stars that I could see his form; his dark eyes above the beard stared down at me expectantly.

To my own astonishment, I stood to my feet and voluntarily slipped my fingers around the bulk of his arm. I felt him tense in surprise briefly. Then, without comment, he took the steps back to the Palace, careful, as he had always been, to match his pace to mine.

9.

Desi was the one who spoke, after all, which shouldn't have been surprising. The Prince had a sharp eye, even in spite of his outgoing nature and the current injury which kept him distracted. He was the one who, in his unwitting way, would start the avalanche on its path. As with all mudslides and avalanches, it remains to be seen, as the earth lurches and barrels forward, where it will end or how the final landscape will be altered and changed. Later, I saw that Fumi used all things for my good, though Desi's words at the time were hardly, in and of themselves, for my good.

Ten days after my arrival at the Palace, the Prince's health was improving steadily and he was able to sit in a deep, well-cushioned chair in his room and watch the gardens. Delophinie read to him for long hours and talked with him, often about news from her home and Alameth. When he grew tired of this, and irritable, she continued the habit of leaving him to my care. Usually after her departure he perked up at once, which led me to believe he feigned irritability just to inspire her to depart... and leave us alone together.

This was the time when he chose to speak.

On that day I was wearing the red cloak again, thrown back and loose at the neck. The servants had brought Desi's mid-day meal on a silver tray and I was arranging this before him on a low stand when his eye caught sight of the cloak thoughtfully. This wasn't the first time he had looked ponderous in his examination of it, so the Prince's first words addressing the cape did not surprise me.

"That cloak —"

I caught his eye, pausing before him. "What of it?"

"That's Jacobe's cloak." He didn't seem to require confirmation of this. "Now that I consider it, I haven't seen him wearing it for nearly two years. You re-sized it."

I nodded, *yes*, wondering where this vein of thought was leading to.

Desi's expression changed. "He's seen you in the past eight years?"

I didn't like the darkness in his tone and spoke to him in a voice that beckoned for reason. "Only once, Desi. He rescued me from a terrible situation in which I was badly injured. Fumi sent him."

His face grew clouded and concerned now as he grasped this. Even in his self-absorption, the Prince did have a caring heart, he always would. "Are you all right? You — are well now?"

I smiled down at him. He was dressed in a silk robe and linen cravat, looking expectedly distinguished even in this. "Yes. Of course." I had no intention of giving him any more information than that.

I moved away from him and took my seat some distance away. I had already borrowed half a dozen books from the Palace's library and luxuriated in their contents in moments like this when Desi was pre-occupied. I reached for one now, expecting him to begin his meal.

But the Prince did not move for his food. He stared out the tall windows before him and over the gardens for a moment. Then he picked up his fork, glanced at his meal, and muttered with displeasure, "I wish he had told me."

I responded to this at once, lowering my book. "And what good would it have done, Desi? Nothing would have changed."

"I could have joined him possibly." The Prince's expression was still dark. "I could have aided him. He's always discouraged any interest in you. In this situation he simply chose not to tell me at all. I've seen how friendly the two of you have grown, most likely because he was there in your moment of need."

I shook my head at him. The relationship between the two men had clearly never changed; if anything, the tension on Desi's part had only increased. I found this surprising, given that he was closer than ever to assuming the throne and Jacobe would then be an insignificant peripheral character in his life. Additionally, I had observed how quiet Jacobe remained around the Prince these many years later; for his part, he rarely advised or interfered with the younger man. Obviously, Desi was no longer his direct responsibility. It seemed clear that the Prince was holding onto an aged resentment of the Huntsman.

"I'm sure your duties as Crown Prince required much more important things of you than to have abandoned all and stormed to my rescue," I told him.

"Things might have been different." Desi was growing persistent and the mood of the moment was quickly changing. He turned to me across the room. "If I'd seen you — thought there was a chance — I might not have ever considered Delophinie and never committed myself to her. Any a number of things could have happened. Jacobe knew this. He knew sight of you, especially sight of you injured and in trouble, might have resulted in a different ending. That's why he said nothing."

"Desi —" I was uncomfortable now. I stood to my feet, as if to leave the room.

His face took on a longing that was difficult to see. "Your eyes look so stricken, Red. Don't you ever think about what could have been?"

I could not answer this, staring over at him. I told myself I needed to leave the room, abandon this conversation. Desi was as easy to love as ever and carried a great appeal in his charm and his attention, but he did not deserve my love.

Sensing my inner struggle, he threw out impulsively, "Marry me, Red. Marry me. I can now; it's possible. Legally I have the freedom to marry anyone I desire."

"*Desi* — " He was so desperate, so earnest. I could see he meant it. "There is no possible way —" I started gently.

"I was only a boy eight years ago," he persisted. "I knew so little about love. I could truly love you now, care for you in a way you deserve. You could be safe at my side for all of your days. *Everything* is possible, Red."

This was the very thing I had dreaded in coming here... and in finding Desi wounded in particular. These very words were the ones I could not bear to hear. Perhaps at some point, before the terrible events with Jamie, I might have given in to the Prince's tender request. My life might have had a different future then. But Fumi's interference had changed everything.

Not for a heartbeat of time did I seriously consider any truth to be found in what Desi was saying. I could see, even then, even now, that he was only thinking of himself. He was not committed to my happiness any more than he took responsibility for Delophinie and the promises he had given her; he was only considering his own need for immediate change. His words would have been different otherwise. Once again, he thought I could save him from a life of boredom and unhappiness. But eventually, even with our rare chemistry and the spirit of easy fun between us, his eye would wander to other inviting shores if I said yes to him now.

"Desi," I told him then, softly; "If you are discontent in your life and your relationship, then you should change it. I can't do this for you; you must fix this for yourself."

A fire lit in his features instantly, but it was not directed at me. I had obviously struck a chord of truth.

His eyes moved to the gardens again; his voice was dull and lackluster. "They all have plans for me, all of them."

I did feel compassion for him; he was not given over to hatred and Evil, as Jamie had been. He was merely weak. And now was my opportunity to tell him the things I should have said eight years ago.

Still standing across the distance between us, I repeated gently, "I can't fix this for you, Desi. You must seize the reins of your own life and master it. One single act of defiance in marrying me will only prove to them all you are a child, not a man, and I would be compliant with it and look just as foolish. I urge you to take control of your own life. I would be very glad for you if you did — it would please me very much if you did so, Desi —"

His soft eyes flickered to mine. I could see at once he'd heard my words and felt my compassion; his mood changed again. "I once told you that you knew me better than anyone. That is still true. I will try, Red, I will try. I've already changed some things, but you're right, of course. There's more." His voice lowered. "I also told you I would always love you, no matter the circumstances. Maybe, after all is settled, maybe I'll come find you —"

He wasn't serious about this final part. Somehow I knew that. The Prince was too prone to get caught up in the moment. Life had been easy for him, and he did not have enough respect for the sacred feelings of the heart. This had been what grieved Jacobe years ago, and was the very quality that had devastated my heart.

I dropped the conversation and moved on, thankful I had not had to crush him and glad I could give him the counsel he really needed. I remained hopeful that my voice, so meaningful to him, would have impact where others had not.

But Desi's attachment to me and his resentment towards Jacobe did not stop him there. These feelings fueled a spite, a jealousy, which surfaced in a way I had never before witnessed in him.

After that first evening where Jacobe and I sat on the edge of the lake and watched night fall, a quiet camaraderie was present between us. He was naturally very thoughtful these days anyway, but that conversation only seemed to deepen it, particularly when he crossed paths with me. I often looked for opportunities to tease him in the hopes of making him smile.

One late afternoon only a handful of days after Desi's confessions to me, I found myself in his room, along with Jacobe, who had entered to deliver a handful of written messages that had arrived from Alameth for the Prince. Every other day or so, I knew, the Huntsman transported himself back to Alameth for messages and interactions with the King and Queen, while also bringing servants back and forth for supplies and errands as needed.

On this day Desi immediately took the notes and began reading them, muttering over various messages he had received. From my position across the room in my usual chair, I could see Jacobe planned to leave now that his task was accomplished. Desi rarely thanked him or acknowledged these small favors.

As Jacobe took the quiet steps to the door, his eyes drifted over to me. There was nothing in his face except the usual thoughtfulness; he was often gauging in these moments whether I was well and safe, I knew. Since I had agreed to this task, he had never discounted the fact that it might prove to be a difficult one for me.

Today I smiled at him, waved briefly, and returned to my book. It was an innocent action, hardly noteworthy, but Desi happened to look up at that moment and caught it. His eyes flickered sharply to Jacobe, who had paused at the doorway after catching my reaction. I will never know if the Prince saw something unusual in Jacobe's expression or he simply flared up at the idea of any friendliness between us at all, but Desi quickly spoke.

"Red, has Jacobe given you his news? I'm sure you've heard by now."

Jacobe froze and pivoted on one heel at once, as uniform as a soldier, facing the Prince down. I looked up in surprise. *What could this be about?*

Desi was smug and bitter. "It turns out he's a prince."

Instantly there was a tension between the two I could not identify.

Jacobe rebuked him, quietly. "Be silent, Desi."

Those low words carried an authority I myself would never have wanted to question and no wise person should have. I looked quickly between the two; Desi showed no signs of obeying.

To assuage the situation, I piped up, "That news is no surprise. I always assumed he was someone important in whatever country he came from." I smiled at Jacobe, hoping this would settle the matter.

But my quiet smile only seemed to fuel Desi more. "Not a prince of his own country, Red," he corrected mockingly, his blue eyes glimmering now at the Huntsman. "A Prince of Alameth. *My father's son, after all.*"

These words fell on the floor between the three of us like heavy stones.

Holding the Prince's eye, Jacobe addressed him in a cool, dangerous tone. "You have no call to complain, Desi." Then he turned swiftly and left the room.

At his departure, I moved almost by instinct, wordlessly dropping my book and hurrying for the door.

Desi called after me plaintively, "Red, don't go — let him sulk —"

I ignored him. He only meant to cause trouble.

Upon exiting Desi's room, I had no idea where to go. The mansion was large and Jacobe could choose any room he liked to disappear into and not be found for the afternoon. I had no idea in what part of the palace he slept, and the grounds outside were enormous. I shot for the nearest exit and headed for the stables. This had always been Jacobe's chosen spot when he and Desi disagreed; maybe he would hide there, where less activity took place.

My instincts proved true. I found him only moments later in *Thunder's* stall, though not hiding. He was saddling the horse and obviously preparing to leave. His movements were self-controlled, not angry or disturbed, though there was something about his expression that would give anyone pause before speaking to him. Jacobe had a deadly purpose when he was disconcerted.

I didn't have to address him. He sensed my presence before it became necessary and glanced over, hands still working the saddle. "I meant to tell you myself," he declared restlessly. "It came to light since the last I saw you."

"I can see it troubles you," I said carefully, watching him.

"It troubles me more that Desi spitefully tried to use it against you and me," he answered. "He deserves a whipping."

This image made me smile, unable to contain myself.

Jacobe caught this reaction and broke into a sudden smile himself; he was tightening the girth strap and paused, shaking his head dryly. "I'm going for a ride. It will help keep me from following through with personally delivering that whipping."

At this I hesitated, uncertain if he welcomed any interference. I wanted to be a friend to him, but he was Jacobe, after all... Even with the growing closeness between us over the past week, I still carried a much greater respect for his desire for privacy.

I decided to try anyway. "I could go with you," I suggested quietly.

This stopped him. A quiet fell in the stall. His head was bent and his hands were on the saddle stirrup before him where he had been adjusting it. He turned to me with dark, wild eyes. I didn't honestly expect him to say yes, but he said briefly, "I plan to ride hard and fast, Red."

I smiled at him. "Then I'll be sure to hold on tight."

We charged out of the front gates of the Palace only moments later. Jacobe wheeled the horse to the North and instantly drove *Thunder* down the shadowed roadway until the animal was at a full stretch. I quickly gave up any pretense of keeping the hood of my cloak on. The wind whipped at my hair and pulled at my clothing, threatening to unseat me. Unthinkingly, I clung to Jacobe as if my life depended on it.

There was something thrilling about the restless energy that fueled this moment. The forested Wood swam past in a blur; the road wound and twisted endlessly. I could feel the Huntsman bend into the wind, the ride, leaning with the horse's motions. His experience as a horseman was in clear evidence today.

For a long while I thought we would ride all the way to Wilsburg or possibly beyond; Jacobe showed no sign of letting up. But there was a moment he suddenly pulled in the reins and sat up, as if he had released the passion he needed to and was returning to his senses now. Still clinging to him, I shifted to an upright position with him. Beneath us, the horse danced and resisted; *Thunder* was ready for more. But Jacobe's direction on the reins was firm, and eventually the animal slowed to a steady pace.

It was then Jacobe asked me over his shoulder, "You all right?"

I nodded, the side of my face pressed between his shoulder blades. "That was invigorating," I breathed out.

He gave no response to this, merely directed *Thunder* back in the direction we had come. I recognized this part of the wood; we had covered a great many miles in just a short time. The roads were darkest here, unable to receive much light through the dense and crowded trees around us. I held no concern, however; Jacobe rode confidently and knew the way.

After a short while, I could sense the Huntsman's mood change. I was beginning to be quicker at reading him, unlike I had always been with Desi, who carried his feelings in his eyes and expressed them quickly to anyone standing by. Jacobe reserved his thoughts for those who counted most. My hands were linked at his waist now; he seemed to become conscious of this and put one hand over both of mine gently as we rode. He said nothing, yet so much was expressed in this one simple gesture.

Finally, he began to speak. "In the days of his youth, when the King was as yet unmarried, he had an —" He hesitated.

"An indiscretion?" I volunteered.

Jacobe was wry. "If that's what you want to call it. I was born from it. I always wondered why my mother spoke of Alameth's king as though she knew him. Later, when I was quickly given a position in the Royal Family as a bodyguard, I began to suspect I had not been told everything."

Silence fell. The only sound that could be heard was the steady clod of the horse's hooves on the dirt road. Jacobe's hand still securely covered my own. I hugged him tightly from behind, enjoying the feel of his warmth.

I said, "One does wonder how this, um, *indiscretion* came to light."

"*Desi.*" Jacobe was immediately dry. "Desi pressed his father until, finally and in a fit of fury, Umgetray confessed the story. This was just after Fumi took you to Shamayim. After the initial shock to the entire household, the news has been accepted rather calmly. Even Desi has been rather pleased."

"Smug," I amended for him. "Desi has been smug."

"Red —" Jacobe's voice was abrupt. "I'm going to be king one day. Probably soon."

For some reason I was shocked. I couldn't explain it to myself in that moment. My thoughts ran back over the past several days — the uneasy, reverential behavior towards him from many of the servants, the increased resentment from Desi whenever Jacobe issued commands. Even the way the household regarded Delophinie, who was not the future king's bride. So many subtle things came to light suddenly.

Jacobe seemed to have known beforehand that this news would have an effect on me. His voice changed and slowed. "Desi abdicated his right to the throne almost as soon as he heard the news. His action is the one everyone remembers far more than the King's. All of Alameth is still shaking their heads over the scandal."

My thoughts whirled again at this, realizing the truth. It had been there all along in Desi's words, in his behavior. In a wild turn of events, he was free now as he had always wanted to be. Free to romantically pursue whom he wanted. Free to live the life he had always dreamed of. Jacobe was the one now bound — bound to the throne, and bound to duty.

Unexplainably, I wanted to withdraw from him. I couldn't understand the entire reason why for this either, but I knew he had become too important. He was too foreign now. This affected the way I looked at him. We could not be friends; he was the future king of Alameth. At the very least, as he took up those duties, we would never relate to each other. Our lives would never again intersect.

With these thoughts, I unlinked my hands and his fell away. I sat up now fully, away from him. I reached back for the low cantle behind me and gripped it.

To cover for my discomfort, I asked, "And you? What do you feel about it?"

Jacobe gave a half-shrug. "I've had mixed feelings, but have finally come to terms with it, I believe. Umgetray — *my father* — " he corrected himself. "— is delighted to have the secret out at last. He is also rather pleased with the conclusion it came to."

Jacobe told Desi years ago that I was no queen. This thought sprang to my mind from nowhere. Somehow I'd never forgotten that. His words had stung then as much as they stung now upon remembering them. My destiny lay elsewhere, he had said.

Why did my thoughts jump to that *just now?* I chided myself.

The two of us rode in silence for the rest of the journey back to the Palace, both wrapped in our thoughts. I was grateful when the pale-stone walls finally appeared, then, shortly after, the gates. Jacobe opened these as he always had with some invisible thought or silent command and they swung open effortlessly. No one was in the courtyard and the windows on this side of the Palace were dark with inactivity. Once at the stables, a livery man exited to offer assistance, but Jacobe waved him away, leading us forward until we stood outside *Thunder's* stall. He extended one arm for me to dismount, swung me down safely, then did so himself.

As his boots touched the ground, his neck pivoted to face me, dark eyes immediately taking me in with a watchful curiosity. "You haven't said what you feel about it, Red. What are your thoughts?"

This made me further uncomfortable. He knew me too well, I thought.

"I — " The words came out painfully slow, another phenomenon I could not explain to myself just now. "I'm surprised, as — as anyone would be. I'm also glad — for you both. Desi is free and —" I raised my eyes to his scarred and painted face. "And you will make an excellent king."

Silence fell briefly. Jacobe's mouth came open, as if he wanted to speak. Several thoughts were in his contemplative eyes. But he did not, and chose to hold his peace.

I could only feel relief, truthfully. I had too many conflicting feelings at the moment. I needed to make a quick escape so I could gather my composure. Then later, I told myself, I would try and decipher the impact this news had had on me. For now, I could barely breathe.

It was towards evening when a knock came to my bedroom door. I had retreated here after my ride with Jacobe and had not surfaced in the few hours since. Upon opening the door, I found a household servant, who bowed slightly.

"Mum, there is a young girl at the gates asking for you. She says she has an urgent message to deliver."

Surprised, I thanked him and closed the door. This had to be a patient call, I thought; that was the only explanation I could piece together. Someone, probably Gran, had guessed I was here after my extended absence from the cottage. Reaching for my basket and my cloak, I hurried out of the Palace to meet my young messenger. Fortunately, I did not see Jacobe on the way; I was grateful for that.

I first headed for the stables for my horse, assuming the call would require some travel through the Wood. Ordinarily I would have referred the girl to Nodden in Wilsburg, but today I was grateful for the distraction. I needed something useful to put my hand to. Desi hardly needed me at this point.

At the stables, I saddled the horse and sought out a livery man to open the gates for me, which he did, and in only moments I led the animal out onto the road. As the servant had reported, a young girl stood there waiting. She was dressed in a plain dress and pinafore, appearing particularly innocent in a set of walnut-colored plaits. I did not know her.

"Are you Miss Red?" she asked.

I nodded. "Did someone send you?"

"Your Gran." Her large round eyes blinked at me with urgency. "She went out for a walk, she said, and fell in the Wood. I was walking by and she asked me to run and get you here at the Palace. She's been hurt real bad."

"Is it far from here?" I asked, alarmed. "Do you mind riding with me on the horse? We'll get there faster."

The little girl nodded acquiescence. "I don't mind riding. It's not too far, back toward Huntsville. But it's off the main road. I can show you."

Quickly, I lifted her small form up on the horse and then swung myself up behind her. We set out towards the west at a quick gait, with the girl directing occasionally. Half-way between the Palace and my cottage was a smaller track that led off into the woods to the north; this road eventually joined two others, I knew, and finally concluded on the main thoroughfare directly into Wilsburg. But the little track wound through a deep, dark part of the Wood and was rarely used. I had to wonder why Gran had chosen it for her walk today.

This brought up a question. "Did my Gran tell you how long she had been out there?" I asked the girl. "Was it just today that she fell?"

She nodded affirmatively, her tiny hands clinging to the saddle horn in front of her. "Just today. That's what she said."

That gave me some relief, knowing she had not been wounded in the Wood for very long. Another five minutes or so passed before we came upon the little track and I quickly took this, wishing at once I had a lantern. The horse could see the road well enough, but I had doubts I could examine Gran very well in this dim lighting. Hopefully she was not so injured that I couldn't get her on the horse and quickly ride us back to the cottage. The distance was not so far...

After several moments, the girl announced, "It's coming up. Just past that tree there —" She pointed into the darkness before us.

Peering ahead, I thought I could make out what tree she was referring to. One in particular grew close to the road, its burly trunk closing in on the path and narrowing the road width significantly. Perhaps Gran had found shelter on the other side of it.

Within only a few seconds more, we reached the spot, which the girl confirmed. "*Here.* She's here."

"On the other side of the tree?" I asked. She nodded.

Immediately I called Gran's name, as I halted the horse and dismounted. "Gran! I'm here! It's Red. Hold on — I'm coming!"

As I turned and helped the little girl dismount, I once again found myself wishing for a lantern. Surely the Palace had one I could have borrowed. The lighting was very dark here, blocked deeply by the heavy trees around us. I could barely make out the shape of the horse. Once the girl was at my side, I instructed her to take my hand and lead the way. I untied my basket from the saddle and left the horse, trusting he would not bolt in the dark.

Together the two of us rounded the tree, being watchful of its entangled heap of roots. These twisted and wound underfoot, making for dangerous footing. Once, the little girl stumbled and I steadied her.

"She's just around the tree," she assured me.

Finally, we reached the other side of the broad, gnarly oak. It was here, I found, the trees parted suddenly and a little clearing formed in the forest. This was unusual for the Wood, but I was thankful for it. Overhead, the light of early dusk lit our way enough that visibility returned. Uniquely, a small plot of grass grew here.

My confidence rose. I looked around us quickly. "Where is she?" I asked. "I don't see her."

The girl pulled free of my hand. Her eyes seemed to be searching the wood around us. "I don't know — she was right here —"

Then, suddenly, she turned and ran from me, disappearing into the trees.

For a moment I was confused, but just as quickly realized something was wrong. I'd lived in the Wood far too long and experienced too much Evil now not to recognize when something was afoot. I told myself I had been too distracted and preoccupied with

Jacobe's news to pay close enough attention. Obviously the girl had led me out here with intention.

Quickly, I turned back to the massive tree, intending to reach the horse and ride out of here as fast as I could. I had no idea what was happening and did not want to wait another moment to find out.

But too late, a pair of yellow familiar eyes glimmered at me in the space just ahead, blocking my way back to the horse. Heart thundering, I stepped back once, twice. My head was pounding a warning signal. The beast, black as night, stepped out from the shadow of the tree and emerged into the gray lighting.

"Hello, Red," he snarled.

The sound of his voice brought back a thousand memories, each one worse than the last. At once an Evil presence moved into the little glade where we stood, like a low fog clinging to the ground. The air was humid, yet perversely cold, as all the Wood was, and I pulled the cloak closer to me for warmth. I did not try to run from him.

"What do you want?" I demanded. "You devised an elaborate scheme to bring me out here; you obviously want something. What is it?"

"Why, I wanted *you*, Red." He was approaching in that proud manner he had always shown, so certain he was the master and I was the prey he could toy with. "Did you think I would let you run off without consequences? It's been *forever. I've missed you.*"

In that moment I did not under-estimate his ability or his power, but I was not afraid. I, who had once been so intimidated by his power, stood fearless. I had always known he would return; I had especially known it when I arrived in Huntsville and found all the wolves had disappeared. He had rallied them and gone into hiding. Fumi had taught me to be unafraid, and courage rose up inside of me now.

"You have no power over me," I announced, "and you know it. The only power you have is the power I give to you."

His reaction surprised me. Once he was three or four feet away, his eyes narrowed and he froze in his tracks. *"What is that?"*

I realized he meant Jacobe's cloak. I had inherited it since the wolf's era. It clearly left him uneasy; he would not approach any further.

"What do you want?" I repeated.

His eyes glimmered again. "I want to talk to you, Red," he said coyly. "You haven't really found the freedom you were looking for, have you? Did you find your way? It certainly doesn't look as though you have. You don't belong in the Wood; you don't belong in the Palace. *Where, oh where could you possibly go?"*

His words were always fear-provoking, I knew that. Though the dilemma he described was real, I refused to let him prey on me in this moment.

"I will find my way," I told him. "Fumi will help me."

The wolf growled. He did not appreciate that name. *"Fumi* can do nothing for you." He became restless and began circling me at a safe distance. His pale fangs were starkly visible as he spoke. "Where is he now? Hiding in the forest?"

"He's here," I assured him. "Would you like me to call him?"

He growled again. "Don't test me, Red. Do you remember what I did to you last time? I can easily do it again. I can snap you in half if I desire to. You're *nothing. Less* than nothing."

I did not turn my back on him as he circled me, but kept watch on him as he glided past slowly a second time. "That isn't true and you know it," I argued. "I'm important. I have Fumi's word on it. I have a great destiny. Just because it has not manifested yet does not mean it isn't coming."

"Oh, please," he snarked, unmoved. "You have nowhere to go. Nothing remarkable is going to happen. Isn't the same thing happening in the Palace that happened last time? I heard the two of you ride by in the forest earlier, you and *that prince.*" Clearly, he didn't appreciate Jacobe either; he spit his title out with a snarl. "I had to come track you down after that. The opportunity was just too delightful not to indulge. You are still going to leave the Palace at the end of the summer empty-handed and adrift, you know. There is no destiny to be found. All the destinies have been taken." He thought this statement was particularly amusing.

I was growing angry, I realized. I repeated again, "*What do you want?*"

At this demand, the wolf snapped his head towards me and growled, "I want *you,* Red. I want *you.*"

"Then you've gone to an elaborate amount of work for nothing," I retorted. "I won't bend, nor break, nor bow. I am not yours and never will be. The plain truth is, *you can't have me, you can't take me, and you won't get me!*"

This, at last, infuriated him. He let out a mighty snarl, tossing his head. He desperately wanted to lunge for me, but the cloak held him back. "What is *that thing?*" he snarled again. "*What is it?*"

"It is what is standing between you and me, obviously," I told him, suddenly grateful for Fumi. He had known all along what I would need, and I had no doubt he orchestrated this from the beginning. Quietly, discreetly, he had been working behind the scenes of my life for some time now. This moved me to tears standing there in the dark deserted Wood pitted against this terrible beast. No matter that Desi had proved to be no different and my position with Jacobe was unclear, Fumi would not let me fail... and I would not let me fail either. I felt suddenly emboldened.

"You will never get near me again," I told the wolf then. "And you will never again convince me that there is no hope, you and your minions. You can turn the world upon me as you did last time, but I will not let go of life. I will not let go of the truth. I will not be deceived again."

Furious now, the wolf threw back his head and howled a piercing cry. The sound cut through the empty forest with a chilling call. Again and again he released the call.

"You'll be sorry for that," he growled.

From the trees around me I heard an answering call, then another, and another. He had called in reinforcements at my words. Slowly, the pack was approaching.

"Am I winning?" I said to him. "Did my words weaken you? Are you losing? You can't handle the situation yourself? Did I prove too invincible?"

"You'll be sorry," he growled again, pacing restlessly before me. I had never before taunted him. "They're coming now. There are too many of us; you won't be able to resist us all."

My courage held until they began to appear one by one on the far edges of the glade, creeping out of the trees with dripping fangs and demon eyes. There were at least twenty of them, as large and massive as Jamie's wolf, each in various shades of mottled gray and black. They had been waiting for this opportunity with glee.

My breath left me. I realized my hands were clenched in fists so tight I could feel the nails digging into my palms. I had no idea how powerful the cloak was, nor how strong my resolve, but I dared not take the chance. I drew one quick breath and screamed, *"FUMI!"*

This both terrified and infuriated them. Every wolf in the glade raised their heads and howled, a terrible demoralizing cry meant to strike terror in the hearts of all who heard it. I raised my hands and covered my ears, nearly weeping at the sound.

They were not yet finished with their cry before what could only be described as an orange fire-bolt exploded from the trees behind me and blasted through the body of Jamie's wolf pacing near my feet. The beast released a scream of pain and slumped, whimpering, to his side. Just that quickly he had been brought to nothing. Another blast came again, and again, shooting across the little glade, striking each wolf it aimed for, tearing through their flesh. These fell where they were shot as well, instantly.

Startled, the other wolves muttered and whimpered in confusion, trying to see their assailant, temporarily trying to decide to run or attack. The smell of burning flesh was strong in the air. A few turned and darted back into the Wood.

Again the relentless fire-bolts came in another round, targeting another four, then five wolves, whizzing past me with a sound like rushing water. Upon reaching the wolves, the bolts exploded through their bodies, destroying them effortlessly.

I turned round now, searching for my rescuer. My heart leapt at once. Jacobe had entered the little glade behind me, his axe in hand,

and was striding towards me slowly and with determination. Even in the failing light I could see his blue cape trailing the ground behind him as he made his way forward. He raised the double-edged blade once again; from it another blast of bolts exited, tearing across the glade, aiming for more of the wolves. These fell with a horrific yowl where they stood.

There were few left now. The wolves were in mad terror as they looked around them, yellow eyes squinting and fearful. Strangely, they looked small and underweight to me now, insignificant beasts who had been stripped of their power to intimidate and torment. Quickly, before the Huntsman could aim his axe again, they scattered into the forest.

I turned back to Jacobe. The little glade had gone quiet, eerie after the terrific sights and sounds of only moments before. He was upon me now, his face bearing an expression I had never seen before. In response, I leapt forward and threw myself against him, bursting into tears.

One arm of steel enclosed me, while the other held the axe away. He buried his face in the top of my head.

We stood there some time until he spoke. "I thought you left," he murmured. "I came looking for you when one of the servants reported that you had gone. I thought you ran away at the news I gave you."

I pulled away far enough to gaze up into his shadowed face. "*No.* I wouldn't run away from you, never. Not like that. I would have told you. How — how did you find me?"

"I was already on my way, but Fumi transported me here when you called him." He frowned over our surroundings. "How did you come to be here?"

I was still clinging to him. "I was fooled. The wolf sent a girl — she said Gran was hurt and needed care."

Mention of the wolf turned Jacobe's gaze away from me and towards the beast lying where he had slain it. His eyes narrowed savagely. "Stand back, Red. He's still breathing."

It was true. As I glanced over, the wolf was drawing shaky ragged breaths, struggling weakly as the last of his life drained from him. Jacobe moved me aside and stepped towards the animal, watching him with a lethal eye. When he stood over him, the Huntsman raised his blade one final time.

"Jacobe, wait!"

He paused, glancing at me.

"Wait," I repeated, holding out one hand as if to stop him, though it wasn't necessary. He waited.

I strode over, breathless now. I don't know what motivated me to think of it — I seemed to be acting purely on instinct now — but in another moment I swept off my cloak. As I threw it down over the wolf, the long folds swirled and rippled in the air, like a waving flag of freedom. It settled on the beast. He let out one last mournful yowl, then a shuddering whimper, and died where he lay.

This wasn't all, however. As Jacobe and I stood over him watching, his body dematerialized. As he disappeared, gone to the hellish place from which he had come, Jamie's body appeared before us in the darkening shadows of nightfall. He was dying; his breathing was as ragged and hoarse as the beast who had just lain here in this space.

I knelt quickly beside him. Astonishingly, his eyes opened and recognition crossed his face. His voice was a rattling whisper. "Red —"

From somewhere within me, a deep compassion emerged. I smiled at him. "Jamie —"

"I didn't — mean it," he said. "Not — not any of it. He took control. I loved you."

"I know," I told him. "I know, Jamie. Sleep now. *Sleep.*"

At these words, Jamie closed his eyes in relief... and drew his final breath.

A quiet fell. I bent my head and wept.

I wept for the life he could have had, the poor choices he had made, and the terrible price he paid because of it. I wept because there was Evil in the world and it still deceived many through their pain and their confusion. And I wept because he was innocent before all this began and there was nothing I could do to save him.

The Huntsman did not interfere; he moved away, quietly, to inspect the other wolves and ensure they were safely dead. Then he disappeared into the trees temporarily and returned with *Thunder* and my own horse, leading them both into the little glade. Still without addressing me, he removed a spade from his saddlebags and began digging a grave some feet away from where I knelt.

By the time he was completed, my tears had stopped. I stood aside as Jacobe wordlessly removed the red cloak, now a dark stain in the night shadows, and lifted Jamie's lifeless body into the empty grave. In just a few moments more, the Huntsman's shovel went to work again, heaving fresh soil until the job was completed.

Afterward, Jacobe and I stood aside and stared at the freshly covered grave in silence. I had no words to say. Words were for the living, not for the dead.

"Let's go home, Red," Jacobe said at last.

I nodded, turning to follow him as he led the way back to the horses. He tied the reins of my mount to a loop on the back of his saddle, then lifted me up on *Thunder's* back. In another instant he had mounted behind me, slipping one rock-hard arm around my waist to hold me steady, with the other free to manage the reins. He felt solid as a pillar behind and around me, I thought, as Jacobe heeled *Thunder* forward. I was exhausted and weary. Before I knew it, I leaned back against him, safe in the circumference of his arms, and fell fast asleep.

10.

I woke in my room at the Palace two days later, aware instantly that Jacobe had put the sleep on me. I was ravenously hungry and needed to use the privy, but these were my only discomforts. I wanted immediately to seek him out. The events of that night with the wolf loomed large in my mind, but even larger was the unresolved issue between Jacobe and me. I had been afraid to confront the truth before the other night, but now, after what had happened, I was ready. As I swept back the plush bed-coverings and began to prepare for the day, I knew it was very possible and very likely that Jacobe and I must part paths. We certainly couldn't draw any closer if there was no future in it. I would not repeat the history I had already lived. Let the truth come out, I thought, whatever it may be; I would face it with courage, and with Fumi's help.

I found him in the gardens later that morning, strolling through the little pathways between the rows of blossoming trellises, flower plants and low hedges. He had not made an appearance in the few hours since I awakened, but I knew this meant nothing. Jacobe always had his ear to the events of the household and seemed to know where every person in it was located. He'd performed this neat little trick with me multiple times since my arrival this summer.

I had requested for my breakfast to be served in my room this morning and had not exited to greet anyone until I looked out my windows and saw Jacobe in the gardens. One of the servants had already delivered messages that Desi was hoping to see me, but I ignored this. He could wait; the Prince was not in danger of any health issues that needed immediate attention and he was no longer the priority after the past few days.

Quickly, I found my way to the gardens, and to Jacobe. As I came upon him from behind, soft-footed, I could see he had abandoned his regular attire and wore long dark boots over black breeches and a loose linen shirt capped by a cravat tie. Even plainly dressed he cut a striking figure. He towered over most men and walked, even deep in thought, with a formidable strength. He had shaved his beard unexpectedly; I realized this as he stopped at once and turned.

"I was wondering when you would emerge from your room," he said.

My eyes caught his. After the intensity of the events with the wolves and the encounter with Jamie, I would have gladly embraced him today. If I had not had control of my impulses, I would have done so. He was my protector and my defender; aside from Fumi, I could count on him the most. This made him infinitely precious to me.

"I have given instructions to the household to leave you alone unless you seek them out," he said then. "I wanted you to have time and privacy. Desi knows there was an incident — he would have guessed even if I hadn't told him — but he doesn't know the details and will hopefully respect any desire you may have for silence. You needn't treat his injury any further if you don't wish to."

He was efficient, as always. I thought he sounded like a prince and future king now more than ever, certainly more than Desi ever had. I could hear it in his tone and see it in his manner like never before. But these were not the words I needed. Jacobe's gold-flecked eyes, watching me closely as he spoke, more obvious now without facial hair, had thoughts in them he wished to say but was holding back.

"Can we walk?" I asked him.

He nodded silently and we moved together through the gardens. A dry breeze whispered past us as it made its way down to the lake. The sun was high, but was already losing its intensity. Already the summer season was winding to a close.

For a moment I breathed in the soft, perfumed air, taking the steps next to him. I felt alive and strong after the events of a few nights ago. I was not afraid.

"There is first the matter of the letter, I suppose," I began. I did not hesitate to think he would tell me everything now, not after the night in the wood. I realized I could get any truth from him I wanted. He had exposed his heart when he had come after me after thinking I had fled from him. "You wrote it."

He could see I was seeking final confirmation. "Yes."

"Did you embellish it any? For the sake of persuading me it was Desi's voice, I mean."

"I understood what you meant." Still moving forward, he pondered this, bare chin low, his tattooed eyes on the ground at his feet. "None of those thoughts had ever surfaced for me until I wrote them. Then they all became very real. At the time you were still a young girl, though your soul has always been much older, wise beyond your years." He paused again. "In the years since I wrote the letter I have thought it was best I left when I did. If those thoughts and feelings had begun to surface — and they were there, in seed form — then it was prudent that I leave."

At my small exclamation, he turned and looked down upon me, his quiet authority always present. "My mother — her suffering through my younger years taught me that. Her heart was broken by the King when he left her. Their relationship had always been an impossibility — the King knew this from the start and yet still pursued her. Not just that, but she was doomed to raise me alone and in shame."

He was nothing like Desi, I thought. The prince, who had always complained he had little in common with his father, was remarkably more like Umgetray than we all knew.

Jacobe's eyes flickered over my face. His next words revealed he was thinking kindred thoughts. "You have been through similar suffering... because of Desi."

I nodded, acknowledging this. But Desi and I were not the point I was driving towards. "And when you saw me these past few weeks?"

He knew what I was asking. His dark eyes sparked. "I was in wonder at the work Fumi had done in you. You were so utterly broken and torn apart the last time I'd seen you. And —" he grasped for the words. "As a woman, you were like fine wine that had seasoned. You were — have been — rather breathtaking, Red."

These words came easily for the Huntsman, all things considered. I doubted he had ever given them to any woman. They were not laced with need like Jamie's had always been, and they rang true, unlike Desi's words, which might have been poetic but were consistently filled with emotion and flattery.

I broke his gaze and turned, resuming my steps. Jacobe joined me silently.

"You said I wasn't a queen," I announced softly. "You told Desi I had another destiny elsewhere."

He was exceedingly sharp, the Huntsman was. Immediately he knew which conversation from so long ago that I was referring to. He released a small breath.

"*Ah.* I see now what has been hindering us. When you drew away at the announcement of me being made king, I feared the worst, I'm afraid. I'd already been hesitant to tell you. I thought it would make you run back to Desi now that he was free."

It was my turn to stop suddenly and face him. "I will never run back to Desi." The words were a vow. "He asked and I said no."

The low heat in my voice gave the Huntsman pause for a moment. He took me in briefly. "I know that now. The other night made me realize the truth. When I visited Fumi, he told me all that you had endured and this should have been enough to convince me that you would never take any of your past back up, but I saw, *felt*, clearly how you regarded me when you — when you clung to me, truthfully. I saw then. My fear was simply that — *my* fear of losing you — and was entirely unfounded." His tone quieted and slowed. His expression changed. "I *did* say you were not a queen, Red. Certainly not Desi's queen. At the time I meant you were something more — it should have been taken as a deep honor I was offering you, not as a criticism."

"I have always understood what you meant by it; that has never been in question. I was disturbed because of the truth in it. If it was the truth then, it must be the truth now," I asserted.

Jacobe's eyes looked haunted for a moment. They fell away from mine. He shook his head. Finally, he confessed his truth at last.

"I can't properly answer this," he said. "Everything in my soul wants you with me for the rest of my life, much more than any desire for a throne. I wanted you well before that revelation emerged, from the night Fumi and I rescued you and you forgave me for writing that absurd letter. You deserved protection, I thought, and safety, and love. I would have gladly seen you with Desi from a young age if it could have spared you suffering, but I realized I wanted to be the one who loved you, no one else. I confessed everything to Fumi when I went to see him in Shamayim; he knows it all." His eyes were intense now, fixed upon me. "But I must take the kingdom, Red — it is mine by right, and mine by destiny. I intend to rule as Alameth's king, as an heir and descendent of Fumi himself. Only you can determine, with Fumi's help, if ruling at my side is your greater destiny. You do have one and I will not willingly interfere with it. I did not see everything back then," he added. "I didn't know all that the future held when I said those words to Desi. Not only that, but I will always think you are worthy of greater things. I'm honored to know you and always will be."

There was nothing to say that could give proper response to this speech. The Great Huntsman had just given me these words. The future king of Alameth. I was moved and struck silent.

Jacobe shook his head again with a low note of sorrow, resuming his steps. "As I said, I can't answer this. I don't stand in an objective position to do so."

I let him walk on, pausing there as he moved ahead. There was only one thing to be done for the moment, I could see that. Only one path was the safe way for my heart to follow until I knew for certain. I had to leave.

Later that day I went to see Desi. I had decided not to avoid him, and needed a respite from an afternoon spent in thought and silent prayer. I was still in need of some definitive confirmation or sign from Fumi, and this had yet to be delivered.

The Prince and Delophinie were arguing when I approached the closed door; I could hear their raised voices and debated temporarily whether to disturb them. I did so anyway. *They probably needed a visitor,* I told myself.

Silence fell briefly. It was Delophinie who answered in a composed voice and bid me to enter.

The two of them were seated in the receiving area of the room, facing the windows. At first sight of me, Delophinie stood to her feet with a concerned expression.

"Red! Are you well? Jacobe told us you'd had some accident and were indisposed."

I had to smile. If Desi did ever decide to put a true heart into his actions and choose her, Delophinie was a good match for him. The two were very alike. Impulsive, given to emotional expression. Beautiful. A trifle spoiled. They understood each other well.

Today Desi's expression was hooded and sharp as he took me in. He understood more than his future bride, though what Jacobe had told him exactly I did not know. At the very least, he did not appear contrite for his behavior the last time I saw him. He'd been spiteful and selfish. That seemed like ages ago now, I thought to myself.

Unheeding of his reaction, I greeted the two of them. "I'm well now, everything is fine. I came to check on the Prince. How are you feeling?"

It was Delophinie who answered for him, with enthusiasm. "He's been improving the past few days considerably. He walked around the room a few times. I'm very hopeful we can still go forward with the wedding this fall."

Unable to hide his feelings at this, Desi shot her a dry glance clear with irritation. This was not a subject he wanted to discuss at the moment. I kept my expression carefully neutral as he glanced back at me. Clearly, he had not acted on my counsel yet.

"If you are both comfortable with it," I announced, "I would like to check the site of the wound. The sutures will probably need removed soon."

They both agreed to this, and we relocated to the bed, where Desi unbuttoned his shirt and I assessed the injury. Delophinie stood over us anxiously.

I thought, again, of how much she cared for him. It was impressive that she loved him even though he would never be king. Instead, he had abandoned the throne at first opportunity. Other women, I knew, would not have been so generous with their hearts.

"It seems fine," I told them both. "You're recovering nicely, your Highness. I think one of your Healers could remove the sutures within the next few days."

This last statement gave them both pause, and Desi looked at me with a question in his eyes. I stood to my feet and moved away from them, as Desi refastened his shirt and Delophinie sat on the edge of the bed, facing me with expectancy.

"I told Jacobe this morning that I must go," I told them with a quiet smile. "I've been away from my patients long enough, and Desi is fine now. I've actually come to say goodbye."

I could see Desi's thoughts were running swiftly at this sudden announcement, but he said nothing. I knew him well enough to know if he had the chance without the Princess present he would try and talk me away from my decision. I would ensure, I purposed privately, not to give him that opportunity. As long as I was here, within his line of vision, I could see he would not take control of his own pathway ahead but would complacently leave it for others around him to decide.

It was Delophinie, surprisingly, who let out a quiet protest. "We will miss you, Red. I wish you didn't have to go. You've been a true support during this time. I thank you."

I smiled at her. She had grown notably warmer towards me since my arrival. "I wish you both the greatest of happiness," I told them then.

They both gave answering murmurs, as they were supposed to, and I began the steps to the exit. The Princess, in another rare gesture of kindness, walked me to the door.

Conversationally, she said, "I've never asked you what your real name is, Red. I didn't assume your mother named you Red from the start of life."

Before I could answer her, Desi spoke from where he was moving, gingerly, from the bed to his familiar chair. "Isobel. Her name is Isobel."

Delophinie started and looked over at me quickly. "A queen's name! How lovely."

It was then some inner bell went off inside of me, as sweetly and suddenly as if the musical chime was here reverberating in the room. I paused suddenly, turned, and stared at her open-mouthed. I could hear Fumi's voice in my head saying, "Your destiny is in your name." How like him to arrange this mystery. I felt a laugh rising up and I was hard put to contain it. The answer had been here all along.

I am certain my behavior was surprising to the two of them as I cried out with a laugh, "I have to go! I must leave. Excuse me, please. *I have to go.*" Then I turned and rushed from the room.

Jacobe saw me running headlong in the gardens before I ever arrived before him. His eyes were dark with concern and one hand came out to steady me when I pulled up short, breathlessly.

"Red — ?"

Today, in spite of the many windows we were exposed to, I threw myself upon him heedlessly. His arms more slowly returned the embrace, but I could hear him laughing softly. *Had I ever heard the mighty Huntsman laugh?*

"What has happened?"

I pulled back, but did not release him, looking up into his bewildered face. "I found my answer, Jacobe."

That was all he needed; my reckless embrace and laughing smile had told him all. Impulsively, as if passion and joy ignited within him simultaneously, he grabbed for my face and kissed me long and hard. In his affection, in that moment of freedom to express all that he had held back out of carefulness, I knew everything about his devotion. Then the moment changed, slowly, and became something even more. We were unable to stop. Still kissing me, one of his hands moved for the back of my neck, offering support. Jacobe would never be a man so caught up that he did not consider me.

He pulled away eventually, looking as amazed as I'd ever seen him... if the Great Huntsman was capable of amazement. "Are you sure, Red? It will be a huge commitment. You are not just marrying me but an entire country."

I laughed. "It's too late. You can't kiss me like that and expect me to change my mind now."

We still hadn't released each other; I felt I could stay here for the remainder of my life if it was possible.

"You do not have to give up healing, Red," he assured me then. "I wouldn't want you to unless you desired it. Anything, *anything at all* that you desire will be yours if I can help it. I may be duty-bound to the throne, but the only duty I desire from you is your duty to me, and I to you. I promise you, I will not let your position as queen encroach upon you as I once told Desi would happen if he married you. I will see to that. You've been through enough."

I didn't know whether to laugh or cry. Every word of Fumi's had proven true. Jacobe sounded like him and loved me with the same love. He was a man among men.

"What happens next?" I asked with great happiness.

Jacobe answered as though he had already considered this, should I say yes. "I thought we could go —"

"See Fumi?" I finished.

He smiled down at me. *"Yes."*

There was no one else I wanted to tell in person as much as the King. I was quite certain he had arranged all of this from the beginning. "When?"

"As soon as you like, my love. This very moment if you desire." His painted eyes turned grave and earnest then. "Let me walk you from this Wood forever, Red. Let's be done with it."

And so we did.

FROM THE DESK OF THE AUTHOR:

Some stories come to us like fairy tales, but stay with us like haunting songs. If Red stirred something in you—if the shadows felt familiar, or the light more radiant—I would love to hear your thoughts. Even a short review helps other readers find their way into this story of wolves, wonder, and a love that never lets go.

If you would like to journey further, I invite you to subscribe to Evie's World The Journal, where I share personal reflections on my music, my stories, and the spiritual work that shapes them. subscribe.evelynmexley.com

You can also connect with me at evelynmexley.com

Thank you for reading.

www.ingramcontent.com/pod-product-compliance
Lightning Source LLC
Chambersburg PA
CBHW071209210726
48293CB00002B/353